Journeys
of
Discoveries

by
Ellis Paris Ramsay

JOURNEYS OF DISCOVERIES
© 2006 BY ELLIS PARIS RAMSAY

ISBN 13: 978-1-933113-43-2
ISBN 10: 1-933113-43-X

CREDITS

EDITOR: Q
COVER DESIGN BY SHERI (GRAPHICARTIST2020@HOTMAIL.COM)

Published by
Intaglio Publications
P O Box 357474
Gainesville, Florida 32635

Visit us on the web: www.intagliopub.com

Dedication

For my Mother
Isabella Paris Ramsay

The bravest and strongest
Woman I know

Thank you for helping make
So many of my dreams
Come true

Acknowledgments

Honestly, my journey would not have been possible without the help of my friends, Gaye and Jude Marshall.

To Gaye who patiently taught me how to use a computer and checked and formatted my writing and punctuation. Her support and encouragement have been worth their weight in gold. And our talks on our morning walks when we can make it helps us laugh more.

To Jude who with her purple pen pointed out how necessary she was to my spelling and application of any given word. She was the one who always believed I could write; it was just a case of when.

To Lee Thornton who helped navigate and taught me how to drive my computer and showed me there was more than one way to do something—and thinks I'm awesome.

To Angela Jury for thinking of running and giving support. Hers is a treasured friendship.

To my dear friend Shelia Keat, who chose Max's last name—and what kind of dog she would have. Her friendship and belief in me is staggering.

To Jocelyn Charlton-Kelly and her niece, Clauda Richardson, for the correct French translation.

To my faithful and loyal clients, who indulge so many of my projects. Thank you for all encouragement.

Thanks to our friend, Dr Tony Poynter, for his medical advice — and he didn't even ask why.

My sincere and grateful thanks goes to David Robinson from The Really Useful Company for his assistance and due diligence. His invaluable advice is a credit to The Really Useful Company.

Thank you, The Really Useful Company, for the use of:
UNEXPECTED SONG from SONG & DANCE
Lyrics by Don Black
Music by Andrew Lloyd Webber
© copyright 1978 & 1982 The Really Useful Group Ltd., London.
All Rights Reserved. International Copyright Secured.

Many thanks to:
Souvenir Press Ltd
43, Great Russell Street
London WC1B 3PD
For allowing me to use a line of poetry from a code poem written
by Leo Marks.

And I couldn't write an acknowledgment page without saying
thank you to:
Katherine V. Forrest
Karin Kallmaker
Claire McNab
For so many wonderful stories that fill our souls and help us to
figure out where we all fit in the universe.
There is one other person I would like to thank for her professional
advice. However, I'm not allowed to name her. Suffice to say, you
know who you are!

Preface

*T*ime had stopped. Everything was in slow motion. Surreal. I started to notice peripheral things—a small violet growing out of the concrete, and a broken light in the lamppost off to the left. The look of horror on total strangers' faces, were they looking at me? The noise was distant, but I knew it was close, and sounded like the funnel from a very large ship. The ripping of steel, the crushing metal against metal like a concertina. How can a few seconds feel like an eternity? Theodora, where is Theo? I was only gone just a minute. Why was my mouth dry and my heart pounding so fast? That scream, where is it coming from? Why was everyone looking at me?

We had planned this trip for weeks. Napier, after being practically flattened by an earthquake in the 1930s, had been rebuilt in Art Deco style, which we love. Plus, it has fabulous wineries. We drove in last night on an early summer's evening and marvelled at how beautiful the ocean looked along Marine Parade. We stopped by the side of the road and got out to watch a few windsurfers enjoy the last of the day's light. There was still a warm breeze, and the ocean lapping the beach sounded wonderful. How I miss that sound, there's something so calming about it, yet right at this moment, I don't feel calm.

The sea is still rolling in. The Parade is full of people, some even breaking out their summer clothes early, as Theo did this morning. She wore shorts and a T-shirt but added a light blouse open over her Tee. The one I really love. It has several different blues that look like waves and looks spectacular over her silvery silk Tee and navy shorts. It had taken us ages to find her blue sandals. She refused to leave until we did; she said something about her black ones would do, but her brown ones would not.

"Someone call an ambulance!"
"Oh, my god, is she all right?"

"Kevin, you stupid bastard. I told you not to drive, you're too pissed, you stupid prick, now see what you've done!"

Shit, that woman's angry, yet I get the feeling she has had a fair bit to drink herself, but she wasn't the one driving.

"I'm sure the ambulance will be here in a moment. Are you with this woman?"

Again, some total stranger is looking at me, who are these people, what do they want from me? Our biggest problem was deciding where to go for lunch. We couldn't decide between ClearView Estate and Te Awa Farm. Did we feel like the sea breeze and a game of Petanque at ClearView or having the best Crème Brule on this earth at Te Awa Farm?

"Maybe we should try somewhere new," Theo said.

"Nah, let's not."

That's the last thing I said to her as I got out of the car to pick up a local newspaper.

"Have you got a phone? Do you want to use mine? Is there someone you should call? Are you all right?"

This woman is talking to me. Do I want to use her phone? Why would I want to use her phone? I have a phone of my own. It's in the car. Theo was about to use it to check up on something at work. Actually, she was using it when I got out of the car. Theo...

Chapter 1

Frances Remy, or Frenchy as her friends call her, hadn't long gotten off the plane. As always, she loved coming home to New Zealand. She loved seeing the Koru on the Air New Zealand plane and being welcomed aboard by stewards with their friendly New Zealand accents. New Zealand hadn't always been her home. Like many New Zealanders, she came from another country to settle here. Frenchy was the first of her generation and likely to be the only as she never had any intention of having children.

She was born in Paris and was the only child of Kirsty and Jean-Paul Remy. Her mother was Scottish and came from Edinburgh and had met Jean-Paul whilst on holiday during a varsity break. They fell madly in love. She didn't return to Edinburgh to finish her Arts degree, and they were married two months later. Frances arrived eight months after that. Their marriage lasted two years. Frenchy spent her life between Paris and Edinburgh—school in Scotland and holidays in France—until she was 16. She chose to live in Paris with her father and go to university there. She was fluent in both English and French. Her mother had gone back to finish her degree and now worked restoring and cleaning masterpieces at art galleries around Scotland; so Frenchy's decision to live with her father was an easy one.

Although her look was androgynous, she was breathtakingly arresting. She had a tall, athletic figure, and her short, dark, straight hair curled in wisps when she got sweaty. She turned heads—both male and female—wherever she went, something that she hated and never understood. Looks meant nothing to her. People were a mystery, and she wondered why they put so much credence on something that was so facile and only skin deep. She thought she looked odd—quite angular like the Amazon women she used to see in her mother's art books. Frenchy never understood the passion and emotion her mother put into her work, and although her mother talked her into doing Fine Arts at university, it was photography that interested her. She liked the voyeuristic life the camera gave her, catching people when they didn't know she was shooting them.

Life with Jean-Paul, as he liked her to call him, was easy. He wasn't the typical dad. He never married again but had a procession of women in his life, and he treated them all badly, which is probably why she did the same. She never loved any of the women she had and no matter how awful she was to them, they all loved her and wanted to see her again. The only woman she had ever loved was Theo, and Theo was the only woman she could never have. Theo was Caitlin's partner for life; it was that simple. Theo met Cat in Wellington nearly twelve years ago and they haven't been apart since. Frenchy met Theo when she was on her big overseas trip and was the reason she came to New Zealand eleven and a half years ago. She took the assignment to photograph the Wearable Arts in Nelson.

By the time Frenchy decided to come to New Zealand, Theo had met Cat, and it was too late. She decided to stay in New Zealand, as she loved the space and the beautiful country and hoped that maybe one day, well… However, she did not expect to like Cat so much and knew that Theo and Cat would always be together. They were just about her best friends, and although they lived in Wellington, they were able to see each other quite often, plus there were e-mails and phone calls most days.

Auckland airport had been fairly busy and while waiting to go through customs, she wondered whether to go home to bed. Then again, she could go to the club and pick up someone to take to bed and get back into the New Zealand time zone as quickly as possible. She was tired and her mind kept wandering back to her time away. *October had been cold in Paris and freezing in Edinburgh. Her mother's flat was on Newington Road in "Auld Reekie" as her mother liked to call it, and there was no point taking the car because there was never anywhere to park. It was easier to take the bus that stopped at the bottom of the mound outside the floral clock on the corner off Princess Street. Her mother was working at the National Gallery at the time. Sitting upstairs on the double-decker bus, she marvelled how the bus kept its ballast going down the icy slope of the mound and remembered her mother telling her that there was an electric blanket under the road that was used in wintertime. She didn't know whether her mother was having her on, but it gave her comfort to think that it might be true.* The customs officer brought Frenchy out of her reverie. "Next."

Frenchy caught a cab home, had a quick shower, and laid out a clean crisp white shirt, black jeans, and examined her collection of toys. She didn't need a bra, as her breasts were as firm as they were when she was eighteen. She finally chose her favourite black nine-inch dildo and strapped herself into the harness, fixing the dildo in place. *Oh, yes, the girls love this one.* Fastening her shirt so there was just a hint of cleavage, she donned her jeans and made sure the dildo was sitting where she wanted it. Going to her drawer by the bed she took out three condoms. Two were 'ribbed for her pleasure,' and one was ice cream flavoured. "Some lucky girl is going to be happy tonight," she said to herself. Coming from France wasn't the only reason she was nicknamed Frenchy, which was something she hoped Theo and Cat never found out about. She checked her watch, and it was still a bit early. Deciding to go to Ponsonby Road and grab a bite to eat first, she picked up her keys to her Renault and left.

She arrived at the club about 9:00 P.M. It wasn't terribly busy yet, but there were enough girls to choose from. She almost wished that she didn't have the choice of all the women there, but she always did. Okay, she avoided couples. Well, couples who looked happy together. She had some scruples, but not many. She had, on the odd occasion, gone with a couple but never found the right combination to make it work for her. Perhaps tonight was the night.

"Hi, Frenchy," Gerry shouted from the bar. "Your usual?"
"Yes, thanks."
Gerry handed Frenchy a Coke in the bottle just the way she liked. Ice waters it down, and in a glass it might be spiked, and Frenchy didn't drink alcohol. She didn't like the taste, and even worse, she hated the feeling of not being in control.
Gerry was the most unlikely Geraldine you would ever meet that's why so few people actually knew. Frenchy only found out one night

when Gerry was showing her a picture of her new dog—a Doberman puppy named Tinkerbelle—her driving licence fell to the ground. Frenchy picked it up and was about to comment when Gerry swore her to secrecy with pleading eyes. Frenchy agreed. She really liked Gerry and knew she had a crush on her, but Frenchy never screwed people she liked. She had very few friends and wanted to keep them. How Gerry could still be her friend after the way she saw her treat other women was beyond her.

"Nice to see you home, Frenchy. How was your trip?"

"Great, thanks, Gerry. A little cold for my liking, but the photo shoot in Paris was worthwhile. It's great having an influential mum when you need one. Being allowed to shoot the models in the Louvre was wonderful. How is Tinkerbelle?"

"Growing every day. It's a good job I don't have a girlfriend at the moment because I don't think I could afford to feed them both."

Frenchy smiled. Gerry was quite cute and had an engaging smile. She was five foot five, bottle blonde, and could handle herself quite well. She'd seen her throw a few very drunk dykes out and live to tell the tale. Frenchy looked around and already several young nubile chicks were looking in her direction. Gerry saw her and said, "You play nice tonight, and try not to leave your usual trail of broken hearts behind you."

"Yeh, yeh," said Frenchy walking away. *I don't break their hearts. I'm always very clear that I only want to fuck them not rent a U-haul.* Frenchy moved to the jukebox and was pretending to study it to see who came to her.

Within thirty seconds, "Hi, I'm Rosy." *And so it begins!* Frenchy turned to find a petite blonde with blue eyes, large breasts, and a tiny waist. She wondered why that was the type that was always attracted to her. "Well, hello, baby. Can I buy you a drink?"

"White wine, thank you."

"Hey, Gerry, a white wine please."

"Comin' up."

Just then Eva Cassidy started to sing 'Fields of Gold.' "Would you like to dance?" She couldn't remember her name and didn't want to, so she just called her 'Baby.'

"Yeh, I'd love to," she said, with eyes wide with delight. *Too easy, too easy.* On the dance floor, she held Baby tight and felt her young firm breasts underneath hers. Her hair smelt of lavender. She guessed it would have been an expensive shampoo, and her fragrance was most definitely French. Just like walking into the Paris Metro first thing in the morning, it beats the hell out of the urine smell in the underground in London.

"I've seen you here before but not for a while."

"Well, this is my local, and I have been away with work for a few weeks; but I'm here now, and let's not talk about work." Frenchy didn't want to know what she did or talk about her work, so she leaned down and kissed Baby on the lips very lightly. Eva had finished singing when Faith Hill started to sing "Let's Make Love." Frenchy had gotten such a good response from the kiss that she leaned down and kissed Baby full on the lips, taking Baby's breath away. The surprise on Baby's face made Frenchy act.

"Would you like to go somewhere a little more private?"

Stunned, Baby whispered, "Yes."

Frenchy took her by the hand and led her to the loo.

As it was still earlyish, the loos were relatively quiet. It looked as if only one booth was in use. Frenchy led Baby into a cubicle, and as she closed the door behind her, she quickly put both of Baby's arms above her head. Placing Baby's left hand with her right, Frenchy held them with her left hand while she gently stroked her face with her free righthand and asked, "This is what you want, isn't it?"

Baby said almost inaudibly, "Yes."

Frenchy leaned down and kissed her hard. She felt Baby go weak. "You'll have to be a little clearer than that," nibbling at her neck. "What is it you want from me?" Frenchy let her hand snake down Baby's torso and settled it on Baby's thigh. As Baby was trying to respond, Frenchy was slowly sliding her dress up until Frenchy's hand rested on the top of Baby's G-string. *G-string! Why is it always a G-string?*

"I want you," Baby replied.

"You want me to what?" asked Frenchy, sliding her finger inside the G-string and again with a kiss that was deeper than before, "you want me to what?"

Baby was having trouble breathing, and she thought her heart was going to jump out of her chest. "I want you to..." There was silence for about ten seconds while Baby tried to focus. "I want you to fuck me."

"Say again. A bit louder."

Baby's eyes almost crossed as Frenchy had just slid two fingers ever so close to Baby's clitoris. Baby moaned, "Fuck me, just fuck me now."

Frenchy smiled, "Not so fast, Baby."

Frenchy let Baby's arms go and in a quick motion lifted Baby's dress off over her head. Frenchy heard an intake of breath as she admired Baby's firm young breasts and flat stomach. Her face, neck, and breasts were red with arousal. Frenchy cupped both her breasts as she kissed her gently, moving her tongue down to her breasts. She sat down on the loo aware of the pressure the dildo was now making on her jeans, and slipped Baby's G-string off, brought her forward, and straddled her on her knees.

"That's better," she said, gently tweaking her nipples as she nibbled around her ears. Frenchy let her hand slide down and with one very quick motion entered Baby deeply. "Oh, you like that, don't you, Baby?"

"Yes. God, yes," she said and gasped with shock as Frenchy removed her hand.

"I've got something for you," said Frenchy as she put her hand in her pocket and pulled out a condom.

Baby looked surprised as Frenchy pulled down the zip on her jeans and pulled out her beautiful black dildo.

Baby's eyes were wide with pleasure. "Oh, my goodness. I've never..."

Frenchy asked, "Would you like to put the condom on?"

"Fuck yes!" Baby expertly tore the packet open with alarming speed and placed the condom on. Before Frenchy could stop her she mounted her black beauty.

"Oh, fuck, oh, fuck me." Placing both her hands behind her on Frenchy's knees, she started to buck like an old time rodeo star. She was making so much noise that Frenchy was sure the whole club could hear her and wondered if there was anyone else in the loos. Frenchy returned her hands to Baby's breasts, focusing on her large hard nipples, which just about sent Baby over the edge. She lowered her thumb and placed it over Baby's clit and after two or three more bucks, and Baby screaming, "Oh, fuck!" it was all over.

Baby, panting very hard, said, "Do you want to come to my place?"

"Sure," said Frenchy. She deposited the condom in the loo while Baby quickly dressed. Leaving the cubicle, there were several women lining the wall watching them.

"I'm next," said the blonde at the top of the queue.

Grabbing Frenchy's hand, Baby said, "In your dreams, sister."

Frenchy dropped a twenty-dollar note on the bar as they left. Gerry, unamused, lifted her head and looked Frenchy in the eyes and said nothing.

Frenchy drove Baby to her flat. She never took women to her home. The drive took only ten minutes and nothing was said. As Frenchy parked the car she removed a tube of lubricant from the glove box. Baby didn't see her, but she knew they all wanted to go all the way in the end. Two minutes later they were in Baby's flat, and Baby was removing her dress and G-string on the way to her bedroom. Frenchy was pleased that she wasn't expected to make conversation. Before she knew it, Baby had her hand in the pocket where she saw Frenchy remove the condom. She picked the ice cream flavoured one, saying, "This will do nicely," dropped to her knees, opened the zip on Frenchy's jeans, and pulled them down just a little over Frenchy's hips. Placing the condom on, she started to suck the tip. Moaning slightly, her hand was pushing down the shaft and Frenchy felt the pressure on her now swollen clitoris, which surprised her. Baby seemed to know what she was doing. She held Baby's head in her hand and watched her black beauty disappear into Baby's mouth and was incredibly turned on. With her eyes closed, Baby was pushing beauty down and down. Frenchy was surprised when she felt Baby's thumb on her clitoris. Frenchy was having trouble balancing and looked for something to steady herself, with the realization she was close to orgasm and wanted to take control.

17

She took Baby's head in her hands and gently pulled her up saying, "On the bed, Baby, on all fours." Baby quickly obliged, and Frenchy entered her immediately with beauty, holding her ass by either side as she rammed herself in quickly, over and over. She knew Baby was close to climax but hers had waned. Five more thrusts, and she heard her come. If Frenchy wanted to come, too, there was only one thing left to do. She put her left hand in her other pocket and took out the tube of lubricant. Removing the lid quickly, she squeezed an amount over her thumb, and while she was still inside Baby, she opened Baby's cheeks with her other hand and placed the gel over her anus. Before Baby could object, Frenchy had removed beauty from Baby's vagina and was slowly but surely entering her ass. Baby's gasp was loud, and before she had time to complain, Frenchy said, "This is what you want, Baby, isn't it"?

Baby answered weakly, "Yes."

Frenchy, not so softly, said, "Isn't it?"

"Yes," cried Baby, "Yes." Frenchy, ever so slowly, increased her thrusts, going a little deeper each time. She could feel the end of beauty against her clitoris, again and again, faster and faster; Baby was shouting, "Yes, yes! Darling, you're nearly there," and with a final thrust, she collapsed on the bed, and Baby curled up beside her.

She was so hot and sweaty she could feel the curls around her neck. She had one more condom left and made use of it before she left Baby's flat at 1 A.M.

Driving home with the window down, she noticed that it was a mild night and was pleased summer was on the way. Entering her flat, which used to be an old warehouse, she turned on a small table lamp. Her flat was sparse but tasteful. Every thing was in its place. No fuss, just as she liked it. She felt numb, flat, as she always did after mindless sex. *Why do they let me treat them like that?* She wondered if Baby had worked out that she had no intention of seeing her again. She remembered that she hadn't listened to her messages before she left for the club, and she switched on her machine. There were a few work-related calls and then Cat's voice. She sat bolt upright when she heard the tone and fear in Cat's voice. *Frenchy, Theo...*

Chapter 2

Aroha Kiriana had decided to pop into work. It was Saturday and her partner, Lizzie, had taken Danny, Aroha's son, off to soccer. Lizzie was so good with Danny. They were real mates. Lizzie had been Danny's second mum since he was two years old. He'd called her Lizzie-mum almost immediately. It seemed to be the easiest way for him to sort out who everyone was. His dad was in the picture, but he seemed more like a playmate to Danny. He always did fun things with Dad, but Mum and Lizzie-mum were the ones he always came to with his problems and when he just needed a hug. He never seemed to be bothered by the fact that he had two mums. In fact, he even said to Aroha that he felt sorry for some of his friends who only had one parent. He was a well-rounded kid who had lots of people and family around who loved him, and he knew it. He loved it when Frenchy came down from Auckland and spent time with him. She was the only one who didn't live in the Wellington area. He thought she was really cool. Aroha felt so proud about having such a well-adjusted son and wondered if she would fare so well in the fast approaching teenage years. *Enjoy it while you've got it, girl; tomorrow's another day.*

The reason she had popped into work was to check up on a not-so-fortunate kid. Child, Youth, and Family did the best they could, but in these days of budget and staff cuts, there was only so much you could do. The burnout rate of social workers in this field was high, and the average length of time people lasted in this job was about two years. This was Aroha's fifth year, and she wondered how much longer she could hack it. If it weren't for the tireless inspiration her boss and dear friend, Theo, gave her, she would have been long gone. Theo was the real reason she had come to work at lunchtime on Saturday. She knew that if Theo hadn't gone away for the weekend, she would have been at work following up on this kid. Lizzie put the extra hours in with her job as well. Secondary school teaching wasn't a cake–walk, especially when you put the extra effort in with the kids you care about. Lizzie often said, "There's no point in doing this job if you don't care, 'cause it's certainly not for the money."

Looking out of her office window over Wellington's harbour, she reminded herself not to spend too much time here on such a beautiful day. Danny's game would be over by 12:30 P.M., and by the time he and Lizzie got home and showered, she should be there by 1:00 P.M. Aroha had promised Danny a lunch since she missed his game. They were hoping to talk him out of going to Mac's and opt for Dockside instead.

The first time Aroha had seen Lizzie was on a hockey field. Cat was playing in a social team, and Theo had been on at her for weeks to come meet this woman who was on Cat's team. "She's really bubbly," Theo said, "and she's such fun. I'm sure you'd like her." Finally, Theo wore her down, and she agreed to go. Theo was very excited and chatted nonstop in the car on the way to the game, relating all the funny things Lizzie said to the point where Aroha believed she wouldn't like this woman, and Theo would have to leave her alone to her life of celibacy. No such luck. Aroha was sucked in and totally mesmerised by Lizzie. When pizza was suggested after the game, Lizzie said, "Only if Aroha comes."

They didn't even notice when everyone had left Lizzie's flat, and with Danny at his dad's till Monday Aroha thought, *well, why not?*

"I don't have anything in for breakfast. Would you mind if we go out for brunch, or dinner, or whatever?" Lizzie looked totally relaxed, but her eye contact was intense. Aroha froze. It took a few seconds to compute what Lizzie had actually said. *Was she saying what I think she is? Fuck, am I ready for this?* Before she could answer, Lizzie took her hand and led her to her bedroom.

When Aroha turned up at work on Monday morning wearing the same clothes as she had on Saturday, Theo could not take the smile off her face, realising Aroha had not been home to change. Aroha felt sure she blushed all day, and when six roses turned up at work—two red, two pink, and two white with a note that read, 'I don't know what colours you like yet, Your Lizzie'—she knew her life was about to change.

Two phone calls later and her work was done. Picking up her cell phone, she noticed that it was actually Lizzie's phone. Aroha smiled as she remembered the day Lizzie came home with a new cell phone. Aroha said "snap" as she took the one she bought herself that day out of her handbag. They even had the same pin number on their voice mail. They laughed when they found that each had chosen their anniversary date, 28 February. Aroha noticed there was a message and thought she better check it in case it was important. "Hey, gorgeous, I was hoping you would change your mind and get 'up close and personal' with me again. Tonight would be great if you can get away. I know you said never again, but it was so good, and you weren't that drunk. Call me. It's Jojo here, just in case you have lots of women ringing you up, you sexy thing."

Aroha reeled, and she just about fell over her office chair. *I have to sit down, I feel dizzy.* With her head between her legs, she replayed that message over and over in her head. *Oh, my God, Danny. How can she do this to Danny and me?* She was unaware of how long she sat staring out of the window. Finally, after several glasses of water, she picked up her car keys, locked the office, and started the drive home, not really sure of what she was going to do. A car horn sounded as she changed lanes. She had forgotten to indicate. When she sat at green traffic lights she realized she was really going to have to concentrate or pull over. She pulled over; she couldn't see to drive anyway because of tears that were streaming down her face. Aroha sobbed for ten minutes before she gave herself a talking to. *For goodness sake, girl, get your act together. You'll just have to confront her to see if there is a way that you can salvage this. Maybe Matt can have Danny after lunch. It's not his weekend, but he might be able to.*

She rang Matt on the way home. He said he was happy to have Danny. Lizzie's car was in the driveway. She felt sick. *Come on, girl, you can hold it together—if not for you then for Danny.* Placing her keys on the kitchen counter and the cell phones side by side, she walked through to the lounge. Lizzie was standing with the phone in her hand and a look of disbelief on her face. "It's Cat, Theo…"

Chapter 3

Willie Te Rangi was pleased it was Friday and school had finished for the week. The staff meeting after final period seemed to go on forever. Their present headmaster had a definite sadistic side, pulling these meetings as often as he did on a Friday.

Lizzie had looked terrible all day and was avoiding eye contact. *I wonder what's up.* He was just deciding whether to go find her when he saw her walking to her car.

"Hey, girlfriend. Are you okay?" he asked.

Lizzie looked up, and as soon as she saw Willie, she burst into tears. "Oh, Willie, I've done something so stupid that I don't know what I'm going to do!"

"Hey, come on, girl, what you do? Tell some pimple-faced teenagers that they were a pain in the arse?" he asked, smiling as if he were an indulgent older brother.

"Oh, god, I wish that's all it was."

"Honey, what's wrong?"

"I'm so ashamed; I can't tell you."

"Are Aroha and Danny okay?"

"Yes, they're fine, but they may not be when they find out."

Climbing into Lizzie's four-wheel drive, Willie took out his laundered hankie and handed it to her. "You better start from the beginning." Lizzie took a deep breath, sobbed one last time, and blew her nose.

"Last night I stayed behind after rehearsal. Jemma has a fabulous voice and every time she sings "Over the Rainbow" I cry. She's going to make a wonderful Dorothy, but she won't learn her lines. She asked me if I could work with her. She's finding it really hard trying to learn her lines and revise for exams and asked me to speak to Mr.

Emerson to get him off her back. As you know, he hasn't an artistic bone in his body and thinks Jemma is wasting time with a silly musical and ought to be putting more effort into her math if she wants to get on in this world."

"Calm down, Lizzie, you're digressing."

"Well, I can't help it. That egotistical, chauvinistic prick of a hetero drives me mad."

"Me, too. Back to Jemma and rehearsal."

"Okay, okay. All the other kids had gone home, but the crew was still there working. You know the backstage set designers, set builders, production, and lighting people. When I was through with Jemma I went over to see if I could help. As it turned out they were just finishing for the night and asked if I'd like to join them for a drink. I was so wound up; I told them I would love to. Aroha wasn't expecting me home till late, and a drink sounded wonderful."

"Well, this sounds all very nice; did you drink too much and make a fool of yourself?"

Lizzie burst into tears again. "Yes, I drank too much and far worse than that."

Willie knew that something really bad had happened and just sat quietly rubbing Lizzie's back till she was ready to speak again.

"Oh, god, Willie, what have I done? You know that substitute teacher, Jojo, who's filling in for Harry while he's off overseas?"

"The Phys Ed girl with the ponytail?"

"Yeh, that's her." Lizzie turned her head away from Willie and cringed trying to find the words she didn't want to hear herself say.

"Well, she's helping with the set building. I was on my fourth wine when I remembered that I hadn't had anything to eat all day. I was taking a rehearsal at lunchtime, and there just wasn't time. So there I was, tossing back another wine poured by Jojo, when she said that she found something in the gym she thought I might find useful for the show and asked me if I'd like to see it. I said sure and thanked her for being so interested in the show. Being a substitute teacher who wasn't involved in my department was above and beyond the call. I thought she was a really sweet kid."

"So, what happened?"

"I went with her to the gym, which wasn't easy as I was having trouble keeping my balance.

24

She opened the door, and I tripped over something and started to laugh. She caught me and as she was steadying me, she kissed me." "She what? Doesn't she know you're married?" "I don't think she cares. I know it sounds lame, but I didn't really work out what was going on until it was all over." "What do you mean?" "Well, she had me pinned against the wall and was kissing me hard. I was trying to work out how to get out of the situation with a little decorum and not make it awkward for us both. Next thing I know, she's pulled my zip down, and her hand is inside my knickers." "You're kidding me!" "No," Lizzie was sobbing continually now. "What was even worse, Willie was I came almost immediately. It was all over in less than a minute. I couldn't believe it, Willie; and to make it worse, Jojo said, 'Wow, baby, you were hot to trot,' with a real smug attitude. I wished I'd slapped her. I was mortified, Willie. Just then we heard some voices. Jojo leaned into me and said, 'We'll have to take a rain check.' I said, 'No, never again!' and almost ran back to where I'd left my stuff and went home. Willie, I came. How could I? I hadn't given this girl a thought. Did I bring this on myself? Did I want this to happen? Aroha and Danny are my life. We have even talked about having another kid." She looked at Willie and smiled. "We thought I should have it this time, and you'd be the father."

"Me!" spurted Willie.

"Yes," laughed Lizzie. "We thought your and my DNA mix would make the child look more like Danny."

"Me!" said Willie incredulously.

"Oh, don't worry, not the traditional way. The old turkey baster job."

"Wow, Cocco would love to be a mum."

They both laughed, imagining the reaction from Willie's partner, Cocco Toshiro. Madam Butterfly himself.

Then Lizzie started to cry again, "But that's not going to happen now, is it?"

"You can't go home like this; you better come to ours. What's Aroha doing tonight?"

"She's staying at work until it's time to pick up Danny from his kickboxing class. They won't be home till about nine, nine-thirty."

"Good, come and have a meal with Cocco and me, and we'll talk this through to see if we can work this out."

Willie and Cocco lived in Hataitai. As they entered the old villa, they were hit with sound waves from the very expensive audio system that was Cocco and Willie's pride and joy. Maria Callas was at the peak of her death scene from *Madam Butterfly*, and even if you weren't into opera, you couldn't help but be enveloped by the surround sound and immediately be moved by the woman's plight. Lizzie always thought of *Philadelphia* when she heard this—the scene in which Tom Hanks, who plays a lawyer suffering from AIDS, tries to reach his homophobic lawyer played by Denzel Washington. Willie had taken Cocco to see the *Madam Butterfly*, and ever since, Cocco had been besotted and refused to believe it wasn't a true story. He'd been sympathizing with the woman ever since and would like Willie to do something about that man Pinkerton if they ever met. Lizzie did so love her 'lezzy boys.'

The boys' house was an eclectic mix of ethnic and cultural influences that included Zen, Buddhist, Japanese, and Maori.

"Hello, my husband. You are home. Oh, and Lizzie darling, sit, I make tea."

Cocco kissed Willie French style, on either cheek, then Maori style, a shared breath. He refused to bow the Japanese way, stating that this was one girl who wasn't going to bow to any man. Willie, of course, didn't want him to anyway and would have preferred he just say "hello" like a normal person. Cocco was definitely different and that's probably why he fell in love with him to begin with.

"Lizzie, you look awful. Would you prefer something stronger?"

Lizzie almost choked on her reply, "No. Tea, please."

Willie and Cocco had met in Palmerston North five years ago. Willie was studying at the College of Education, and Cocco was at International Pacific College. Cocco's family was happy to send their son overseas, as he was an embarrassment to them. The further away the better. Money wasn't a problem, so Cocco had a very comfortable, but unhappy life in New Zealand. He didn't get on well with the other Japanese students and preferred to live in town. He found a house to rent on Te Awe Awe Street in the suburb of

Hokowhitu. It was halfway between the city and the IPC and as it turned out very close to the College of Education. He didn't go to IPC much, preferring to spend most of his time playing the pokie machines in a bar in town. That's where he met Willie.

He was spellbound the day he saw Willie in the bar playing pool with some friends and was astounded when Willie looked over at him and smiled. Cocco had never seen such a beautiful brown man before. He was tall and very well built. Muscles showed through his shirtsleeves. Cocco had forgotten to breathe, and when Willie walked over and asked, "Are you all right, mate?" he just about died. *Mate. He called me Mate! This beautiful god called me Mate.* Not one to miss an opportunity, he swooned and said, "Not really."

Willie helped him to a chair. "Can I get you a glass of water?"

"Thank you. That would be kind!" Batting his long eyelashes, he couldn't take his eyes off Willie. Willie continued to play pool while Cocco looked on, feeling happy for the first time since he had been in New Zealand. When Willie asked if he would like a lift home, Cocco graciously accepted and insisted Willie come in for tea. Willie could see that the house was far nicer than his grotty flat that was messy and untidy, due to his two lazy flatmates, and had no trouble saying yes. Cocco insisted on a proper tea ceremony for his guest, and Willie enjoyed the ceremony that was just for him. He had never met anyone quite like Cocco.

Cocco was wearing his kimono, not a formal one that you see depicted by Geisha women, but just a simple cream silk with a delicate design of a blossom of fuchsia and cerise pinks. His long black hair was pulled back into a ponytail and he had a cream and pink coloured miniature orchid flower over his right ear. He placed three bowls, a bamboo brush that Lizzie always thought looked like a rejected shaving brush, a small basket of green tea, his favourite teapot with a cane handle that went over its top, and a small Japanese patterned cloth on the table. He was kneeling in front of the coffee table and motioned silently, with a wave of his hand across the table, for Willie and Lizzie to sit. It was always best to respond immediately when Cocco did this, as he was extremely serious about the tea ceremony. Also, it was a delight to be part of the magic, and even with Lizzie feeling like hell, it was an honoured distraction that she welcomed.

"I do not like to see my friend look so sad, Lizzie." Cocco had, of course, served the master of the house first, then Lizzie and had only just poured himself tea when he voiced his concern. "My Willie will help you, I will cheer you up. I will dance for you. No, no. I will make you laugh. I tell you my three most memorable sex times with Willie. I so lucky, he has such big cock, Lizzie."

Lizzie just about choked on her tea, and Willie blurted, "Cocco, no."

"Oh, don't be silly, my Willie. Lizzie our friend. She be proud to know she have man friend of such large stature and be happy for me. The first time I saw my Willie's beautiful brown cock was when he brought me home after I met him in pool bar."

"Cocco, you can't tell her that."

"Oh, quiet, my husband."

Lizzie was still laughing. She couldn't imagine what was coming next. Willie was holding his hands over his face groaning, while Cocco continued.

"Well, I made him tea, and I sat on the floor while he drank it. I don't think he cared for the tea first time, but he a good boy and drank it anyway. When he finished he said he must be going. So I said to him right then, that I was good girl and could not have sex on first date."

Lizzie gulped and asked, "So what did he say?"

"He say, and he looked surprised, 'Okay.'"

So I say, "I just give you blow job, no sex."

Lizzie burst out laughing. Willie was still covering his face with his hands, "No, no."

"So I lean over and undo his zip. This time I got surprise when his huge brown cock jumped out of his pants. He tell me later that he had no clean underwear and was not expecting to meet anyone."

By this time, Lizzie was in hysterics.

"Lizzie, I was so happy, I never seen cock so big. Willie, show Lizzie your cock..."

Lizzie thought she was going to split her sides.

"Take your pants down, Willie."

"No, I will not."

"Anyway, I give good blow job and invited him to sex and dinner next night and he come. Boy, he come! Willie like blow job so much, he tell me about this fantasy that he had. He would like to drive car so fast along road while someone give him blow job. So when his birthday come I say he can have it. He tell me Foxton straight, between Foxton and Himatangi, be best place. So we make a date. I pack a picnic, and we go down to Foxton Beach and have picnic and walk along beach. Oh, Lizzie, it was so romantic walking along the beach with my big Willie."

Lizzie looked at Willie who was smiling at the memory.

"I had on my sarong, covering my breasts, you know, the pretty one with the red flowers, and a straw sun hat. Willie just had long shorts on and was showing off his manly chest. I was so happy. Willie had borrowed friend's old Holden Belmont car, because they have a long seat across the front and what Willie says is called a column change on the wheel, so no gear stick or brakes get in the way. Anyway, we wait till sun go down and road's a bit quieter. We got in car, and I say to Willie, 'you have to take your pants off. I no fight with them and steering wheel.' He say, 'I'm not sitting in the nude.' I say, 'put on your T-shirt' and he did."

Lizzie looked incredulous. "You sat in the car without your pants on?"

Willie looked sheepish and nodded yes. "There was a lot at stake here."

"I cuddle up to Willie, and he had his left arm around my shoulder, and I started to give him hand job with my left hand."

"Too much detail, Cocco," Willie protested.

"Lizzie has to get picture, Willie," Cocco said. "Anyway it didn't take long for Willie to get an even bigger cock, so I leaned down to give him his birthday blow job. I could tell from the sound he making he happy as Larry. I could feel car going faster, which made me work faster. Then I hear him shout, 'Oh, god, Oh, god, Oh, Nooooooo,' which I thought funny as he had not come, and next thing I hit my head on steering wheel and fell to floor. Willie was braking and car stopping. I say, 'Willie, what you do, you not there yet.' He say, 'quick, quick, sit up and put your hat on.' It was then I heard the siren. I no hear before as Willie was playing Ricky Martin singing "She Bang, She Bang" very loudly on stereo. So I sit up and put hat on. Willie is sitting frozen to spot, and his hands gripping wheel. I wanted to laugh 'cause he still had very big hard on that poke his shirt out. I covered mouth and giggled like schoolgirl. Then police officer came to window of car and said, 'Good evening, sir, do you know what speed you were doing?' Then he saw me and leaned in a little and said, 'Oh, good evening, miss. I didn't know there was anyone else in the car.' Then he saw Willie's hard on, and the look on face and said, 'I see, the old Foxton straight run. Sir, do you know how dangerous that is, and how much risk you were putting your young lady in?' I giggle. He knew I was nice young lady. 'Sorry officer,' Willie said. 'It's my birthday.'"

Lizzie, who thought she couldn't possibly laugh any more, repeated. "It's my birthday! You're kidding me?"

Willie cringed and said, "It's the best I could come up with considering how much embarrassment and discomfort I was in."

Cocco continued, "The officer say, 'Well, in that case, I'll let you off if you promise never to do this again and take better care of the young lady.' I glad I have my legs waxed. 'And Miss, you wear your seatbelt at all times and make him keep the sex to bedroom. Trust me, it's a lot safer there.' I giggle again and made out I too embarrass to look at him. 'Thank you officer,' said Willie, 'it won't happen again,' and the guy walked away smiling.

"So you never got your birthday fantasy?" asked Lizzie.

"Of course, he did," said Cocco. "As soon as officer had gone and Willie started to drive again I lean over and finish my job. Willie was so nervous, he almost couldn't come, he able to keep up long time. He had really good come."

"Cocco, too far," said Willie. "You go too far."

Lizzie wiped the tears from her eyes.

"Good to see you smile, Lizzie, you want one more story?"

"No more!"

"Yes," said Lizzie.

"I promise three stories to Lizzie and three she get. You know I cook..."

Lizzie thought this was an understatement, as Cocco was a superb cook...

"I always try variety in my cooking, and on Valentine's Day I was cooking everything pink or red, which included Borsch soup. I had set the table all pretty. Pink tablecloth, red candles, and Willie's aunt's silver cutlery that she gave us. Little red heart sprinkles, heart-shaped little chocolates, red roses, and a bottle of Rosé chilled, just the way he likes it. I put on my red shiny Chinese dress; you know the one with the splits up the sides."

Lizzie was still amused that out of Aroha, Cat, Theo, and herself, Cocco was the most feminine in a un-PC way. "I put Bette Midler's *Bette of Roses* on and waited on my man hand and foot. He carry me upstairs after dinner. He so romantic. I thought I gonna die from happiness. Now I always like to lay on my back when Willie make love to me. I like to look at his face, and it's not ladylike to go doggie, but I so happy I want make my big Willie happy, so I go doggie for him."

"I am not going to be able to look Lizzie in the face ever again, Cocco."

Lizzie said, "Of course, you are, sweetheart. It's just my bottom I'm going to keep away from you and old Holden cars."

Willie covered his face again and said, "This isn't happening."

"Oh, hush, Willie. You proud of your manhood. Willie is very excited about me going doggie. He say he can fit more of his big cock that way."

"Cocco!"

Lizzie was laughing so hard she was sure the neighbours would hear her.

"He go on and on. He such a virile man, and the tension was really building. I shout, 'Willie, Willie, I so lucky' and just then the borsch took effect, and I blew Willie across room. Lizzie, I horrified and say, 'no more borsch ever again.'"

Lizzie was rolling about the floor killing herself laughing, Willie was in the kitchen checking on the food in the oven, shaking his head, and Cocco was kneeling back on his legs looking very happy with himself. After dinner, Cocco discreetly removed himself and went off to bed leaving Willie and Lizzie to talk.

The next morning Willie went off to watch Danny play soccer, and when he got home for lunch Cocco was able to get the whole story out of Willie, as Willie knew there would be no peace until he did.

Cocco was crying. "Poor Lizzie, poor Aroha, poor Danny. Oh, Willie, our family is hurting. What can we do?"

Ellis Paris Ramsay

"Lizzie is going to tell Aroha next weekend when Danny is at his dad's. We'll just have to wait and see and hope Aroha will deal with it and just accept it as a stupid mistake."

Just then the phone rang. Cocco, still tearful, picked it up. "Hi, CC." He was the only one to call Cat, 'CC.' Then he let out a gutwrenching yell, "Nooooo…"

Chapter 4

Maxine Lawson was walking her dog, Ozzie, along the beach at Paekakariki. Now that she was retired, she took great pleasure in her twice a day constitutional, as her father would have called it, with Ozzie. The Kapiti coastline had an endless beach, so it was really up to her mood as to how far she walked. It was such a joy to do after years of working in stuffy rooms listening to other people's problems, not that she hadn't enjoyed her work as a psychiatrist, especially in the later years when she stopped teaching and went into private practice. It was a privilege to do the work she did; at least that's what she thought. It's just that she was tired and missed her husband Callum very much—cancer had taken him when he was sixty-one years old, which was far too young to die. Now five years later, she could stop taking the commuter train into Wellington every day and just enjoy their home. After all, Wellington was only forty minutes away by train or twenty-five minutes in the car. There was no need to keep the flat on in Wellington as she could always stay with her niece, Caitlin, and her partner, Theo. They had a lovely modern house in Roseneath with plenty of room, and they didn't even mind her bringing Ozzie.

Max's own house on the beachfront in Paekakariki was originally built in the fifties, and she and Callum had bought it in the sixties before the beach became popular. Most of their friends thought they were mad, but they loved it and spent twenty years doing it up and adding a second storey, which gave them a fabulous view of the Pacific Ocean and Kapiti Island bird sanctuary. On very clear days, one could see the tip of the South Island straight ahead to the left and Mount Egmont up the coast to the right. Although Egmont's name had been changed to Mount Taranaki, she still thought of it as Egmont. Her early life had been spent in Australia where she was brought up in the outback, and she remembered well the first time she had seen the ocean. She was twenty-two years old, out of university, and on her way to New Zealand to pick fruit for the summer. Sydney's harbour had looked spectacular, but when she saw the ocean from Nelson Beach at the top of the South Island, she knew she could never not live by it.

She met Callum fruit picking and never returned to live in Australia. Apart from the occasional visits, the only Australian thing in her life was Ozzie, a blue-haired Blue Heeler. "Come on, Ozzie, time to go home for lunch."

At sixty-five, Max could no longer run with Ozzie but had no problem walking at a cracking pace, which is why she still had a good figure, and her hairdresser of twenty years kept her hair looking as red as it was in her twenties. She had plenty of suitors, but she wasn't interested in a permanent relationship. Callum had been the love of her life, and although she didn't believe in celibacy, she had no interest in washing and cooking for anyone else on a regular basis or sharing her newly found freedom. This was time for herself. "Now, what shall I have for lunch, darling?" she asked Ozzie as she scratched behind his ears. She was sitting on her doorstep taking off her shoes and wondering what Cat and Theo would be having for their lunch in Napier. They were both working too hard and badly needed a holiday, so she hoped that a weekend away would be better than nothing.

She had her head in the fridge, trying to decide what to eat, when she heard the phone ring. "Who could that be, Ozzie?" She smiled to herself, thinking of what she would say to a client who talked to his or her pets like they were human.

"Hello, Max Lawson speaking. Cat, what on earth's the matter, dear?"
"There's been an accident, a terrible accident!"
"Cat, are you all right? What kind of accident?"

"It's Theo, Max. She's in the hospital." Cat was sobbing so much that Max could hardly hear her say, "I don't know what to do."

"Cat," Max said in a clear, even-toned voice, moving into professional mode, "first, tell me where you are and what happened."

It took Cat a few seconds to reply. Max could almost hear how much Cat's brain was not engaging. And while her heart was breaking for her niece, if she were to be of any help, she needed information.

"Um, I'm in the hospital. Hastings Hospital. Theo was in the car, and this drunken guy ran into the car while it was parked."

"What are the doctors saying, Cat?"

"Um, I don't know. I haven't heard yet. Max, she was unconscious all the way here from Napier. That's like half an hour or more by the time the ambulance got to her. Oh, Max, what am I going to do? If anything's wrong with Theo or…"

Max knew that Cat couldn't voice her fears.

"Honey, I'm on my way."

Max was able to find out that Cat had rung Lizzie, and she, Aroha, Willie, and Cocco were on their way to pick her up in Lizzie's big Prado, so they could all go together. This meant she had about twenty, twenty-five minutes to pack a few things and make a few phone calls. Ted would take Ozzie. She rang a motel in Hastings and made bookings for them all, wrote down the address of the hospital, and made flasks of tea and coffee, all the time trying not to think the worst.

She'd have to be strong for Cat. Cat had been her brick when Callum died.

Chapter 5

Thery found Cat sitting bent over and studying the floor. They stopped, gave each other a collective look, and prepared themselves for the unthinkable. There had been no contact with Cat since her initial phone calls, as cell phone usage was not permitted in hospitals.

Max was ahead, and the first to speak. "Honey, I'm here. What's the news?" Max sat by her side as Cat slowly lifted her head, taking in her surroundings and looking at her friends, one by one, as if in a dream. If, by any chance in a million, she had not realized the severity of the situation she could see it clearly in the looks on her friends' faces. She took a few seconds to reply, which seemed like an eternity to all present.

"I don't know. They are still with her."

Max rose immediately saying, "I'll go see what I can find out."

Aroha sat to Cat's right and Cocco to her left. Willie and Liz stood in front. No one really knew what to say; what could they say? She'll be fine? When no one knew if she would. Aroha finally spoke, holding her friend's hand. "Cat, can you tell us what happened?"

"We were in town." It was several seconds before she spoke again. "We were deciding where to go for lunch. We were parked, and I had gotten out of the car to pick up a local paper to see what was on, and this car…this car came from nowhere and slammed into our car." Cat started to sob very quietly. It was a few minutes before she could speak again. "He drove straight into the car, just behind the back right hand seat. The impact threw Theo forward, and because we were parked, she didn't have her seat belt on, and she hit the windscreen and then her body snapped back. I couldn't get the door open, Aroha. I tried and tried." She was crying much louder now. "They had to get the Fire Brigade to cut her out. She was unconscious."

Max returned, "Okay, there will be a doctor along in a moment to speak with Cat. She's alive, but that's all I could find out."

Cocco burst out crying, "Oh, thank you, Buddha." He closed his eyes and crossed himself. If it had been another time or place, it would have been funny. Willie grabbed his hand and gave him a look. Cocco was not catholic; he just loved the dramatics of it all. However, Cat did make an attempt to laugh as they all did, anything to lighten the moment.

Five minutes later a doctor approached them. "Ms. Craig?"

Cat stood up, and her legs gave way. Aroha and Cocco each held an arm. Max moved to her side and said quietly, "It's okay; we can do this."

"So far, Ms. Gray is stable." Everyone gave a sigh of relief.

"But we are not out of the woods yet. She has sustained a heavy blow to her head, and we think whiplash to her neck, and a possible spinal injury. At the moment there is swelling in her spinal cord and her brain. We won't know what damage there is until the swelling subsides. Meantime, we are taking X rays, which will tell us if anything is broken. We won't do an MRI scan unless it's necessary, but we are doing a CT scan. We can't do a neurological exam, as Ms. Gray has not recovered consciousness yet. There are other tests we can do after we get the results from the X rays and CT scan. When the swelling reduces, it is possible the patient will have nothing more than a bad headache and a sore neck and back. Ms. Craig, I always find that telling relatives the worst they can expect to happen usually means that when they get the final results they are relieved. As soon as I have the results, I will tell you, and we can discuss options." Cat was stunned and speechless.

It was Max who spoke, "I shall stay with my niece."

"Thank you, Doctor Lawson; I'll be back as soon as we have the results."

"Willie," said Max, "why don't you get us all some coffee? I'm sure we could all use it."

"Sure," said Willie.

"And I'll help you," said Lizzie.

They left in search of coffee and were grateful to have a few moments to take it all in. "She's gotta be okay, Willie, she just has to be."

"This is the longest day of my life, and it's not over yet," said Willie.

"Cat looks ten years older. How can someone age ten years in a day?"

"When it looks as if you're going to lose your life partner."

"Maybe I will, too, if Aroha doesn't forgive me."

"You're still going to tell her then."

"I have to, Willie, or it will just hang over me for the rest of my life. I'll be forever wondering if she knows. Anyway, I can't think of that at the moment; we're here for Cat and Theo, not me."

"When did you eat last, Cat?" asked Max.

Realizing that Max was speaking to her, "Um, breakfast, I suppose, but please, Aunty Max, don't make me eat anything. I couldn't."

"Okay, honey, but you must keep drinking water. It's so hot in here, and we can't have you dehydrating." Max was a little stunned; it had been many years since Cat had called her 'Aunty,' which probably meant that she was happy for her to take control. Not that she wanted to, given the feeling in the pit of her stomach; but if she went into professional mode, she probably could. Well, at least till she was on her own. She wished that the hospital surroundings did not remind her so much of Callum's death. *Come on, Max, Theo is not going to die. She's far too young and healthy.* "Aroha, would you go find some water, please?"

"Sure."

Cocco was still sitting beside Cat, stroking her arm and gently humming a sweet melody that Cat had often heard him hum before. She imagined it was Japanese but didn't ask. She felt really numb. Looking around the room as if something or someone was missing, she turned to Max. "I've left a message on Frenchy's machine. I don't know what time she gets home today."

Willie and Lizzie arrived with the coffee, and there they all sat, waiting.

It was 2:00 A.M. before the doctor appeared. "Ms. Craig."

"Cat, please."

"Cat, there is some good news. The spinal injury may be just temporary paralysis. There is no sign of damage to the spine, so we are fairly confident that when the swelling goes down Theo will be able to walk, although that will take a little time. As for her head injury, we'll know more in the morning."

"Can I see her?"

"Certainly. They're taking her to ICU. The nurse will come for you when they have her ready. Just two at a time."

"Thank you, doctor," said Max. "We appreciate your candour." It was nearly an hour before a nurse came for Cat. "I'll go with you, honey. I'll be able to explain all the equipment."

Cat walked into the unit where Theo was. There were three other patients, two nurses, and a doctor in the room. *Theo, was it really Theo?* Her face was calm but her brow was bandaged. "The monitor," Max said, "shows her heart-rate, breathing, blood, and intracranial pressures, and cerebral blood flow. The wires are for an EKG, and a catheter allows nutrients and medicine to go into the veins. There's a urinary catheter, also, as they don't know how long she'll be unconscious."

"The ventilator, Max. Can't she breathe on her own?"

"It'll only be precautionary; it will be removed the moment she wakes up. Don't be frightened by all this, Cat, they're just covering all eventualities."

Tears welled up in Cat's eyes. Max took her firmly by the shoulders, "Not in here, Cat. Theo needs to hear positives, not negatives. Just sit down, and talk to her. They say that unconscious people can often hear you, they just can't speak."

"What will I say?"

"Oh, sweetheart, say just what's in your heart. I'll start. I'll tell her what Ozzie found on the beach today. That will make her laugh."

They each took turns at sitting with her, and at 6:00 A.M. in the morning, Frenchy arrived. As usual, all heads turned as she walked down the passage. Even after driving all night and lack of sleep, she still looked breathtaking.

"Where is she? How is she? Is she going to be all right? Can I see her?"

"Wow, slow down, girlfriend." Willie was on his feet. None of them had ever seen Frenchy so out of control. They all knew why. It had always been obvious that Frenchy was in love with Theo. Only Frenchy didn't know that everyone else knew.

"Okay, you can start breathing again. I'll fill you in, and then you can see her."

At 7:00 A.M., Max had finally talked Cat into going to the motel, having a shower, and getting a little sleep. Willie and Lizzie had already gone to the motel in Napier to get Theo and Cat's stuff and had taken it to the motel they now had in Hastings. "Frenchy and Willie are going to take the first watch, then Lizzie and Aroha. Cocco and I will stay with you. If there is any change at all, they will call right away." A broken and exhausted Cat finally agreed. "Just an hour or two. You promise you will call straight away."

Ellis Paris Ramsay

Chapter 6

Frenchy was sitting in a chair next to Theo's bed. She was absolutely gutted and way past exhausted. At least driving through the night had meant the roads were light on traffic. She knew she had driven far too fast, and it would not have helped if she had ended up in an accident herself. Not that she would have minded, a life without Theo in it was not one she cared to live. After she got off the phone with Cat she quickly had a shower, berating herself for not checking her mail first. Plus, she could not have gone near Theo smelling of another woman. It might have been the quickest shower she'd ever had and certainly she was not totally dry when she dressed. She took a light sweatshirt from the drawer, black slacks, and her toilet bag from her unpacked suitcase. Running towards the door, she backtracked and grabbed a black T-shirt. Hospitals and Napier/Hastings in the Hawkes Bay are renowned for being hot places. She was probably out of the door ten minutes after listening to Cat's message, stopping only for petrol and black coffee. She bought two as she did not want to stop again, and she figured a second cup might be necessary, regardless of it being hot or cold.

The person in the bed didn't look like Theo. She had been ventilated, her face was puffy, and the bandage around her head showed signs of blood. They would not know if there was any damage to the spine until the swelling went down. Frenchy wanted to scream and shout; she was so angry, but instead she was almost having an out-of-body experience, as if she were sitting in a cinema watching a Film Noir. Willie would be back in a moment with coffee; he had just popped out for a cigarette. *Stay with it, girl; you can't freak out.* But her mind was wandering back to the first time she had ever set eyes on Theo.

It was in Princess Street Gardens in Edinburgh on a beautiful summer day. While she was 'people-watching' with her camera in her hands, Theo walked past her lens. She almost dropped the camera. She had honey-gold coloured hair that waved just like the Mona Lisa and startling blue eyes. She wore a sky blue V-necked blouse with a pair of stone-coloured denims. On her back she carried a small day backpack and hanging off one of the zips was a small Kiwi on a key ring. Just then the one o'clock gun went off, and Theo just about jumped out of her skin and hit the deck. Frenchy burst out laughing very loudly, and when Theo lifted her head, she looked in the direction of Frenchy.

"Ha, bloody ha," said Theo. "What the hell was that?"

As she approached Frenchy, Frenchy was again stunned by this woman's beauty. "It was the one o'clock gun. It's fired every day from the castle to let workers and visitors know the exact time if they want to check their watches."

"They might warn people."

"Well, it's a well-known fact, unless you're a visitor who hasn't done her homework. Then we know who you are."

"I suppose that's this Scottish humour and sarcasm that I have been hearing so much about," Theo said, with her hands on her hips.

Frenchy had never felt as alive as she had at that moment and was trying to think of a way to keep this woman talking.

"The answer is yes, but the other half of me is French, just as rude, but I'll fling in coffee and be your tour guide if you like."

"You're on." Putting her hand forwards, Theo introduced herself. "Theo Gray from Wellington, New Zealand."

"Frances Remy, born in Paris, educated in Edinburgh, live between them both."

"Lucky you."

"Probably, but it does leave me with a feeling of not belonging anywhere in particular. I'm told all young New Zealanders who travel abroad do so on the smell of an oily rag. If it wouldn't offend you, I'd like to buy you lunch."

Theo tucked her hair behind her left ear, looked Frances up and down and in her best American accent that she could muster said, "Why, I've always been accustomed to the kindness of strangers."

Frances smiled, "Great. I know a place in George Street where the food is pretty good."

"Lead on, maestro, I'm all yours."

They chatted on endlessly as Frances led the way to the café, swapping stories about their lives. Theo told her, she was travelling with two friends who she had left in London. Theo wanted to come up to Scotland, and they wanted to go and sun themselves on a beach in Spain for two weeks. She thought she could go to the beach as often as she liked in New Zealand but probably not get to Scotland when she wanted to. "So I hopped on the train, and here I am. Couldn't return to New Zealand without seeing 'Bonnie Scotland,' now could I?"

After a very long lunch, Frances took Theo sightseeing.
"The castle, I think, to start with, then down the Royal Mile." As they walked up the rampart, Frances pointed out that this was where they held the Tattoo every year.
"Oh, I've seen that on the TV. Wow, here?"
Frances was enjoying being a tour guide and loved how Theo responded to everything. "Gosh, I hope you're not going to stiff me with a bill for being such an informative guide."
"No, but it might take me a few days or weeks to do justice to this city and Scotland, that is, if you'll allow me to do so. I have a car."
Theo stopped in her tracks and looked at this woman for a moment. "Maybe we could discuss the terms over dinner, we'll go dutch."
Frances was happy and did her best to point out things that she thought Theo would find interesting in the castle. "No one has been able to date the castle, or say when it was built, by whom, or why on top of volcanic rock. Nor do they know when it was first used as a settlement, but it was long before the Romans sailed up the Forth and landed at Crammond."

She took Theo into the tiny Norman chapel of Saint Margaret's, which is the oldest building in the castle, dating back nine hundred years. "Members of the castle garrison still have the right to be married here, and I've even heard that anyone with enough money can hire it for a wedding."
"You're kidding me," said Theo. The look on her face was incredulous.
"No really," said Frances. "I kid you not."

She took Theo to the witches well, "If you were found to be guilty of witchcraft this is where you would be put to death at the stake."

Shivering, Theo replied, "And who exactly decided that?" She shook the thought out of her head that there really was no answer to.

They walked down the castle rampart to the top of the Royal Mile, which was also named High Street, and entered the Camera Obscurer. Theo thought the view from the castle was spectacular, but this was something else completely. You could almost see any part of Edinburgh you wanted to by looking in this oval, arched, glass table and moving it around.

Walking down the Royal Mile to Holyrood Palace, they passed all the ancient houses—most about five stories high—and Frances explained why Edinburgh was nicknamed "Auld Reekie." "Edinburgh was the first city in the world to have high storied buildings. In fact, it was the first international city in the world, if you like, and was known to have many secret passages in and out of the city. This was most useful for fugitives and in particular fleeing French aristocracy who were escaping the guillotine. They moved into the fourth and fifth stories of these buildings while everyone else filled the second and third. Animals and the very poor mostly lived on the ground floor. They had no sanitation, and that's why the aristocracy preferred to be higher up. No one ever walked down the streets near the sides of these buildings; instead one walked in the middle of the street as all effluence was flung out of the windows with the shout, 'Regardy Loo!'"

"No shit!"

"Oh, plenty of that, me thinks."

"Yuck!!"

There was so much to see in the High Street that they were both pretty tired when they got to the bottom at Holyrood Palace. They decided to make this the last stop of the day. One painting in particular blew Theo away; it was painted by an unknown artist during the fifteenth century and was of an unknown woman who was the spitting image of Princess Anne.

"Things must have been pretty incestuous back then, huh?"

"Well, the Royals didn't have that big a pool to draw from; she's probably an illegitimate daughter."

"Here's some coffee," Willie said, as he handed a cup to Frenchy. "Has she moved or anything?"

Frenchy, shaking her head out of her reverie, "No, nothing. Willie, what if she doesn't wake up?"

"Now, come on, girl, it's highly likely she'll be fine. We can't write her off yet. She's a fighter."

"I know, Willie, but it's such a shock." Tears welled up in Frenchy's eyes.

"You need to sleep. Lizzie and Aroha will be here as soon as they get something to eat. Then you and I should do the same. I wonder if Max and Cocco have been able to get Cat to sleep." Frenchy closed her eyes, and her thoughts returned to Theo in Edinburgh.

Frances had taken Theo to a pub in Rose Street for dinner.
"At least the Scots have their lager cold, not like the English.
So would we split the cost of the petrol?"
"If you like."
"Accommodation?"
"B&B's, I think."
"This is so weird, Frances. I feel as if I've known you forever."
Frances turned to Theo, taking a few seconds to reply. How weird would it be if I told her I loved her? *"Me, too. We must have known each other in another life."*
"That will be it."

After spending two more days in the city, they took off for the highlands. Frances had travelled there many times before, but this felt different. She loved seeing it through Theo's eyes. The Isle of Skye, from the Kyle of Lochalsh, Orkney, and Shetland Islands, Oban, Inverness, and driving along the side of Loch Ness was breathtaking. They even went to a Celidh. The time went far too quickly. When they got back to Edinburgh, Frances had arranged for them to take the tour through the old Edinburgh of Rabbie Burns days, where the streets of cobblestones and ancient street lamps remained hidden underneath the new town and could only be accessed through tunnels with permission. It was a wonderful way to spend her last day in this magnificent city. Frances had insisted Theo stay with her at her mother's flat and not return to the backpackers. She gave Theo her bed and slept on the sofa in the lounge. Not that she slept. Theo was leaving to return to New Zealand the week after. She wished that she had met Theo before, at the beginning of her trip, not the end. She remembered how Theo looked when she got out of the water after they went swimming in the Loch. The water streamed down her body, and her costume hugged her tightly around her beautiful figure. She moaned as she thought of what it would be like to touch her, and those lips, what she wouldn't give to kiss those full lips. She touched herself, making up for all the nights lying beside Theo in the B&B's when they shared a double bed because there were no twins. How she wanted to touch her, how she ached and thought she would die if she didn't. Then, worst of all, she was leaving the next day. They had never discussed their sexuality, and Frances was too scared to say anything in case Theo ran a mile. Two weeks with this goddess was better than none.

That morning came all too soon, and then there they were down at Waverly Station, standing on the platform not knowing what to say, wasting the last few precious moments. Frances, with her head bowed, and not wanting to sound too needy said, "You will keep in t..." She was shocked as she realized that she had lost control. She was fighting with herself when she felt Theo lift her face. She took it in her hands, making Frances make eye contact, and kissed her full on the lips, probing with her tongue in a kiss that lasted a full two minutes. She remembered losing her balance when Theo removed her lips. Theo looked her straight in the eye and said, "Well, there was a waste of two weeks if ever I saw one!" With that, she spun around, walked down the aisle, and boarded the train without looking back. With a wave over her shoulder like Sally Bowles in Cabaret, *Theo was gone.*

"Frenchy, are you okay?"

Frenchy jumped physically. "Yes, I am, but Theo isn't."

Just then, Lizzie and Aroha arrived. "Any change?"

"No," said Willie, and the girls followed his eyes to Frenchy who was sitting distraught in her chair.

"Come on, Frenchy, let's get you something to eat and off to bed."

Frenchy looked up alarmed, "I can't go."

"You have to, sweetie; you're no use to anyone like this."

Aroha put her hand on Frenchy's shoulder. "Off you go. I'll call if there is any change at all. I bet you haven't had any sleep since you left the U.K. When was that, two, three days ago?" Paralysed to the spot, Frenchy answered, "Yeah, something like that."

"Go, we'll call."

Ellis Paris Ramsay

Chapter 7

Aroha and Lizzie were sitting either side of Theo's bed. It was 10 A.M. The nurses monitored Theo all the time, and the doctors checked at least every thirty minutes. Theo had occasionally moaned and twitched, but she was still unconscious.

"I don't know what I'd do if it were you lying there, Aroha," Lizzie said, looking at her partner with great affection.

"Really," replied Aroha.

Lizzie was stunned by Aroha's indifference. "Yes, of course. What on earth would make you think other?"

Aroha shrugged, "Nothing." She rubbed her eyes, "I'm just tired, Lizzie. As we all are."

Lizzie was still reeling from Aroha's out of character retort. "You sure there's nothing else, honey? You're not sick, are you?"

Finally, looking Lizzie in the face, "No, I'm fine. Just a little ragged."

Aroha looked at her hands. *This is not the time. That's my best friend lying there on her deathbed, and all I can think about is myself. How selfish is that?* "Max says we should be talking to Theo, that she might be able to hear us. Why don't you tell her how the show is going? You know how much she loves musicals."

Lizzie seemed pleased to finally have a purpose and talking about her show was something she never tired of. "Oh, Theo, just wait till you hear Jemma sing. She'll make you cry. How a sixteen-year-old girl can have such a mature voice is beyond me. The wardrobe team has had such fun with the munchkin costumes, and the first years are really enjoying playing them. They all have stripes going across and no heels on their shoes, whereas everyone else has diagonal stripes and heeled shoes. You know that idiot Kyle I'm always telling you about? The one who always acts up in class and never does his homework? Well, he's playing the Wizard of Oz himself, and he is

51

absolutely brilliant. And that little witch, Torri Jacobs, is playing the Wicked Witch of the West. Talk about a match made in heaven or hell, depending on your beliefs. Oh, and you'll never guess. You know how I was having trouble casting the good witch, Linda, 'cause no one wanted to play such a sugary sweet person? If that's not a sign of the times, then I don't know what is, anyway, the ditsy/hippie art teacher wants the role. The kids think it's hysterical, and she's just over the moon. Go figure, huh?" Lizzie talked on for ages while Aroha just sat and wondered what it would be like not to have this woman in her life. *Will I ever be able to trust her again? Have there been other women?*

"Theo, you have to get better fast," said Lizzie. "You can't miss the show. You have three weeks till opening..."

"Lizzie," said Aroha, "we have to talk."

Lizzie practically spun on the spot and had this really sick feeling in her gut. Frozen to her chair, she looked at Aroha who was pale.

As if saved by the bell, Cat walked in with Cocco. Lizzie didn't know whether she was pleased to see her or not.

"Any change?"

"No," answered Aroha. "There has been a little groaning and twitching, but the nurse says that's quite usual."

Cat, who still looked like death warmed up, said, "Okay. Max has gone off to find a doctor and ask what the possibility is of having her moved to Wellington. Why don't you two go get some rest? I'll be in touch as soon as there is anything."

Cat and Aroha embraced and held on tight, both taking comfort in each other's warmth and friendship.

When Aroha and Lizzie emerged from the hospital the sun was shining. Aroha was struck by the knowledge that no matter how beautiful this day was, it was winter in her heart, and she couldn't go on another minute without facing her fears.

"Let's get some coffee and something to eat and take it to the park. As I said, we need to talk." She half-heartedly smiled at Lizzie who looked frightened. Fifteen minutes later, they were sitting on a rug that Lizzie kept in the boot. Neither of them had said a word, which indicated to them both that they knew what it was about else Lizzie would have been asking two thousand questions by now. It was cold comfort to Aroha that they often knew exactly what each other was thinking. They finished each other's sentences sometimes and didn't even have to speak because they were so in sync. *So how could this have happened?* "Lizzie, please don't even consider lying to me." She turned and looked her straight in the face. "This is something I never thought would happen to us."

"Oh, Aroha, I'm so, so, sorry. It's all such a dreadful mistake. I never meant for it to happen."

"But it did happen, Lizzie. How long has it been going on? Who is this Jojo? And why have you let her into our lives? What is it that she gives you that you can't get at home?" Tears were running down Lizzie's face. She felt as if her life was running downhill at jet speed, and she had no brakes. How on earth was she going to explain this when she couldn't explain it to herself?

Aroha took her silence to mean that she had no defence. "I thought we had a future; I thought all the game playing was over. That we had a life that was full and had meaning."

"We do. It is. We have. Oh, Aroha, darling," Lizzie said, reaching out to take her hand.

Aroha immediately flinched and withdrew her hand. "Don't. Oh, god, what am I going to tell Danny?" This time it was Aroha who was crying. "He loves you, Lizzie, this will break his heart".

"Darling."

"Don't call me that! This is not something you can cajole me over."

"Look, Aroha, this is a mistake."

"You're damn right this is a mistake," Aroha's voice was now bitter. "And one that is probably going to change all of our lives." Lizzie was stunned. There was so much to say, so much to tell her. If she could just describe how it all happened, surely she would realize that nothing was planned, and nothing was meant to happen. She was just tired, drank too much too quickly, and if anything, was just naïve.

"Look, Aroha, I was going to tell you, ask Willie if you d…"

"You told Willie? You told Willie, but not me?"

"Honey."

"Don't."

"Aroha, please. I was only going to wait till the weekend when Danny was with Matt."

"I can't believe you told Willie. That means Cocco will know, too."

"No, I never."

"Don't be bloody stupid; of course, Cocco will know. Willie will have told him. THEY tell each other everything. Look, it's what two people who respect and care for each other do."

Aroha stood up and started to walk away. "I need to walk; I'll meet you back at the hospital."

"Aroha, please."

"Not now, Lizzie. Not…," she was unable to finish the sentence.

Lizzie had never fainted in her life, but every nerve in her body was buzzing. *Oh, my god, oh, my god, what is happening? Theo is lying in hospital dying, for all we know, and someone just changed the channel on my life without my permission. I want to turn the clock back. This can't be happening. My life is spinning out of control; this can't be the end. I have to fix it.*

Chapter 8

Cocco was holding Theo's hand. She had been moaning and twitching a lot more. Max and Cat had gone to speak to the doctor.

"Theo, I must speak to you while I have this moment alone with you, and you must listen very closely, wherever you are. I am going to tell reasons why you have to get well and soon." His voice was very sincere, and it was obvious to anyone watching how much he cared for this woman. "Theo, you are rock which our family built on. You are foundation. You keep all together and care for each of us. How CC put up with it, I don't know. If my Willie gave as much of himself to others I would not be happy, and he would know it."

Normally, Cocco would have smiled as he said that, but he was deadly serious. "You never forget birthdays or anniversaries. You bring flowers; you bake. It's you who organizes our dinner parties, picnics, our theatre trips, and our weekends away. And when we go away anywhere without you, you water plants, pick up mail, and even organize CC to cut lawn. If we pop in to visit without calling you always drop everything and tend to us. My Willie say you make best coffee. Theo, to CC you the sun that shines, and the air she breathes. You are mentor to Aroha, who shines light and shows way in a life, she never had that before. To Lizzie, girl, you voice of reason and purity. When you two girls sing together it like listening to angels. And to my Willie, you comrade, ah! He know you always stand by side, you there for him, and you talk about work things I don't understand. He need that. Maxine need you, too, as you have heart of most precious thing in her life, CC. This, you know, but maybe you don't know why I need you."

Cocco took a deep breath and stared at the bed cover as if he had found something there that didn't belong, as if he were searching for a reason. Then he spoke, finally putting voice to the words that had never been said before. "Theo, I not had happy life. But that okay 'cause my Willie worth all bad things I go through. My father very wealthy man, very powerful from very old family in Japan. He marry my mother 'cause she come from good family, too. My mother never work, she marry man her parents tell her to. She only eighteen and very beautiful. My father older, and he like to show her off, gave him great position 'cause she from good family. She scared of my father. She like butterfly, very fragile. She had three children, I youngest. First born my brother, Lyndon, he named after American President. My father very impressed with American powerful men. Lyndon like my father, very serious, and he go into my father's business. He powerful man, too. My sister, Yoko, is married and give father grandsons. He very happy, just what daughters should do.

"I was born much later, my sister ten years older, my brother twelve. My mother allowed to choose my name, and my mother allowed to bring me up any way she want. My father have his son and his grandchildren, he no care about me, he no need me. Theo, I love my mother very much; she so beautiful, and I may never see her again." Cocco was very close to tears and took a moment.

"My mother not let me out her sight, we do everything together. I was first thing she allowed to have all to self. That why I have such good taste in clothes. I got to be with ladies. She taught me to do Sado tea ceremony; and all the women would talk about their men, and how to look after them. I could have been Geisha, I tried on all ceremonial gowns and kimonos, I love it, and I love being with my mother. I hardly saw my father, and my mother was only required for official functions. It wasn't until I thirteen and he wanted to see school reports that he notice me, and then he shocked. I had good marks, but no mention of sports or activities he thought I should be doing. He didn't like mention of things I really good at like dancing, cooking, sewing. He thought I too feminine, and he blame my mother. So he sent me away to schools, away from my mother. Schools he thought had manly curriculum like fencing, football, and polo.

"Theo, it broke my mother's heart, and I very unhappy. I cry every night. I want to go home to my mother, so I get into trouble at school, so they send me home. This make father very angry. He say I embarrassment to him, and he banned mother from seeing me, and send me away to another school. This time I got caught giving blow job to boy in school, and my father was so angry; I thought he gonna kill me. When I was eighteen, he decided to send me to college in other country. I had no choice. He wanted me out of Japan and out of his life. My mother so sad, Theo, she beg him not to, but she had no say; even Lyndon, who no like me, say he thought it for best.

"So I come to New Zealand and go Palmerston North. Very strange place after Tokyo. So small, and not many people, but after while I think not so bad. I miss my mother, and when I try to call, I told she not home, or she not available. My father see to that. So I have to wait till my mother visit sister, and she call me then, or I call her. At end of my first year, I receive money from my father, telling me to travel for holiday. He already give me weekly allowance, more than I need, so I no really need money, but he send lots. So I go rent house as I no like living at college. I fill house with lots of lovely things, buy clothes and lots of flowers, and take class on cooking. I even pay rent, year in advance. Landlord very happy, say he no have tenant as good as me I keep house tidy and very quiet.

"My father have business trip in Australia next year and come see me. I was very surprised, as he no like me, but he had plan. He went to IPC and spoke with master then took me out to lunch. He get out package and lay it on table. He say he has paid for another year at college and has put enough funds into bank account to last me two years. Then he push package towards me and say, 'this is yours. You will never return to Japan again and never speak with your mother. You know I am man of my word. If you return or try to contact your mother, your life will be over.' I so scared, as I know my father has connections. You do not get to be powerful man without them. He mean I be dead. He say he never wants to see me again, and if I need help gaining citizenship to this country or any other contact his P.A. He will be instructed to help. He stood up and said that is all the money I receive, and there be no inheritance. Then he left me sitting in restaurant.

"When I got home, I counted money. It was $NZ800,000. I never seen so much money, I just stare. Then I got really sad, 'cause for first time, I realize I never see my beautiful mother again. I know she be sad, too, as father probably never told her what he do. Next day I go to bank and never touch money. I put it investment scheme. Not that I want to make more money, I just don't want to see it every time I get balance. I don't know whether to tell my mother or not. I no want to make things more difficult for her.

"Then I met my Willie, and for first time, I happy since I was taken from my mother. My mother always knew I was gay, she never minded. She just say I have good heart and beautiful soul. You would like my mother, Theo, and I know she like you. I sometimes think I sneak into Japan and meet my mother somewhere, but Willie say if my father that powerful, he know I back in country. I would have to get passport under false name. I have money to do that, but Willie say too dangerous. My father probably would not let my mother go anywhere on her own anyway. So I just have to settle for stolen conversations with my mother when I can. I tell my mother about Willie and my friends, and she so happy for me. She say I have more good friends than she was ever allowed in her whole life. I finally realize that I lucky one. I got away from father. My mother never can."

There was a tear running down Cocco's face. "You, Theo, have shown me true friendship, without prejudice or condition. I love Willie, that's no secret. CC, Aroha, and Lizzie could not be dearer to me than they are. I love them like I should have loved my sister. But you, Theo, always make sure I'm comfortable and are sensitive my culture and know when I don't understand any inferences to local sayings and jokes. You are what a friend should be, always there for each other. Someone should write a book on friendship and use you as model. This is why you have to wake up and get well. We need you, I need you, and most of all, your beloved needs you. You need you. So if there is a bright light beckoning the way, you say 'no, no, I go home, I needed!'"

Max and Cat returned not looking very happy. Cocco sat silently and waited. They were having trouble saying whatever they had to say. Cat walked over to the bed and leant over and kissed Theo gently on the lips and sat beside her with her head resting on the bed. Cocco looked over to Max.

"The doctors…" Max was having trouble speaking. She coughed. "The doctors say that they thought Theo would have awoken by now. They are concerned about a blood clot. They are going to monitor more closely tonight and run a few more tests. If there is no improvement by tomorrow, she will be flown to Wellington in the rescue helicopter. There she will be operated on. They might have to drill holes to relieve the pressure."

Cocco was stunned; he had not expected this. He wanted desperately to say something to CC, but what? He had the feeling that their lives were never going to be the same again. He wondered what he had done in his life to deserve all this bad Karma. Max looked awfully tired. He got to his feet and made her sit. He wished he could make tea for them and have something useful to do; it would make him feel better.

Ellis Paris Ramsay

Chapter 9

Aroha had walked for well over an hour. She had not returned to the hospital but had instead found herself back at the motel. Her face showed her distress, and she did not want Cat to see that. *Thank the goddess for cell phones.* At least she could be contacted in an instant if there was any change. Willie was sitting reading at the table. He was just about to say something to her, as she rushed past him with her head bowed.

"I just have to go to the loo, won't be a moment."

Inside the bathroom, she held the basin with both hands after she had turned the cold tap on full. She knew she was going to cry but was unprepared for the howl that came from her very soul. She was practically choking on the tears, and she could no longer breathe through her nose. She felt bile in her stomach and was glad the loo was next to the basin. She threw up. When she was finished, she sat on the cool tiles for a few minutes. Getting to her feet, she caught a glimpse of herself in the mirror and was horrified. Who was this person? Gone was her usual smile and sparkling eyes, which had always been her best feature. Instead, this gaunt face looked back at her. *What am I doing? Whatever might happen to Lizzie and me is not here. This is not the time to examine our relationship or reflect on past relationships. She is not Matt; she is my best friend and to the best of my knowledge has never done anything willingly to hurt me. I am a grown woman, and right now Cat and Theo need me to be strong for them. Lizzie and I will sort this out when I get home.*

Ten minutes later, after having a shower, she returned to the lounge where Willie was sitting with a freshly poured cup of coffee. "I've popped a little brandy in it; you looked as if you could do with it." They had managed to get a family unit for the four of them. Lizzie and she had one room, and Willie and Cocco had the other. There was a pull-down sofa in the lounge that Frenchy could use. Cat and Max had a room next door, but right now Frenchy was sprawled across the queen-size bed in her room. She was lying on her front on top of the sheet as if she were climbing a mountain. She had on a pair of jockey knickers and matching top in a soft grey colour, which only just covered her breasts. Her hair curled in wisps around her neck, and she was dead to the world. "God, even sound asleep, isn't she the most beautiful woman you have ever seen?" Willie laughed gently, "Yes, and she's the most beautiful man I've ever seen, too, but don't tell Cocco."

Aroha smiled. "Well, there's no need for any of us to be jealous; we all know she's in love with Theo and how desperately unhappy she is. I wonder how Cat and Theo cope with that."

"Aroha, do you mind if we talk?"

"Its okay, Willie, I'm all right now."

"Even so, I could do with a chat."

Aroha sat down, gratefully sipping at her coffee.

Unsure of what Willie was going to say, "We shouldn't be too long. I want to get back and see Theo."

Willie took a deep breath. "I know it's none of my business, but I can see from your face that you know what happened to Lizzie at school."

"At school? I didn't realize it was at school. Was it a student?"

"No, no, don't be silly. Obviously, my dear and stupid friend hasn't been able to tell you, probably because she is still in shock. I don't think she's come to terms with it herself." Willie spent the next ten minutes telling Aroha what happened, and in an attempt to cheer her up, he even related some of what Cocco had told Lizzie.

"Aroha, no two relationships are the same, and no two people love the same. Cocco's love for me is almost an obsession, and I think Lizzie's love for you is the same." He turned to the coffee cup in his hand, as if searching for the right words. "I love Cocco and am happy to be with him. But sometimes his love frightens me, and I feel a great responsibility by it. He doesn't want anything or anyone else in his life bar our friends and me. That seems to be part of the package deal. If I ever left Cocco, I don't mean to be dramatic, but I think he would kill himself. He had the most dreadful upbringing akin to something out of a Dickensian novel. He can never return to Japan, and he has no one else in his life. Now I'm not saying that I'm going to leave him or want to, it's just that I feel I'll never have the choice."

Aroha was sitting silently listening to everything Willie said. *This is a side of Willie I've never seen.* It wasn't that they weren't close; it's just that Lizzie was closer to Willie as she was to Theo.

"What do you mean he can never return to Japan?"

Willie told Aroha a little of Cocco's story.

"$800,000. You're shitting me!"

"No, really. So that's how much his life was worth to his father."

"Fuck, I could never put a price on Danny's life."

"Yes, but you love Danny. The only person in the world who loved Cocco before he came here was his mother. And she was more or less taken from him at age thirteen."

"Do you think his father would have him killed?"

"Yes, I do. Anyway, what I wanted to say, Aroha; is that Lizzie would never have an affair and would never do anything to hurt you or Danny. You're all she ever talks about. She drives me mad sometimes." Willie smiled coyly, as if he had a secret. "Besides, Cocco and I want to be parents."

Aroha gasped in astonishment, and laughing, she said, "She told you, didn't she? Shit, is there anything she doesn't tell you?"

They were both laughing as Lizzie walked through the door.

Relief was written all over Lizzie's face, "Oh, good, you're here. I went to the hospital, and Max and Cat hadn't seen you."

Lizzie's eyes never left Aroha. "Are you okay?"

Lizzie had the mark of someone who had been doing a lot of crying herself. Willie went in to his bedroom.

"Yeah, I'm okay. Willie has been talking to me."

"What about us, Aroha?"

"We are here for Cat and Theo; we can wait till we get home."

"It's not great news from the hospital."

"What?" asked Aroha, bolting upright in her chair.

Willie came out of his room, "What's the news?"

"They thought Theo would have been awake by now. They think there is a blood clot. They are going to do more tests, and if there is no improvement by the morning, she'll be flown to Wellington hospital tomorrow."

"How's Cat?"

"She's a mess. The doctors say they want nobody there between six and eight tonight. Max will bring her back here and asked if we could have a meal ready, nothing too heavy, so we can discuss what happens next."

"Willie and I will go to the supermarket and get a rotisserie chicken and some bread and salads. You stay here for Frenchy when she wakes up."

"Where is she?"

"Out cold on our bed."

'Our bed,' she said 'our bed.' She's still thinking of us as a couple. That's gotta be good. "Sure, I'll round up plates and set the table."

At 5:15 P.M., Max and Cat returned to the motel. Cat looked dreadful. Frenchy finally woke up and could not believe how long she had been asleep. She had wanted to go to the hospital immediately, but Lizzie talked her out of it.

"Wait till you speak with Max and Cat. They'll be here soon." Lizzie made Frenchy tell her all about her trip home and her assignment in the hope of distracting her, but it wasn't really working for either of them.

Dinner was a very quiet affair; no one really wanted to talk. Everyone was walking on eggshells around Cat. Max was doing her best to get her to eat something and not really winning. Although they were in one of the best wine producing areas in New Zealand, everyone preferred to drink brandy.

"Okay," said Max. "Frances, you go back with Cat at eight. I'll go with you but return here as soon as the doctor has given us the news. Willie and Aroha will go in later. Lizzie, you had better rest since you'll be driving tomorrow. Cat will fly in the helicopter with Theo. If you guys leave at ten tomorrow morning that should have you back in Wellington about two, two-thirty. Frances and I will stay with Cat until the helicopter leaves at noon, then we will follow, and I will stop at home to change and see to Ozzie. He'll be quite happy with Ted, but I better just stick my head in." She was about to continue when someone caught her attention at the door.

"Excuse me, Ma'am. I'm Detective Brown, and this is Detective Jamieson. We are looking for Ms. Caitlin Craig."

Cat stood up and turned around. "Yes."

"Ms. Craig, I wonder if we could have a word in private."

"This is my aunt, and these are my closest friends, I don't need privacy. Please sit down." The two detectives sat on the edge of the sofa.

"Ms. Craig, we have had some interesting developments in Ms. Gray's case. The man who drove into the car, a Mr. Kevin Johnston, refused to be breathalysed at the scene of the crime. It was pointed out to Mr. Johnston that he would have to accompany the police officer to the station where he would have a blood test taken. If he refused to do so, he would be arrested on suspicion of driving a vehicle whilst intoxicated and causing grievous bodily harm. Mr. Johnston did finally agree to accompany the officer to the station. Afterwards, he was released pending the blood test results. We had his name, driver's licence number, and his address. The blood test was sent off to the lab. This is all just procedure. This afternoon we had a visit from a Mr. Johnston of the same address who had been away in New Plymouth for the weekend. He stated his car had been stolen from his home in Napier, and it turns out that he keeps his driver's licence in the car."

Everyone at the table sat in disbelief.

"The constable taking the stolen property report had been the officer who attended the accident and informed the CID immediately. It turns out that he was, indeed, the correct Mr. Johnston, and the man driving the car involved in Ms. Gray's accident was not. He was probably the man who stole the car and licence."

"Detective," said Max, "surely the photo on the licence would have told you he was not Mr. Johnston."

"It appears that he bore a striking resemblance, plus he had a light beard that he said he had grown since the photo was taken." Both the detectives were looking a little sheepish at this point. "The young woman who was in the car with the driver also gave a false name and address. Proof of her identity was not required as she was the passenger."

The detectives moved awkwardly in their seats. "We were able to get the blood results back from toxicology early, and there was surprising news."

Everyone was sitting rigid, wondering what was coming next.

"It appears that the driver of the car was not intoxicated. There was no sign of alcohol in his body at all. Ms. Craig, did Ms. Gray have any enemies?"

"Dear God," said Max, "what are you saying?"

"We have had the scene inspected by experts; and given the angle and positioning of the cars on the road, the impact, and the fact the driver was not intoxicated, we believe this might not have been an accident."

Cat was mortified. "You mean you think someone was trying to kill Theo? Why?"

"We were hoping you might be able to shed some light on this."

"Oh, my god," said Aroha. "Oh, my god." Everyone turned to look her way.

Aroha was trying to form her thoughts. "I'm Aroha Kiriana. I work with Theo. She had been working on a fairly nasty case. We work at CYFS in Wellington. I can't give you details without a warrant, but I can tell you it involves violence and sexual abuse, and Theo had to remove a child from his home for his own safety. He was only seven. The father threatened her, but that's not unusual in these cases. There was a police officer with her at the time."

"And you think this could be the man?"

"I don't know".

"Could you describe him?"

"No, I wasn't with her."

"When are you returning to Wellington, Ms. Kiriana?"

"Tomorrow. We all are. Theo is being flown to Wellington. Her condition is critical."

"We will hand this over to the Wellington CID, and I'm sure they will be in touch tomorrow. Perhaps the officer in Wellington who accompanied Ms. Gray will be able to identify the driver."

The detectives rose to leave. "We are sorry to bring you such disturbing news. We hope Ms. Gray improves very soon. Good evening." Detective Brown handed Cat and Aroha his card saying, "Please don't hesitate to call if we can be any help."

Chapter 10

Aroha turned over in bed and sensing Lizzie was awake asked, "What time is it?"
"Five to six. Can't you sleep?"
"Not much. Have you been up? Who's here?"
"Max and Frenchy left about an hour ago when Willie and Cocco got back. They have gone to bed for a couple of hours. I'll have to call the Head about seven, seven-thirty to say we won't be in today. He'll love that, not!"
"Matt's taking Danny to school, and I'll have to go straight into work and face the furore of a warrant."
"Do you think it will be this guy?"
"I don't know, but who else could possibly want to hurt Theo?"
"Aroha, are we okay?"
Aroha sat up in bed. She was awake now, and there was no point in going back to sleep; there had been something bothering her.
"I don't understand, Lizzie. Willie said she duped you into going to the gym under false pretences, kissed you, unzipped your jeans, you were drunk and your reactions were slow, and then you heard voices. She said, 'let's take a rain check,' and you said, 'never again.' Now I would have been annoyed at that, but that's all. So what is it that he didn't tell me? What is it that's making you act so guilty?"
Lizzie felt sick again; it was becoming a permanent feeling.
"She um…," Aroha was looking her straight in the eye, but Lizzie couldn't see that as she had her head bowed, searching for strength and how to tell her something she didn't understand herself.
"Um…," she knew she couldn't lie.
"Em…she had her hand down there long enough to make me come." Lizzie screwed up her face; she was so ashamed of herself.
"She what? How long?" Her reply was angry and loud.
"Em…a minute or close to."

"You never come that quickly. You must have been really attracted to her. A whole minute! Lizzie, you could have stopped her. Why didn't you?"

Aroha was out of bed and crying again. She was so angry and hurt.

"I promised myself I wasn't going to do this till we got home."

She left the room and closed the door behind her. Lizzie couldn't move.

The door opened again ten minutes later. Aroha said, "You better stay with Cat when we get home. I don't want you near me. You can tell her you don't want her to be alone."

"But Danny?"

"You leave my son to me!"

She left and closed the door again. Lizzie could not have been more wounded. *But Danny? I won't see Danny.*

By 9:30 A.M., they had all checked out of the motel and gone to the hospital. There was no improvement in Theo, so the transfer was still going ahead. They all arranged to meet at Wellington hospital at 4:00 P.M. Theo and Cat would be there by 1:00 P.M., but by the time the doctors did their assessments; it would be at least 3:00 P.M. or 4:00 P.M. before they could see her. "Okay, you lot," said Max. "Drive carefully, see you soon." She hugged and kissed each one of them. "My niece is so fortunate to have such wonderful friends." Max and Frenchy returned inside to join Cat.

Aroha had sat in the back of the Prado, insisting Willie sit in front beside Lizzie. She professed to be tired and wanted to sleep, as did Cocco. Although her eyes were closed she did not sleep. *A minute and she came.* She could not get over that fact. *How can I ever be with her again? How can we ever make love again? I will always be timing her. What am I going to tell Danny? It will be all right while Theo is still in hospital, but then what? Oh, god, Theo! What if she's not all right?*

"Do I have to go through Palmerston North, Willie?"

"No, after you go through the gorge, you can turn left at the other side of the Ashhurst Bridge, then take Old West Road, which joins up with State Highway 57. That will take you through Shannon and back onto State Highway 1 at Levin; it saves about ten to fifteen minutes."

"I always like going home through the gorge more than going over it north. It's a hell of a drop, and I always worry about slips." Lizzie was pleased to be driving. The concentration was helping taking her mind off not going home to her own home and not seeing Aroha and Danny every morning and night.

"It's okay, Frances," Max preferred Frances to Frenchy. She always thought it rather rude, and Frances did not mind. "There will be a doctor flying with Theo and Cat. They'll be fine. It's we who have over a four-hour drive in front of us. Mind you, with your driving and your car, it may be considerably less." At least Frenchy had the good grace to smile.

The helicopter left on schedule, and Max and Frenchy were on the road before it left their sight. Frenchy loved to drive, and she preferred to listen to haunting melodies. They were in Dannevirke before she knew it. They had been listening to Mark Knopfler's *Screenplaying*. Max had fallen asleep, which was fine with Frenchy; she didn't feel much like talking anyway. Max was still a very attractive woman, and Frenchy couldn't help but wonder what she would look like herself at that age, if she made it. Max started to sneeze and couldn't stop.

"Have you got any tissues, Frances?" and without waiting for a reply, she opened the glove box.

She came across several tubes of lube. "What on earth would you want this for?" Frenchy was sure she was blushing from her nipples upwards.

Trying to change the subject, she asked, "Do you think Theo is going to be all right, Max?"

"I hope so, Frances, she has to be. I think, perhaps, this operation will make the difference. Relieving the pressure might bring her back to us."

"What about this stolen car business? Do you think someone really tried to kill her?"

Max shrugged, "Well, if what Aroha told us is true, I guess that boy's father could be after her. Theo would have had to apply to the court for an order to remove the child. Then her name and details would have become public knowledge to anyone who wanted to find out."

"So you think its work related then?"

"I guess," Max frowned. "Unless..."

"Unless what?"

"Oh, nothing dear. How much further?"

"I think we're halfway there." Frenchy was trying to work out what Max might be thinking but didn't want to push as she might ask about the lube in the glove box again.

As it was ten minutes north of Wellington, Lizzie dropped Aroha off at their home in Johnsonville on the way into the city. Aroha wanted to change and get her own car to go into work. As she got out the car, she turned and said, "I'll bring a bag for you to the hospital. It will save you doubling back. See you there at four."

Willie and Cocco shouted, "Bye."

Oh, my god, this is actually happening.

Willie said, "It's a good idea for you to stay with Cat, Lizzie. I'm sure she'll appreciate it."

"Yeah," said Lizzie. "Yeah."

They had made good time. Willie and Cocco insisted Lizzie come in and have lunch while they got changed. Lizzie suddenly realized that she may not have a home to go to anymore. Four days ago she was as happy as anyone could be. She had a job she loved; she was doing what she loved. She had good friends, and best of all, she had a partner for life whom she loved and who loved her, and Danny. She had a son and the possibility of another child. Now she had what?

"Tea or coffee, Lizzie?"

"Coffee, please"

"I know we should be talking about what might happen with Theo," said Willie, "but I can't think that way. We just have to deal with whatever and be there for Cat."

"Thank the good lord for Max," Cocco said.

Willie looked over at Cocco, "Don't you dare cross yourself."

Cocco stopped in his tracks. Willie was wagging his finger at him, and Cocco was feigning displeasure. Lizzie laughed.

"Don't encourage him, Lizzie."

"What religion is he anyway?"

"Oh, whichever suits his mood of the day."

Frenchy pulled into Max's driveway at 3:30 P.M. "I won't be long, Frances. Make yourself a drink, I just want to check in with Ted and say 'hello' to Ozzie." Frenchy moved to the window and realized she had forgotten what a magnificent view Max had. The road ran right in front of Max's house, but it did not interfere with the view. The beach was just the other side of the road. Paekakariki was a small place and close enough to Wellington. *Maybe I should consider moving down this way and being closer to everyone. Yeah, and let everyone find out who I really am.*

The phone rang. "Should I get that, Max?"

"Yes, thank you, dear," Max shouted from her bedroom.

"It's Cat, Max. They're going to operate now."

Max stood at the door and closed her eyes as if she were saying a prayer.

"We'd better go then," and she moved over to Frenchy and embraced her. Max held her tight. *Fuck, she knows I love Theo.*

All hell had been let loose at Aroha's work by the time she got there.

She was met by one of her colleagues. "The police have been here since first thing this morning. They want to see you as soon as you arrive." A policewoman was waiting at her desk. "Hello, are you Aroha Kiriana?" Aroha was stunned by this lyrical soft Irish brogue and the vision in front of her. "Yes."

The woman leaning on her desk was about five feet ten, nearly as tall as Frenchy, had sparkling blue eyes and blonde layered hair. Her taupe jacket and trousers were obviously very expensive and fashionable. Under her jacket she wore a soft green almost grey round neck stretch top, which exaggerated her ample breasts, and a simple silver chain. With hand outstretched, she said, "I'm Detective Inspector Sarah Adams."

Aroha shook her hand, "Detective Inspector." She made an admiring face.

Sarah smiled. "Any news on Ms. Gray, Ms Kiriana?"

"Aroha, please. She was flown to Wellington Hospital as you probably know."

Looking at her watch, she said, "We are all meeting there at four." Aroha was impressed that the officer asked about Theo first before getting to business. "Detective Inspector, huh? We've gone up in the world since Hastings."

"Well, if Ms. Gray doesn't make it, we are looking at murder."

"Murder?" Aroha fell to her chair. "Murder? Theo dead?"

Aroha put her head in her hands. It had finally been said. Theo could die.

"Are you all right, Aroha?"

"No, I am not. You have just pointed out that my best friend could die."

Detective Adams was on her feet, "I'm so sorry, I did not mean to upset you."

"It's not your fault that I haven't faced up to that fact yet. How is the investigation going? Have you caught the bastard yet?"

"Our enquiries are ongoing, but there have been no developments yet. We are bringing the father of Ms. Gray's client in now, and he will be questioned. Also, the officer who attended the accident in Napier will see if he can identify this man."

Detective Inspector Adams spent half an hour talking to Aroha and was only just finishing up when a colleague interrupted them.

"Aroha, there's a call for you on one, they said it was important."

"Hello, Aroha Kiriana speaking. Okay, Cat." She stood. "I'm on my way. Is Max there yet? Okay, see you soon."

Aroha replaced the phone and turned to Detective Inspector Adams. "It's Theo. They're taking her to surgery now, I have to go."

"Sure, would you like a lift?"

"No, thank you. I have my car downstairs."

For 3:30 P.M. on a Monday, the traffic was fairly light, but Aroha could still not get there fast enough. She looked at Lizzie's bag sitting on the passenger seat and felt cold. *How can life change so fast? What brought us to this point?* She remembered when she left Matt. She was ready and knew she was doing the right thing, but with Lizzie, this was different. She still loved her. *How could she do this?*

Chapter 11

C at hated hospitals. She had tried so hard to fight the memory away when they were in Hastings Hospital, but now, with Theo going into surgery, she was back there. *Her mother was in surgery, and her brother was dead on arrival. Everybody was shouting; people were rushing past. A policewoman was sitting by her side asking questions she couldn't hear. She didn't know anything. She knew her stepfather was dead. They had taken him to the mortuary. At least that's what she thought she heard. There was so much blood everywhere. She looked down at her school uniform. The white blouse and skirt were all bloody. She meant to take it off when she got home from school but had read her book and forgotten. Hours seemed to go by, and no one came to tell her about her mother. She had no idea how long she waited. People were whispering all around her. Someone had brought her a fizzy drink in a can. She held it unopened. She was thirsty but couldn't seem to move. She should feel sad. She didn't care for her stepfather very much but loved her younger brother, Fraser. Oh, God, Max. Where are you?*

Aroha arrived first, "Cat, what's happening?"

"They took her in about fifteen minutes ago. There's definitely a blood clot, and the pressure is building. They're going to use burr holes to remove the clot."

"Come here, sweetie." Aroha took Cat in her arms. "I'm sure it's going to be all right."

"What, you feel it in your water?"

They both made an attempt to laugh. It's what Aroha's mother always said.

"She's a wise old broad is my mother." Aroha was trying to think of something to distract Cat. "The police were at work waiting for me."

"Yeah. Did they have anything to say?"

"Not yet, but let me tell you about Detective Inspector Sarah Adams. She's gorgeous, nearly as tall as Frenchy, has eyes of blue you could dive into, and the most engaging soft Irish accent."

"Really, do you think we've finally found someone for Frenchy? She is gay, I take it."

"I don't know, my gaydar is usually spot on, but I'm not sure about this one."

"Was she wearing a wedding band?"

"I don't think I noticed."

Cat looked at her watch.

Aroha rubbed her back. "Did they say how long it would take?"

Cat shook her head. "At least an hour, but it could be two or more."

Aroha took her hand and looked along the corridor, willing the others to arrive.

Max, from the other end of the corridor shouted, "I'm here." Willie, Cocco, Frenchy, and Lizzie were right behind her. They met in the car park.

"I'm here," she said again as she approached Cat.

The two embraced, "Oh, Aunty Max, it's just like when Mum and Fraser died."

Cat was crying so hard now she was having trouble breathing and talking. "She's going to die in there, just as Mum did."

"There, there, Cat, this is nothing like what happened to your mother. Theo is going to be all right."

Everyone else was stunned. They had never seen Cat cry like this, and they had certainly never heard of her mother or someone called Fraser dying in hospital. In fact, they had never heard Cat speak of her family at all. They had all assumed that she either had no family or chose never to speak of them. Max was her family, and she never seemed to need anyone else.

Cocco asked, as quietly as he could, "What did Cat's mother die of?"

Everyone looked at each other and shook his or her head. Nobody knew. Aroha filled them in on what was happening to Theo.

An hour had passed and everybody was coffeed out. Cat kept checking her watch every two minutes. Max had tried to explain to all what was probably happening to Theo.

"She could very well be fine after this, you know."

In Cat's mind, she was back in London waiting for someone to come and tell her how her mum was. She was thirteen years old, and in her first year of secondary school. Her brother, Fraser, who was actually her half-brother, was ten. *She sat rubbing her skirt, trying to get the blood off. She looked down at her shoes—there was blood on them as well. She wondered if it was her mother's or Fraser's. Everybody kept asking if she was okay, thinking the blood was hers. Finally, a surgeon approached and removed his cap. His green scrubs were covered in blood. The police officer sitting beside her rose and approached the surgeon. He was shaking his head while he was talking to her. The police officer looked sad and after a few moments came over to her and sat down. She said, "I'm very sorry; your mother didn't make it. Do you have any other family in London?" She hadn't thought about other family. This morning she had a mother, a brother, and a stepfather. She shook her head.*

Frenchy looked around her friends. Something was up with Aroha and Lizzie. Normally they were inseparable, and now they couldn't seem to get far enough away from each other. Lizzie looked sad, but Aroha looked angry. Frenchy's world was falling apart enough without there being something wrong with those two and Theo and Cat. *Imagine Cat losing her mother and her brother and none of us knowing anything about it! I was meant to be the reclusive one, yet everyone knows whom my parents are, and that they both live in another country. Max is looking so tired; this is really taking a toll on her. I wonder if she knows how I feel about Theo. I have always tried to be so careful. If anything happens to Theo, I don't know what I'll do. Even Cocco, who is always making them laugh, is very quiet.*

Willie said, "I'm going out for a fag; I'll be back in a minute."

"I'll join you," said Lizzie and followed him out.

It was just after 5:30 P.M. and still a very pleasant warm breeze was in the air. Lizzie was just an occasional smoker. Willie was used to her cadging the odd fag and never minded.

"She's thrown me out, Willie. She told me she doesn't want to be anywhere near me."

"You're kidding me!"

Lizzie shook her head, too scared to speak in case she started to cry again.

"I thought she was going to be okay. She insisted I finish what you didn't tell her."

"Oh, shit."

"You can say that again."

Willie put a brotherly arm around her shoulder. "You'll sort this out, kid. In a week or two, this will be behind you."

"I don't know, Willie. When I asked her about Danny she said, 'leave my son to me.' I felt as if I had been slapped in the face. Danny's my son, too, but I don't have any rights." Lizzie looked away, "What if she won't let me see him, Willie?"

"Look, she's bound to be very angry. Just give her a day or two to get over this, and then I'm sure you'll see Danny. Come on, we better get back inside, there may be some news."

Willie sat down beside Cocco. They were quite a striking pair, and both had long dark hair. Cocco's was sleek and very shiny; Willie's was more bushy and fought to get out of the bone hair-clasp that held it back in place. Cocco was trying to take his mind off this infernal waiting by redesigning the corridor and the waiting room.

"What a soulless place this is, Willie. There's no colour, no music, and what awful uniforms the nurses have to wear."

Willie looked at Cocco and didn't know what to say. While he found Cocco's comments inappropriate, he was perfectly right.

Frenchy and Lizzie had just got back from another round of coffee fetching when they saw the surgeon. Frenchy practically dropped the coffee, but instead she burnt her fingers and dumped the coffee in the bin. As if in replay mode from Hastings, Cat had trouble standing, and again Max and Cocco were by her side. Aroha had inadvertently taken Lizzie's hand and immediately dropped it as soon as she realized what she'd done.

"The operation seems to have gone very well. We have been able to remove the clot successfully. There doesn't appear to be any spinal injury. However...," Max steeled herself and felt Cat lose her balance, "it's early yet. At this point, we have no idea what damage, if any, Ms. Gray has sustained. We expect she should come out of the anaesthetic very soon, and we'll have a better indication of how she's doing."

"Can I see her?"

"Shortly. They're just taking her into recovery. When Ms. Gray awakens, we will be able to do a neurological exam."

"What's that? Will it hurt her?" Cat couldn't stand the thought of Theo in any more pain.

"Not at all. It's a series of questions and simple commands to see if she can open her eyes, speak, and move. Questions like 'What is your name?' 'What day of the week is it?' 'Can you wiggle your toes?' 'How many fingers?' That sort of thing. That way we can measure her cognitive function. After that, we can talk about recovery and aftercare. If you'll excuse me I have to go. The nurse will come for you."

They didn't know whether to laugh or cry.

"That's good news, right?" asked Frenchy.

"I think so," said Max. "Do you want me to come in with you? Or would you rather be on your own?"

Cat looked at Max, processed what she said, and finally answered, "I think on my own."

It wasn't very long before a nurse came for Cat. She had to don a gown and mask. *Theo looks so peaceful now, and she's off the respirator, too.* She sat down beside her and picked up her hand. "Hello, gorgeous. Love the turban." *Theo would hate the bandage around her head and the bruising around her eyes.*

"Hey, I miss you. If you don't wake up soon, I'm never going to be able to go to sleep. Not just me either. You have a room full of people who haven't slept in days. Honey, I'm no good without you. It's time to wake up. We never got to have lunch or enjoy our weekend away. Theo, there's something I have to tell you. Something I should have told you a long time ago, something no one knows, except Max. I don't know why I've never told you before. I guess it's too painful to talk about, but I have to tell you now. You being in hospital and just about dying has made me realize," she looked thoughtfully at Theo, " that I'm ready."

Theo stirred. Cat sat up, "Theo, darling, can you hear me?".

A moan escaped from Theo. Finally, with her eyes closed Theo spoke, "Shut up."

Cat got such a fright. She jumped up, "Theo, can you hear me?"

"Would you shut up, woman? You're giving me a bloody headache."

Cat was stunned. Theo spoke! But Theo hardly ever swore.

She didn't care. Theo spoke! Cat laughed, "That's the most wonderful thing you've ever said to me. Theo?" There was no reply. Cat went to find a doctor who came immediately.

"She spoke to me, then she stopped." The doctor took her pulse and smiled.

"She's fine, she's just sleeping."

Cat ran out to tell the others.

"She said what?" laughed Aroha.

"Would you shut up, woman? You're giving me a bloody headache."

"No."

"Yes."

"That doesn't sound like Theo."

"It's not unusual with that sort of head injury for morality, manners, and irritability to be altered," said Max.

"Really?" asked Frenchy.

"Yes, we may have a different Theo on our hands."

"Well, I don't care. I'm pleased to have her alive," said Cat.

"And so say all of us." Cocco silently crossed himself, and Willie gave him a look.

"What now?" asked Frenchy."

"I'm going back in to sit with Theo. I imagine she will sleep a bit longer. Why don't you guys go get something to eat, and I'll stay with Cat," said Max.

"I'll stay, too," said Frenchy.

"Bring Frances, Cat, and me something back. I doubt that they will let us all stay. Maybe it's time you got some sleep and started your lives again," said Max.

Willie, Cocco, and Aroha left at 9:00 P.M. Theo woke again about ten o'clock, but she was still very irritable and wanted to go back to sleep. Although she was slow to answer the doctor's questions, she was most definitely responsive. She even told the doctor to take his hands off her, or she'd have him for sexual harassment.

Max talked a very reluctant Cat into going home. "Lizzie will be with you, and Frenchy and I will stay here and phone you the second anything goes wrong, but it won't. You'll need all your strength tomorrow, and it's likely that Theo will sleep through the night."

"What about you, Max? You must be exhausted."

"I'm all right just now. I'll go home as soon as you return in the morning. Frances will take me, won't you dear?"

"Of course."

"Off you go. I know Lizzie will take good care of you. The sooner you go, the sooner you'll be back."

Max smiled, It's the kind of thing you say to a child. She wondered how much longer she had to play the parent and worried about what might lie ahead for Theo and Cat.

Ellis Paris Ramsay

Chapter 12

Lizzie was trying to get Cat to eat some breakfast before she went to the hospital. "You might as well, Cat. It's only seven fifteen; they're not going to want you there this early."

"I can't believe I slept this long; I wanted to go earlier."

"Look, Max and Frenchy are there. They would have rung if Theo had woken up. You're not going to be much use to Theo if you become sick, are you?"

"No, I suppose your right. A piece of toast wouldn't do any harm. I can't get over how you guys have been so wonderful." Cat's eyes welled up. "You know I couldn't have gotten through this without you, don't you?"

Lizzie went over to Cat and gave her a bear hug. "You know we all love you and Theo. You're our family."

Just then the phone rang. Cat nearly tripped over her chair getting there. "Oh, hi, Danny. How are you? Yeah, she's right here. Oh, thank you, sweetie. I'm sure she'll be home soon. Hang on, here's Lizzie-mum."

Lizzie's stomach took a tumble at the sound of Lizzie-mum. Danny didn't often call her that much any more, usually when he wanted something or to make it clear whom he was talking to.

Lizzie ran to the phone. "Hi, squirt."

Danny laughed, "I keep telling you I don't squirt any more."

"What's up?"

"Mum says you might not be home for a while and that you're staying with Cat till Theo comes home."

"Yeah, that's right." Lizzie wondered if Aroha had said anything else.

"Does that mean you won't take me to soccer practice tomorrow night?"

"Hell no."

"I'll tell Mum you swore."

"Do and you die. I'll be there tomorrow, and I'll take you to your game on Saturday as well."

"You still owe me lunch at Mackers."

"I still owe you lunch. I never agreed to Mac's."

"Am I still going to help you backstage when your show's on?"

"You betcha, kid."

"Mum wants a word."

Lizzie's heart jumped.

Aroha came on the phone. "How's Theo? Anything further?"

"No, we haven't heard, so we presume all okay. Cat is just about to go in."

She could hear Aroha shout, "Danny, brush your teeth, we have to go soon."

Lizzie didn't think she could miss such a mundane routine so much...

"Um, I'm sorry for the crack about Danny yesterday. Danny shouldn't suffer just because..."

"Can I come home?"

"I don't know, Lizzie. I need time to think, and you still have to tell me why."

Lizzie wanted to scream, "I don't know why."

Instead, Aroha said, "See you at the hospital at five," and hung up.

Frenchy and Max left as soon as Cat got there. There had been no change. They both looked absolutely exhausted, and she felt guilty for having slept. Max had told her to expect Cocco at 8:30 A.M. "Willie will drop him off on the way to school. He's bringing lunch and lots of glossies," which is what Cocco always called expensive magazines. Cocco didn't have to be there but had insisted. He said, "I can't leave you to stare at those awful walls and unshaven legs all day by yourself. My dear, what are friends for, if not to carry some of burdens in life with you." Lizzie had rehearsals at lunch and after school but would pop in afterwards.

Cat saw Theo was still asleep and went in search of a doctor. "She slept fairly peacefully last night. We think you can expect a full recovery. However, you should be aware of a few behavioural traits. Often patients, after this kind of injury, can be confused about where

82

they are and what has happened. She may not even remember the accident. This could cause her to lash out, yell, swear, and maybe even bite. This should not overly concern you as, in most cases, it passes. Sometimes we use soft ankle or wrist ties as restraints."

"No! You can't do that to Theo."

"Let's hope that's not necessary. Just remember this behaviour is not intentional."

Cocco arrived armed with magazines and crosswords. Cat tried hard to do a crossword but just could not concentrate. Cocco was reading out gossip from the magazines, trying his best to keep Cat amused. He had a hard job today.

Finally, at 10:00 A.M., Theo woke. She was very thirsty. Cat held the mug with the straw for Theo to drink from, as her motor skills were slow.

"Where the hell am I? I don't think much of this hotel."

"Honey, you're in hospital in Wellington."

"Wellington? I thought we were in Napier."

"We were, but you had an accident. Do you remember?"

"No."

Cat spent the rest of the morning explaining to Theo what had happened. It appeared Theo was having trouble grasping everything.

"Where's Cocco? I want to speak to him."

Cat went to fetch Cocco.

"I just wanted to tell you, Cocco, that Cat and I are going to Japan."

Both Cocco and Cat were stunned.

"But Theo, you know I don't travel overseas."

"Well, I'll go my bloody self then. I will go see your mother."

Cat frowned, "Why?"

"Because Cocco can't."

"Why can't Cocco go?"

"I can't remember why, Cat; I just know I'm going, and you can do what you like."

This is so unlike Theo. I can't get upset; I can't get upset. She's alive and on the road to recovery.

"Theo, you heard me!" Cocco shouted.

Both Cat and Theo looked at Cocco.

"Of course, I heard you, and I'm not scared of your father."

Just then the nurse came in and asked them to step outside as rounds were about to start. Still a little shell-shocked, Cat sat in disbelief while Cocco told her all he had told Theo.

"So how often do you get to speak to your mum?"

"Not often. Once a week if I'm lucky, but she has to be very careful. If father find out she call me from Auntie's, he put a stop to her visits. I have sent Aunty computer and web cam so hopefully sometime I can speak to her live and see her beautiful face. But Mother and Aunty no too good with computer and hours are different, don't always suit. I have suggested they go to course for computer. They say, 'see what we can do.'"

"Cocco, that would be wonderful."

Cocco smiled at the thought of seeing his beautiful mother. "Yeah, it would be good."

After rounds were finished, Theo was brought lunch. She took one look at it and said, "I'm not eating this. I wouldn't give this to a dog." Cat was still standing in the corridor and cringed. She didn't know whether to laugh or cry. She was not used to Theo being so ill mannered. Cocco rose to his feet, grabbed his large 'Kete' bag. His favourite one that Willie's mother had given him. He had glued black feathers and Paua shells around the top, which had turned it into a very fashionable and expensive bag. "Don't worry, darling, I have lunch for you." He removed the food tray from Theo's bed tray and pulled out a small white cloth from his bag and placed it over the bed tray. Dipping into his bag, he pulled out a silver, single-stemmed vase, and placed a rose from one of Theo's floral bouquets in it and set it on the tray. He brought out a white linen napkin and a black glass plate. "Now, I thought finger-food today, little bits of this and that."

Cocco didn't stop talking to Theo with bits of gossip as he spread pate on fresh ciabatta bread fingers, slivers of smoked salmon with a little cream cheese, and little slices of fresh melon. "We're going to have to sort out Lizzie and Aroha. Uh uh, trouble in paradise there, girlfriend." Cat was walking out the door to catch the doctor and made a mental note to ask Cocco what that was all about. She wanted to ask the doctor when Theo might be able to come home with her.

It was lunchtime at school, and Lizzie was at rehearsal. She was dreading this as they were so far behind, and she couldn't imagine how they would catch up. She was absolutely gobsmacked to find out that Torri Jacobs had taken over rehearsals when she was away and had been a little tyrant. She had called rehearsal all day Sunday and into the evening and a chorus rehearsal Monday night, telling the leads to spend that time learning their lines to go script free today. Lizzie had to sit down. The idea of this little Goth getting everyone to 'follow the yellow brick road' was more than she could take in. She was such a 'pain in the arse' in class and hadn't realized the extent of her musical ability.

"Well, Ms. Beck, when Ms. Toomey rang to cancel rehearsals and I got out of her the reason why, I just told her I'd do it." *I can just hear the conversation, and Torri being like a dog with a bone would not have let her off the phone without having the full story.* "After all, we sisters have to stick together." Lizzie did a double take and wondered if she had meant what she thought she'd meant. Before she had time to go down that road someone had asked her a question.

Back at the hospital, the doctor told Cat, "If Ms. Gray continues to improve at this rate, you may be able to take her home on Saturday. We'll have to talk about outpatient therapy though."

Ellis Paris Ramsay

Chapter 13

Max couldn't remember when she last felt so tired. Frenchy had just dropped her off and refused breakfast, as she needed to get some sleep herself. Max had offered her a bed, but she said she was going to bunk down with Willie and Cocco. "I'll be nearer to the hospital, and Cocco wants me to tell him all about the photo shoot in Paris and about my visit with my mother. He's promised to cook me a French meal," she crossed her eyes, "if I spill the beans."

"Well, I'm afraid I can't match the French meal so go in peace and in slumber."

They hugged and Frenchy left.

Max looked around her house, feeling very happy to be home. She made herself a cup of tea and sat down. She was just about asleep but wanted to wait till Ted brought Ozzie home. She had rung him that morning and told him what time she should be home. She was a little early, as she did not take into consideration Frances' driving. Sitting on her sofa with her legs up and looking at the sea, she reproached herself for not making Cat tell Theo about her family. By not facing up to it, it has made it so much harder to do now. She should have known better. After all the counselling she gave her when she brought her home, it just seemed too much to push. She broke her own rules about counselling her own family, but Cat had been through so much. She still, to this day, remembers that frightened child she met in the Vancouver bus station who wouldn't speak. She was thirteen years old and had already seen more than any human being should ever see, and now this. *What if Theo is a different person? I wonder how it would affect their relationship.*

"Hello, anyone home?"

"Ted, I'm through here."

Ozzie came pounding through and jumped up on the sofa, barking and licking Max's face.

Max started to scratch behind his ears, "Well, hello to you, too. Did you miss me? Yes, I missed you. What a fine fellow you are."

"Thank you," said Ted.

Max turned and laughed. "And you, too." She flung her legs over and went to stand up. As she did, she felt dizzy and fell back down.

"Max!" Ted was at her side. "Are you all right? Shall I get a doctor? Should I call an ambulance?"

"No, no, I'm just so very tired. I haven't had much sleep for…," Max thought, "three days. I'm just exhausted, Ted."

"Are you sure? You don't look all right to me."

Ozzie was barking. He was concerned as well.

"Look, you fellas, I'm fine. Nothing that a good night's sleep and some TLC wouldn't cure."

Ted smiled, "Okay, I can do that. Shall I cook dinner tonight?"

"Yes, please, but here. I don't want to go anywhere for a while."

"You're on. Why don't I take Ozzie for a nice long walk, and we'll both come back later."

"Perfect. You're a dear."

Ted pulled the comforter that was on the end of the sofa over Max. "I'll close the door on my way out and use my key later."

"Ted, have you taken your Viagra today?"

"Pardon?"

"You heard me."

"I don't need Viagra," he said, quite put out.

"Yes, you do. I'll need lots and lots of TLC tonight, after dinner."

"Really, Maxine!"

Ted closed the door quietly and left.

A few hours later, Max woke to the sound of Itzhak Perlman playing Bruch's Violin Concerto no. 1, her favourite piece of music. The sounds of the strings filled her house. She was reluctant to wake, but if she had to this was the way to do it. Ted had read her mood perfectly. She turned over and smiled when she saw there was a white rose with pink edges in a little bud vase on the small side table beside her. There was also a glass of brandy in her favourite Swedish crystal balloon, and she noticed an empty space in a packet of Viagra. Max gently giggled. As she came more awake, she could smell the wonderful aroma of chicken cooking and a strong smell of garlic and olive oil.

Ah, Ted must be cooking his pasta dish. I love that he always uses fresh pasta. She sat up, as did Ozzie who had been lying at her feet. She looked over to the kitchen, and there was Ted, standing cooking with her plastic apron on that read, '*My most favourite thing to make for dinner is reservations*', and she noticed that he had nothing on under it.

Ted noticed that Max was awake. "How about a soak in the spa before dinner?"

"Ooh, yes, please, what time is it?"

"Five-thirty."

"Boy, I'm starving," and just as if Ted had read her mind, he produced a small platter of cheeses, salami, and tomato on wafer thin biscuits.

"That should keep you going. I've got a lovely bottle of Sauvignon Blanc chilling for dinner."

"Just what I like, a man who thinks of everything."

"You scared me a little today, Max. You're always so strong, and nothing gets you down."

"None of us are as young as we used to be. But don't worry Ted, I was just tired."

She leaned over and kissed him softly on the lips, "I'll prove it to you later," she said, arching her eyebrows, "that I'm at my peak. Ooh, I love this piece. Just when you think Itzhak and Bruch have climaxed for the last time they rise again."

"Is that a challenge?"

"I do hope so. Come on, let's have that soak."

Sitting in the spa, sipping her brandy, she felt at peace for the first time in days. Ted was exceedingly good company, the water was warm, and the view was great. Watching the sea lap the shore through the gaps in the punga's was magnificent.

"Is your niece's partner, Theo is it, going to be okay?"

"Physically, yes, but as yet, it's not clear if she will be the same person she was before what part of her brain, if any, has been affected."

"You said Cat still had some demons to face."

"Yes," and Max told Ted the whole tragic story.

"And Theo doesn't know this?"

"No, Theo and their friends don't know."

"Won't Theo be offended that she hasn't told her before now?"

"The old Theo would probably understand, but I don't know now."

Ted left Max soaking in the spa deep in thought, while he finished preparations for the meal. The pasta was delicious; it was not too heavy but was filling. The wine was exquisite. Ted went to open another bottle, and Max stopped him. "Why don't you put that one on ice, and we'll have it later?"

Ted smiled, bowed, and said, "I'm at your command."

"Just as it should be," and with that, Max led Ted to the bedroom.

Chapter 14

Aroha had gone to work early to try to catch up on some of her cases and was getting nowhere fast. She had just gone to get herself the second coffee of the day, and when she returned to her desk, Detective Inspector Sarah Adams was waiting for her.

"Good morning, Inspector."

"Good morning, Ms. Kiriana. How are you today?"

Sarah was dressed once again in a business suit, but today it was a dark grey, almost a blue charcoal. Her top was sapphire blue and was cut straight across at the neck. She wore a silver necklace again, but this time there was a solid silver pendant that held a large piece of Paua shell that hung from it. Aroha was trying to look at her left hand, but Sarah was leaning on it.

She followed Aroha's eyes and stood up. "I'm sorry. Was I sitting on something?"

"No. I was just wondering if I had left my last empty cup there. How are things going? Any news?"

"Actually, that's what I have come to see you about Ms. Kiriana."

"Aroha, please."

"That's such a pretty name, what does it mean?"

"It means love."

Sarah smiled. "It suits you."

"Is that a touch of the Irish blarney, Inspector?"

"I'm going to need your help, Aroha. Can I buy you a decent cup of coffee while we talk?"

"I'd love to, but I'm snowed under here."

"I spoke with your boss earlier, and as of now, you have been relieved of all your other work and are mine alone."

Aroha was about to flirt and realized for this to happen it must be pretty serious.

"Is Theo still in danger?"

"We don't know yet. Come on, I'll buy you coffee."

Astoria Café on Lambton Quay used to be old public toilets, but now it was a very 'in' place to go. They sat outside in the sun. It had been a long winter and now sunny, spring days were to be treasured. Even the birds were happy.

"So Inspector, how can I help?"

"The boy's father is a dead end."

"Really?"

"Yes. He was in a fight in a pub Friday night, he messed up this other guy real bad and was in a cell till yesterday morning."

"Could he have gotten someone else to do this for him?"

"We considered this, but he doesn't seem to make or have any friends, and he has no income or savings to speak of. Also, he was questioned by one of my officers yesterday, and unless he is the world's best liar, I don't think he is intelligent enough. He doesn't even know who Theo is or remembers, in his words, 'the bitch who took his son.'"

"Where does this leave us?"

"We are going to have to go through all of Theo's cases, say in the last six months. As you stated, she often got threatened. How many cases do you think we are talking about here?"

"In any given week we could be handling forty cases."

"Shit, and I thought my workload was heavy."

"But the kinds of cases you're talking about, I would guess ten or twelve."

"It's going to be a long day then."

Sarah was holding her coffee cup, and Aroha noticed there was no ring on her left hand. *Doesn't necessarily mean a thing.*

They spent most of the day going through papers and in the end came up with only three possibles.

"Well, that looks a lot more doable than this morning. Not a wasted day then?"

Sarah smiled. "Not at all. I've enjoyed your company."

"Thank you."

Aroha looked at her watch. "I have to go to the hospital to see how Theo's doing."

"I'm pleased to hear she is recovering."

"We all are. Do you get to go home to someone nice now?" Aroha could not help herself.

Sarah smiled again. "Back to work for me, and no, I don't get to go home to someone nice."

"Hmm, *what does that mean?* So you're not married or in a relationship then?"

"No, I'm not married or in a relationship. My work makes that very difficult. I don't date within the job, and apart from villains, I don't get to meet too many people. What about you?"

"I have a son, Danny, he's eleven. His father and I split up nine years ago. We're divorced now. He has a new family, but Danny sees him regularly. And I...," Aroha looked at the floor, "and I've been in my present relationship for eight years now."

"So you have someone nice to go home to."

Aroha smiled this time. "Actually, she's staying with Cat at the moment, while Theo is in hospital."

Changing the subject quickly as they were walking out the door, she asked, "How do you feel about blind dates, Sarah?"

Sarah groaned as she playfully hit Aroha in the arm.

At 5:10 P.M., Willie, Lizzie, and Aroha were all back at the hospital.

"She's a lot better but still very grumpy. Cocco is dealing with her much better than I. She's so irritable with me. Cocco is just sarcastic to her and that seems to shut her up. I've never been any good at that. The doctor says she may be able to come home on Saturday. I'm meeting with him tomorrow to discuss aftercare. Aroha, she wants to see you right away."

Aroha went into Theo's room and was pleased to see her friend sitting up. "Now there's a sight for sore eyes." Her arms were outstretched, as were Theo's. Cat couldn't help but notice that Theo hadn't once reached out for her.

"Theo, you had us so worried."

"I'm sorry, couldn't be helped. Tell me about work."

"You'll never guess. I think I've found someone for Frenchy. It's the police officer who's in charge of your case."

"Oh, tell me more."

They had all decided to grab a quick meal together at a nearby café, and share their day's news.

"You first, Cat."

"Well, the doctor says she could be home Saturday if she continues to improve as fast as she is, and I think she's determined to as she hates being in hospital. I'm taking a month off work. I have the leave owing, as Theo and I could never seem get our schedules to coincide for a holiday. I'll pop in tomorrow for a couple of hours to see to anything urgent and then just delegate."

"Oh, the joys of working for the government."

"What kind of help do you think you'll need?"

"Maybe none, I don't know yet."

"Mum says she can do a day a week," said Willie.

"And mine," said Aroha.

"I can do a couple," said Cocco, "I only go into café two days a week."

"Thank you," said Cat. "Max, of course, says she can do a day, but I'm hoping Theo will be improved enough for me just to cope." *I'm sure I can physically manage Theo, but I'm not so sure about mentally.*

Willie asked, "Lizzie, what's this I've been hearing at school today that Torri Jacobs took over rehearsals while you were away?"

"Yeah, who'd a thought?"

Lizzie then went on to describe the good job she had been doing. "And Jemma is nearly word perfect!"

Saturday. Theo might go home Saturday. I wonder if I get to go home. But what if Aroha asks me why it happened, why I didn't stop her? What the hell am I going to say, because I don't know? I wonder if I should speak with Max, or is that a cop-out? Lizzie had tried to make eye contact with Aroha, but it was not happening. She wasn't going to get out of this one with her winning smile.

"Willie, you have booked us best seats?"

"It's a hall, Cocco. It doesn't really have best seats."

"Hmm," said Cocco. "Well, I bring cushion and make me higher. I don't want to miss anything."

"I'm not sure whether my news is good news or not," said Aroha. "I spent the day with the lovely Detective Inspector Sarah Adams at my work..."

Lizzie got that sick feeling in her stomach again and tried not to show it. *Aroha doesn't normally describe other women as lovely.*

"It's definitely not that boy's father who tried to kill Theo. He was in a cell all weekend and does not have the will or wherefore to get someone else to do it for him."

"So who is it?" asked Willie.

"That's what we tried to find out today. We went through all of Theo's cases and narrowed it down to three that the police are going to check out tomorrow. Let's hope they can find him before Theo leaves the hospital."

Cat was suddenly very alert. She hadn't thought of that.

Aroha noticed and said, "Don't worry, Cat. I'm sure the police will be on to that, and I'm sure Lizzie can stay longer."

This was shocking news to Lizzie, and she couldn't hide it from Aroha. Fortunately, Cat seemed to be the only one who did not notice Lizzie's reaction.

Aroha stood up to leave, "I'd better get home. I have to pick Danny up from one of his friend's houses and get him home to bed, it's a school night 'n all. I take it you'll pick him up from school tomorrow, Lizzie?"

"Yeah, we'll go get something to eat then I'll take him to practice and bring him home."

"See you all tomorrow. Give Theo a kiss from me, Cat." She leaned down to Cat and kissed her.

"Night all."

What I would give for that kiss. Lizzie stood up next, looking at her watch. "I have to go to rehearsal before Torri takes over completely. See you at yours, Cat. See you in the morning, Willie. Bye, Cocco."

Cat watched her friend walk away and turned to the boys and asked, "What's going on? Am I the only one who doesn't know?"

Cocco told Cat the whole story. "Fuck, if it doesn't rain, it bloody pours. I've been so wrapped up in my own life; I didn't even notice what was going on all around me. I only just found out about Cocco and his father."

"Ah, that old news," said Cocco, dismissing it with a hand wave. "No point going down that road. You work on getting Theo well, and we'll work on Aroha and Lizzie."

"I'm not sure we should interfere, Cocco," said Willie, with an earnest face.

"Don't be silly, darling. What are friends for?"

Willie and Cocco went home, at Cat's insistence, and she returned to the hospital to find Theo asleep. She sat by her bed and watched the peaceful face of the Theo she knew, asleep.

Chapter 15

Sarah was sitting at her desk chewing the end of her pencil. "Are you sure you've checked all three thoroughly?"

Sitting beside her were Detective Doug Spicer and Detective John Fergusson. "I'm telling you, Sarah, it could not have been any of these guys. Brown has been back in prison for the last three months, Bailly is in the South Island working on a farm far from civilization, and Dexter is in Australia."

Sarah picked up Theo's file and started to go through it for the fortieth time. "There is nothing in her background to suggest anything."

"Normal growing up stuff in Paihia, Auckland University, O.E. for two years, work in Wellington."

"Your overseas check, Doug. That didn't come up with anything?"

"Nadir. Not even a parking or jaywalking ticket."

"So who would want to kill Ms. Gray?"

"The scene investigation team is sure this is no accident?"

"Absolutely. They say if the driver were drunk, unconscious, or having a heart attack or a fit possibly, but otherwise, it was no accident. Plus the guy absconded without a trace and left no fingerprints anywhere."

"Okay, let's take a break. I need some fresh air." She looked at her watch. "Let's meet back here in half an hour and go through all this again, or see if we can come up with another angle."

Both the men groaned but were happy to have the break.

Sarah drove in to town. She really wished she could go for a run but didn't have the time, so a coffee in the fresh air would have to do. She was thinking about Aroha. She had so few friends and would love to have Aroha as one. She said her partner was staying with Theo's partner till Theo came home. Well, that's only three days away; they would have to have come up with someone by then, or it would mean protection, which would blow the budget. Theo's partner, Cat... "Shit!"

Sarah almost knocked the table over as she stood. She ran to her car and drove way too fast. She was almost tempted to use her siren. She bounded up the stairs two at a time. Bursting into her office, she said to Doug and John, "The accident report, where is it?"

Doug handed it to her. "What is it, Sarah?"

She ran her finger down the sheet. "There! Blue Ford Mondeo, registered to Ms. Caitlin Craig. They're not after Theo; they're after Cat. What time is it, four-thirty? I'm off to the hospital. Doug, start a file on Caitlin Craig."

Chapter 16

Cat was feeling very tired. She hadn't slept a night through since the accident. *What accident? They really should start calling it what it is, an attempted murder. Maybe I should try to talk Theo into changing professions after this. Who am I kidding? Theo loves her job, and she'll just write this off as 'it goes with the job.'* Theo had slept most of the day. She was exhausted after all the questioning Inspector Adams had put her through last evening. Cocco and Frenchy had kept her company today, until Willie came for Cocco, and Frenchy had gone for a run. She said she needed to let off some steam. Max had just arrived and seemed to be in great spirits. She had gone to find the doctor, as she wanted to check what Theo might need at home. *Aroha was right about Inspector Adams. She's gorgeous and would be just right for Frenchy.* Theo thought so, too, and was in cahoots with Aroha to set it up.

Everything at work was fine. She was assured that her work would be taken care of and not to give it a second thought. The P.A., Ngaire, even gave her a hug and told her to take care of each other. *All I want to do now is get Theo home and take care of her, but what if it's not safe? How can I take care of her? Maybe we should stay with Max for a while. Maybe Inspector Adams will have some news.* She was just walking back into Theo's room after visiting the loo when she saw Sarah walk towards her. She didn't know whether to be hopeful or scared. They certainly could do with some good news. However, the look on Sarah's face told her this might not be the case.

Theo brightened immediately as they walked into her room.

"Well, hello, Inspector. You have some news? Have you apprehended any villains today? Am I safe to walk the streets again?"

Sarah stood at the doorway, not knowing where to start or what to say.

"Hello, you must be Detective Inspector Adams. I'm Maxine Lawson." Max was standing behind Sarah. She stood aside and allowed Max to enter the room.

Sarah shook her hand. "Oh, yes. Ms. Kiriana mentioned you."

"Do you bring news, Detective Inspector?"

"Yes I do, but not what you're all expecting."

Sarah had everyone's attention.

Looking thoughtful and taking a deep breath, "We have eliminated all suspects in Ms. Gray's case. We no longer feel she is under any threat."

"So how do you explain the attempt on her life in Napier, Inspector?"

"We now believe the intended victim, and has been all along, is Ms. Craig."

"Pardon?" said Cat.

"You're joking, aren't you?" asked Theo. "Cat is a political analyst for the Ministry of Social Development. Who the hell would want to kill Cat?"

"I was hoping Ms. Craig would have some insight on this."

Everyone turned to Cat. She was rocking in her chair, white with fear.

"No, no, this can't be happening. Aunty Max, he's come for me, he always said he would. No, no! He said he'd get me no matter how long it took. He's going to kill me just as he killed Mum and Fraser and my stepdad. No, no!"

Cat started to dry retch. Max was by her side.

"What the hell are you talking about, Cat? Who is going to kill you, and what do you mean kill you like your mother and who's Fraser? Cat, what's going on?"

Theo was trying to get out of bed. Max was holding Cat as she bent over the hand basin. Sarah had to help Theo as she stumbled out of bed. Theo, who was now crying, asked, "Cat, darling, what is it?"

Cat let out a long moan that was almost primeval and chilled Theo to the core. "Cat, darling, speak to me."

"Theo," said Max, "I don't think she can. I will tell you."

Sarah, who was silently watching this drama unfold in front of her, felt helpless and could only assist Theo back to her bed. She didn't know what to expect when she came to the hospital, but it certainly wasn't this.

"Cat," said Max, "Cat, can you hear me darling?" Cat's eyes were rolling back in her head.

"Inspector, find a doctor. We need a sedative here."

Sarah had no trouble complying and had left the room before Max had finished asking.

"Theo, calm down. As soon as we have Cat seen to, I'll tell you everything. Cat was going to anyway when you got home. She has tried to tell you for years but has never been able to."

"Max, you're scaring me."

"I'm sorry, honey. I don't mean to, but there are things about Cat you don't know. No one knows except me. Things she has hidden inside herself that she doesn't want to remember, and I can't blame her. She's has been through so much, more than anyone should, let alone a thirteen-year-old girl."

Sarah returned with a doctor.

"She's in shock. Help me get her on to the other bed. She just needs a sedative doctor, and I'm sure she will be fine."

"Has this happened before, Dr Lawson?"

"Once, when she first came to New Zealand when she was thirteen."

"Came to New Zealand?" asked Theo. "You mean she wasn't born here?"

"No, dear, she was born in England."

"England, but she never said."

"I'll tell you all. Inspector, why don't you get us all a hot drink? There's a machine at the end of the hall. It's a bit of a long story."

Sarah was out of the room and halfway down the hall before she realized that for the past ten minutes Maxine had been calling the shots. *Oh, she's good; I like this woman. I have no idea what's coming next.*

With Cat settled and Sarah back from getting coffee, they sat waiting for Max to continue. "This all happened a long time ago. It was the worst and best time of my life as it brought Cat in to it. She was a frightened thirteen-year-old girl who would not speak. She had witnessed the death of her stepfather, her mother, and her younger half-brother, Fraser. She was very nearly killed herself. This is a story that should have died with her family twenty-six years ago, and I would not be telling you now if it weren't for the fact that Cat's life is obviously in danger. My husband knew, of course, and a couple of people in the New Zealand government of the day. I thought I was the only person who knew Cat was in this country. Clearly that's no longer so. So I had better start at the beginning."

Chapter 17

I know very little about my sister's second husband," Max said. "Catharine was five years younger than me. She met her first husband, an American, on her overseas trip in London. He was a thrillseeker and tragically died in a climbing accident. He was Cat's father. I doubt that she remembers him. She was not quite two when he died. He was Eugene Yates from Denver, Colorado. I don't know if he had family, Catharine never said. I begged her to come home. I didn't like the thought of her on her own with a small child. I think that she was going to, but then she met Jimmy Campbell. The police told me all they knew about Campbell—what they found out themselves and what the media dug up on him. Anyone who knew him was interviewed. It was a very big story at the time.

"Jimmy Campbell had never been able to keep a job in his life. His good looks had helped him so far, but his youthful charm had long gone. He had left Glasgow eleven years earlier, and he knew he could never return. He had left behind debts and had done the dirty on too many people.

"Almost immediately, his luck changed in London when he met a young Australian widow, my sister Catharine Yates and her pretty two-year-old daughter Catharine, or Cat, as she was called. He fell in love with Catharine immediately. He had never loved anyone in his life before and was completely beguiled and enchanted by her. Jimmy had no family to speak of, at least none who wanted any part of him. He was out on the streets fending for himself at age fourteen.

"He started by running errands for the local bookie, and it wasn't long before he started to run a book trackside. He did well to begin with and got used to the high life. He had a flashy car, any amount of girls he wanted, and money to spend. He opened his own shop, and as far as Jimmy was concerned, he owned Glasgow. He was unpopular, but he did not care. He got greedy, and the day came when he was robbed. He had stepped on too many Glasgow big boys' shoes. It was time he was taught a lesson.

"Jimmy had never bothered with insurance. He felt immortal and wouldn't waste his money on something he didn't need. So when he couldn't cover a big win the next day, he knew he had been set up. He sold his car, but that did not come close to what he owed. So he left town in the hope that whoever had set him up would be happy just to have him gone.

"When he met Catharine, he was determined to get a job and become a family man. He married Catharine one month after they met and within another month she was pregnant. When his son Fraser was born, he couldn't have been happier. His dead-end jobs never lasted more than a couple of months, but he did not care. As his family's needs grew, he was financially unable to cope, and he found himself more and more at the other end of a bottle. He still loved Catharine but felt that he had let her down and couldn't bear to see the disappointment in her face. He drank mostly at the local pub at the end of his street. Two of the regulars were Frank Corolla and his son, Tony. They were the local heavies, but Jimmy got on well with them. Not much could scare a Glaswegian.

"The Corollas liked Jimmy; he was one of the few men who was not intimidated by them, so Jimmy started to hang about with them. They offered Jimmy a job as a delivery man for their dry cleaning business, and it wasn't too long before Jimmy worked out that the dry cleaning was just a front for the very lucrative drug trade the Corollas ran. Jimmy didn't care; he had money and was able to buy for his son and a growing Cat. Catharine was happy with the regular income, and they even spoke about visiting me. Life was looking good for the first time since he met Catharine.

"As the years passed, Frank's other son, Dean, joined the business and things changed. He was young and arrogant and felt Jimmy held too high a position in his family's business. He felt he should take over Jimmy's work. Frank was able to mollify Dean most of the time, but Jimmy knew there was going to come a day when he would be out of a job. So he made a plan.

"On Thursdays, when he delivered to Dockside, he passed an old deserted warehouse. There was always a lot of money on Thursdays. He decided to hide the money in the old warehouse and tell Frank that he had been done over and that he was fairly sure that he had been followed after he dropped off the cocaine. He would carry on as usual, and when the heat was off, he would get the money, take his family, and disappear overseas. He had arranged for someone to do him over a bit, so it was more realistic.

"When the day came, everything went well; there were no hiccups. He hid the money and took the beating that he had paid for. He was purposely two hours late returning to the Corollas, and told them that he had been knocked out. Frank and Tony were immediately in their car chasing the Dockside contacts, accusing them of stealing the money back. The Corollas swore they would never do business with them again until they got their money back. To show that they meant what they said, they shot and killed one of the contacts. Dean was suspicious of Jimmy straight away and demanded to search Jimmy and his house. Jimmy protested his innocence and told Frank he was welcome to search his house. Frank said no, that he trusted Jimmy, but Dean felt sure Jimmy knew where the £500,000 was. Jimmy had no idea that's how much money there was.

"Three months later, Jimmy arranged to get some time off to take his family on holiday. He was going to take the family to Scotland for Christmas, he told Frank, but his plan was to drive them all to the airport and leave for good.

"It was a Friday morning, and he was doing his usual rounds. He had started the day early, as he had to fit in a visit to the warehouse. He didn't want to be late on his regular Friday routine and throw suspicion on himself. He then drove to his house and hid the money.

"He continued on his route for the rest of the day and finally finished at four-thirty. He parked the van at the back of dry cleaners and was surprised to be met by Frank, Tony, and Dean. Dean was wielding a baseball bat. A very angry Frank asked, 'Where is it,

Jimmy?' At least, that's what an eyewitness heard." Max seemed distant for a moment, then continued. "I, of course, never met the man, and Catharine was always vague about his background. All I know was he was from Glasgow, was very handsome, and he loved Catharine very much. It was this family, Frank Corolla and his son, Tony, who killed Jimmy, Catharine, and Fraser." Max's eyes glazed, and you could see the sadness in them. "Cat is lucky to be alive. If the police had taken any longer to get there," Max paused again, "she would have been killed, also."

"I was upstairs in my bedroom, reading," Cat's voice startled Max, and she turned to her.

"Cat, are you all right?"

Cat was sitting up, a little woozy. "Yeah, it's time I told what happened, Max. I was lying on my bed reading. I was supposed to get changed and pack a bag to be ready to go on holiday, but when I got home about quarter to four, the book was lying on my bed, and as there was lots of time, I picked it up and started to read. Later, I heard this noise coming from the back of the garden. There was a small access road to all the houses there. It runs along to the end by the school. It was dark. I looked at the clock by the bed. It was five-thirty. I jumped up, as I thought I'd better get moving, or Mum would hit the roof. I was always reading and not doing what I was supposed to. I looked out the window. There was a street light by the lane, so I could see quite clearly. Frank and Tony Corolla were dragging my stepfather. They held him under each arm, one on each side, and his feet were dragging along on the ground. They came up the path and in through the kitchen door.

"Mum was ironing in the living room, and Fraser was watching TV. I looked over the banister and could see them as they dragged Jimmy into the living room. His face was all bloodied, and his eyelids were swollen, as were his lips. He couldn't stand because they had broken his legs. My mother screamed, and Fraser stood up behind her. 'Where is the money, Jimmy?' they asked."

Cat was silent for what seemed to be an eternity; no one dared speak. "Jimmy tried to talk but most of his teeth were broken and just a gurgling sound came out. Tony pulled Fraser away from Mum and shot him in the head. Just like that. I let out a scream, but they didn't hear me for my mother's screams. She was hysterical. Jimmy was trying to crawl to Fraser. 'Where is it, Jimmy?' Frank yelled, and they shot him in the back of both knees. I thought Jimmy was dead, but he had just passed out. Frank turned him over, and Tony went to the kitchen and got a pot of water. I didn't know what to do. Tony came back and threw the water over Jimmy. He came round, and Frank said to him, 'Jimmy, you've got one more chance.' He grabbed my mother by the hair. She fell to her knees. She was screaming uncontrollably."

Cat looked over to Max; she had her hand over her mouth trying to quieten her sobs. Theo was still looking shocked and had tears in her eyes.

Sarah spoke. "Do you want to take a break, Cat?"

"No, no, I have to do this now." Sarah walked over and took her hand.

"Again, Frank asked, 'Where is it, Jimmy?' Frank was holding a gun to my mother's head. Jimmy was trying to speak but nothing came out. Frank shot my mother in the back of the head. Tony started to kick Jimmy, calling him a piece of shit. Frank was pacing back and forth saying, 'I trusted you, Jimmy, and this is how you repay me.' Then he just shot him, again and again and again. 'He's got to have hidden the money here,' Frank said. 'Let's rip this joint apart.'

"I could hear them banging around downstairs, and I realized that they would come up, and I had no way of getting out. I kept telling myself to move, but my legs wouldn't. Then something took over. I can't explain it. I was helpless and couldn't think, but somewhere inside me someone took over and told me what to do. I just followed the voice inside my head that said, 'Go hide in your wardrobe. You have to survive so they can be punished.'

"The wardrobe in my bedroom was kind of funny. It looked ordinary, but it had an extra bit you couldn't see. The extra bit went into the bottom of the hot water cupboard that had been blocked off from the hall. I had found it when I was a kid and used to hide there. It took Mum weeks to find out where I was hiding. I had to make myself really small. This voice in my head was telling me not to make any noise, 'be very still.' I heard them going through the house and ripping it to pieces. I heard Tony in my bedroom. 'Where's that brat of a kid, you know the girl, what's her name?'

"Frank came into my room, 'Cat. She's not hiding somewhere is she, Tony?'

I could hear Tony move the clothes along in my closet. 'Nah, she must have a paper run or something.'

Frank said, 'Maybe she knows where the money is. Maybe we should wait and ask her.'

I wanted to scream, 'No, go away,' but instead this voice in my head was humming to me. 'You're going to be okay.' I should be dead, I was thinking, but this voice kept humming.

Frank said, 'I'll go and get a sledge hammer and we'll start ripping these walls out.'

I thought, I'm dead, I'm dead, they'll find me. Then I heard a siren in the background. I held my breath because Tony was so close to me. The siren was also getting closer.

'Tony,' Frank yelled, 'we gotta get the fuck out of here. We'll come back later and search. Come on.'

"They both left. I could hear their car start about the same time the police arrived. I was too scared to move. This voice in my head was saying, 'it's okay, you're all right now. You can get out now,' but I couldn't move. My legs were cramped up, and my head was bent over. I heard the police saying things like 'Bloody hell, are they alive?' and 'That's just a kid!' I could even hear one of them retching. I wanted to call out, but I couldn't. A couple of them came upstairs, 'What a mess,' I heard one of them say. 'I wonder if they found what they were looking for.'

'No,' I heard myself answer.

I heard a woman say, 'Shit, did you hear that?'

I said, 'Hello? I'm in the cupboard.' I still couldn't move.

She asked, 'What's your name?'

'Cat,' I said.

She said, 'Just keep talking to us pet, we'll find you. Don't be scared. Are you hurt?'

'I don't think so,' I said, and then I could see a policewoman on her knees looking down at me. 'Can you get out pet? Can I help you?'

'I don't think I can,' I said.

The policewoman said, 'That's okay. I'm going to sit beside you while Jeff goes for help. Jeff, hurry! It's very cramped in there.' She sat down and stroked my face. She said, 'You were very clever getting yourself in here. Is this where you used to hide when you were small?'

'Yes, but I'm too big now,' I said. I could hear the other policeman bound up the stairs saying, 'Yes, she's alive, and we think unhurt. She's stuck in the bottom of this cupboard.'

I could hear a lot of noise and then the wall opened up. They had to remove a shelf, but then I was free. The policewoman just took me in her arms and held me. She stroked my hair and said I was going to be all right. Apparently I was humming."

"You always hum when you're nervous," Theo said.

"How could I be all right? My mother was dead, so were Fraser and Jimmy. I wondered what I had done wrong. I should have changed when I got home. I had to go downstairs to get out. When I saw my mum, I tried to get her up. The policewoman had to drag me off her.

"They took me to the hospital, and I sat with the policewoman. My mother was still alive; she lived for a couple of hours. But I was told that if she had survived she would have been brain-dead. I thought, better she go with Fraser. They actually kept me in hospital that night. The policewoman stayed with me. The next day I went to the police station and told them everything I had seen and heard. Two very surprised men, Frank and Tony Corolla, were arrested.

"The court case was ten weeks later. I stayed with foster families a few days at a time. The police were afraid that someone might try to kill me. Not that they told me. They just said they were keeping me safe. After I told them about Frank and Tony, I stopped talking. They didn't know about Max till I was taken home one day to get some clothes, and I picked up the mail and handed them a letter from Max. It wasn't a long trial. They were worried I wouldn't identify Frank and Tony as I wasn't talking, but this I seemed to be able to do. When it came time, I just did what this voice in my head told me to. I just wanted them put away, and then I didn't speak. They got three life sentences each."

Cat looked very scared as she told what happened next. "As I left the court, Dean, Frank's youngest son, came up to me before the police could stop him. He was with his younger sister, Maria. Their mother had died years before. Dean said, 'I'll get you ya bitch. If it takes me the rest of my life, I'll get you.'

Maria was being restrained. 'You're dead!' she said. Then the police got me out of there."

Theo was crying more audibly now and tried to get out of bed. Cat stood up and walked to her.

"You've been living with this all this time, and I didn't know. Oh, Cat, honey, why didn't you tell me?" She reached out to Cat.

Cat went willingly to her arms, "I just couldn't, Theo; it would have made it all real."

"Oh, baby, come here," and Cat lay on Theo's bed with her.

Sarah stood and looked at Max, "Do you feel like getting some fresh air, Dr. Lawson?"

"Oh, I think we're on a first name basis now, dear, don't you?"

Sarah smiled, "Yes," and offered her arm.

Chapter 18

Max and Sarah found a bench in the sun. "Max, you look pretty shaken. Are you all right?"

Max took a hankie from her pocket. "I'll be all right in a moment, dear. It's just that I never knew all the details before. When the police rang me, they just said that Cat had witnessed all the murders, and she was, of course, their prime witness. I said that I'd come over immediately, and they said no."

Sarah looked surprised. "They said no?"

"They thought Cat was in real danger of retaliation, and it would be better for her to come to me after the trial, if that's what I wanted. I said, 'of course that's what I wanted'; Callum and I couldn't have children. I had missed out on knowing Fraser, and there was no way I couldn't not have Cat. They said if I came to get her it may leave a trail back to New Zealand."

"So how did she get here?"

Max laughed just a little. "Oh, it was very Machiavellian. I sent some money over with half of it in Canadian dollars. It took a little help from the British and New Zealand governments and one of Cat's schoolteachers."

"I'm intrigued now, Max."

"After the trial was over, there was a school skiing trip to Canada. Cat wasn't going back to school, and I'm not too sure she had much interest in skiing, but it was a way to make it work. The ski trip was in Banff in the Rocky Mountains with a day trip to Calgary, which included a trip to the zoo and shopping for souvenirs. She went to Canada with her passport that said she was Catharine Campbell. With the help of the government here, I had a passport made for her in the name of Lawson on the condition that we hand it in when we arrived in New Zealand."

"So Caitlin Craig isn't her real name."

"No" said Max. "Her real name is Catharine Yates, although all her life, since she was two, she was known as Catharine Campbell. Jimmy never officially adopted her, but they wrote Campbell on all her documents and school things. It was me who chose Caitlin. As you would know, Sarah, it's Irish for Catharine."

"Indeed, I do," said Sarah. "And a fine name it is, too."

"And Craig was her mother's and my maiden name. Anyway, the day they went to Calgary it was arranged with one of the teachers—only he knew, no other teacher or kid on the trip knew—that he would slip away with Cat, get a taxi to the bus station, and put her on the next bus to Vancouver where I would be waiting."

"With the passport in the name of Caitlin Lawson?"

"Yes."

"Very clever."

"He was instructed to make sure Cat had food and water in her day backpack, a change of clothes, and only one personal item. Cat was told not to speak to anyone or get off the bus till she got to Vancouver. They used cash, so there was no record of Cat on the bus. I just stayed at the bus station and met every bus that came from Calgary till Cat arrived. I had no trouble recognizing her; apart from being the only frightened girl on the bus, she looked just as my younger sister did when she was thirteen."

"Max, do you think the Corollas are after Cat?"

"I don't know, Sarah. Who else could it be? You are sure that it is Cat?"

"Yes, I am."

"Well, I can tell you that it's not Frank or Tony."

"How do you know that?"

"About five or six years ago, I hired an investigator on the net."

"You can do that?"

"Yes, it was relatively easy."

"Why did you want an investigator?"

"Well, it had been twenty years since the Corollas had been jailed, and I wanted to know if they were still in prison or if they had been paroled."

"What did you find out?"

"I found out that Frank had died in jail from cancer. Tony had been paroled but had been killed shortly after his release. It was drug related; a payback for a killing he had committed twenty years earlier with some business associates in the docklands area. At least, that's the report I got. There wasn't much information on Dean. The dry cleaning business was closed down, and he had been in and out of trouble with the police, then nothing—as if he just disappeared."

"So it could be Dean?"

"I guess so."

"How was Cat when she got off the bus in Vancouver?"

"She was pale, withdrawn, and her eyes were dead, as if she had no soul. I don't think she had any difficulty recognizing me either. My sister and I looked similar, I'm taller and my hair is redder to her darker auburn, but we still look very much alike. She didn't speak. I had to control myself really well. All I wanted to do was take her in my arms and hold her and cry, but I knew I had to be careful. I did hold her, and she did return the hug, whether it was for the likeness of her mother or what she wanted, I didn't know. I took her to my hotel for the night while I confirmed bookings and made arrangements. She just lay on the bed in the fetal position and watched TV. She wasn't angry or resentful; she just wasn't there, and she wouldn't speak. She would nod the occasional yes or no, but that was all."

"How did Cat take to your husband?"

Max got a wonderful smile on her face. "He was simply marvellous with her. I don't think he could have loved his own daughter any more than he did Cat. He was so patient with her. We arrived in Wellington, and Callum was there to meet us. He brought the dog we had then, Honey, a golden Labrador. He couldn't have done anything better. Cat sat in the back of the car as we drove to Paekakariki with Honey by her side. It was instant love for both of them. She still wasn't talking. Honey and Cat became inseparable after that. She slept on Cat's bed. Cat could run along the beach faster with Honey than Callum and I could. Callum taught her to play chess; it's how they communicated. Otherwise, we just went about our lives and made sure Cat knew she was loved. I told her that we would not send her to school until she was ready. I took leave from work because I was able to do some from home, and Cat spent most of her days walking the beach with Honey and reading.

"One day, about three months later, she strolled in from the beach and came up to me and said, 'I'm ready, Aunty Max.' I'm sure my mouth must have dropped open, but I tried not to show my surprise and said, 'good. I'll call the school.' I wanted to jump up and down and ask her two thousand questions; instead, I just went back to what I was doing. She wandered over to the window and stood looking out and finally said, 'I wish Fraser could see this.' Sarah, I thought I was going to start crying, I could feel the tears, and I told myself, 'too much, Max, get a grip.' Instead, I just said, 'me, too,' and after a minute, because I couldn't help myself, I said, 'any time you want to talk, anytime, I'm here.' She turned to me, nodded, and said, 'I know.' To shut up was the hardest thing I think I've ever had to do in my life.

"When Callum came home and walked in the door, Cat and Honey were lying on the floor watching television, and she just looked up and said, 'Hi, Uncle Callum.' Callum was great. He didn't miss a beat; he just put his hands over his ears and said, 'Ooh, an English accent. Ooh!' Cat just started to laugh, actually giggle, so Callum went over, and they just started to roughhouse with each other and Honey. Honey was barking so loud, and her tail was wagging, and all I could do was cry and laugh at the same time. That's when he started to call her 'Sport.' She loved it.

"Cat started school in Wellington the next week, and we went back to the apartment during the week and to the beach on weekends. It didn't take very long for her to catch up on her schoolwork. She was very bright. Callum would encourage her to talk about politics or anything that was topical. When the Rainbow Warrior was blown up, he and Cat had their own theories long before anyone else. I tried, on the odd occasion, to get her to talk about her past, and she would, but only up until the murders. She told me about her mum and stepdad. I don't think she was overly fond of him, but he was kind to her. It was obvious that he really loved Fraser, but she said that was okay because she and her mum were very close. Apparently they even talked often about coming out here, and she thought that they were. But I never pushed her to talk about the murders." Max turned from Sarah and said, with a shaky voice, "It must have been awful."

"Max, I don't know how much protection I can get Cat. It's all speculation, and I don't know if I can make it fly at work. We'll certainly look into finding this Dean Corolla, but without evidence that it's him…" She shrugged and put her hands in the air.

"I'll insist that they stay with me at the beach, and I'll get Frances to stay, too. The more, the safer I think. Have you met Frances yet?"

Sarah looked slightly uncomfortable, "No, not yet."

"Oh, I think you two will get on very well."

"So I hear. We had better go back in and speak to the girls."

Ellis Paris Ramsay

Chapter 19

Cat was lying in Theo's arms, feeling at peace for the first time since she could remember.

"I guess this is going to take time," said Theo. "I feel as if I don't know you. So how did you get from there to here?"

Cat told her about the ski trip, the schoolteacher, and Max in Vancouver.

"So your name isn't even Caitlin?"

"No, it's not. Apparently my birth father insisted on me being named Catharine, after my mother, and believe it or not, my American grandmother. He said he loved how the three most important women in his life were all named Catharine. Mum said he was a real romantic but with a Peter Pan complex. Everything was a game to him, and he was destined not to make old bones. He refused to ever consider his own mortality and always stared death in the face. My real name is Catharine Shelly Yates. My dad was a poet as well; but ever since I was two years old, I've been called Catharine Campbell. Cocco isn't the first one to call me CC. I used to get that all the time at school when I was a kid. I like Caitlin though, I feel like a Caitlin. Max did well, and I couldn't have been luckier to have Max and Callum for parents."

"Did your mother ever talk about your American family?"

"I don't think she knew them. I don't think that she knew any more than I've just told you."

"Have you ever thought about trying to find them?"

"Not really. That would have meant getting a passport and going to America."

"So that's why you never wanted to travel overseas, I always thought you were afraid to fly."

"I know it has been twenty-six years, but the Corolla family has long memories, and I'll never forget what Dean said, 'I'll get you ya bitch, no matter how long it takes.'"

Cat went rigid, "Oh, Theo, it's because of me you were nearly killed, I'm to blame."

"You're not to blame, Cat, but the Corollas are and possibly your stepfather, Jimmy. Tell me about your childhood. I can't believe I'm living with a Pom."

Cat dug Theo in the ribs. "My mother was Australian, my father American, my stepfather Scottish. I was born in England, but I live in New Zealand."

"Oh, my god," said Theo, "I'm living with a mongrel,"

Cat laughed. "No, not really. Just a typical Kiwi, and I am a Kiwi. We lived in a three up and two down in London's East End. We weren't rich. Not many people were where we lived and where I went to school, but once Jimmy started to work for the Corollas, we didn't go without. We had summer holidays, unlike a lot of kids at my school. Mum used to love the beach, so we often went to Bournemouth, Plymouth, or Devon and took a September holiday in Blackpool and spent Easter in Scotland.

"Jimmy really loved Fraser and spent as much time with him as he could. I was always welcome to join in, but I was happy being with Mum. Most girls at school would do anything to avoid family time, but I loved it. Jimmy would take Fraser to school football on a Saturday morning, a pub lunch, then off to watch the local team in the afternoon. That left Mum and I to go shopping, have lunch up town, and then either take in an art gallery or a movie, or if we could afford it, a matinee at a musical."

"You were so lucky to be close to all that wonderful theatre, Cat."

"I know. Most of my mates thought I was mad. It sounded like torture to them to be stuck in a theatre with their mum. Maybe it was because Mum was from the Australian outback and never had the opportunity to go when she was growing up that she loved it so much, and so did I."

"When did you know you were gay?"

"I think I always knew even from when I was four or five. Not that I could have named it then. I remember watching movies or TV programs and never understanding why the leading lady went off with the guy. I always wanted her to go with the other woman."

"I can't believe I'm only now having this conversation with you, Cat, after we have been together for eleven years. It's like starting all over again."

"Well, maybe that's not a bad idea. Theo, you know I love you, but we haven't been exactly close lately."

"Oh, that's just the pressure of work."

"I don't know that it is. You've seemed unhappy to be with me."

"Oh, don't be so melodramatic. Tell me more. How old were you when you had your first crush on a girl?"

"And like that. You always change the subject."

Theo looked annoyed.

"I was nine, she was the babysitter. Her name was Louise, and she was fifteen."

"You always did like older women then?"

"You're only two years older than I. She used to let me brush her long hair for hours. I thought she was beautiful. It broke my heart when I saw her go out with boys."

"What about your first kiss?"

"Twelve. Gwyneth Davis. She lived three doors down. She didn't go to the same school as I did, she was catholic. Her mother worked till five, so she used to come to our house after school, till her mum got home."

"Did you kiss her, or did she kiss you first?"

"Really, Theo, you're like a kid. She kissed me. We were bragging about what good kissers we were going to be, and she suggested we practice on each other."

"Oh, what a great line. I wish I had thought of it."

"Seriously, Theo, we need to talk."

Theo sat up; she was not happy. "I don't think this is the time or place, Cat. We have plenty of time to talk when I get home."

"Theo, we haven't made love for over two years. Do you still love me?"

"It hasn't been that long." She was really pissed off now. "You count? Well, that takes all the spontaneity out of it now; do we have a schedule that I don't know about?"

"Theo, I don't want us to argue. I just want to know where I stand with you."

"You're so needy and sensitive sometimes; I don't see why we have to tell each other that we love each other all the time."

"Once in a while would be nice."

Theo didn't say anything but picked up a magazine and leafed through it.

"Theo, you show more affection to our friends than you do me."

"That's ridiculous, Cat. Of course, I love you. We have a good life together, don't we? I'm just not the demonstrative type."

"Theo, I'm not talking about when we are with other people, I'm talking about when we are alone."

"I'm comfortable with you, Cat, and sometimes my job takes so much out of me it's all I can give. What we need to talk about is that you are in danger and what's to be done about it."

Cat knew there was no point in pursuing the conversation, just like always. "I don't think we should go home, Theo. If he followed the car then he probably knows where we live. I've been home the last two nights."

"I know, and I feel quite sick when I think how vulnerable you were."

So she does care. "Maybe we should stay at a motel or something. I don't want to put anyone at risk, including you, Theo."

"Oh, no, you don't. We stay together; I doubt that I'll be back at work for a week or two."

"Now that the police know who they are looking for they may catch him soon."

"I hope so. He is only eight years older than I. I wonder if I would still recognize him. We were always invited to the Corolla's parties and barbeques."

"I didn't know that England ever had good enough weather for barbeques." Theo tried to keep a straight face.

"You can say that after the summer we had, or not as it were, at the beginning of this year?"

"True," said Theo. "I hope it's a better one ahead of us."

"Well, it's been a great spring so far, so let's cross our fingers."

Sarah and Max entered the room and found Cat and Theo asleep on the bed.

"Wow, they fit perfectly, don't they?"

"I always thought so."

"When did you find out Cat was gay? Did you mind?"

"When she was sixteen and asked if she could take her girlfriend to the school ball and if I could help her do something with her hair."

"Really? What did you say?"

"I said I'd take her to my hairdresser and asked her if she wanted to wear a suit or a gown."

Sarah laughed. "I have to ask, what did she say?"

"She said she'd check with her girlfriend. And no, I didn't mind. In my profession, you learn to value happiness wherever you find it."

"Did your husband feel the same way?"

This time Max laughed. "He put his hand on my shoulder and said, 'Sorry old girl, there might not be any grandchildren, but look on the bright side, you get another daughter.' 'What about you?' I asked, 'you'll miss out, too?' Callum said, 'No, I won't, if Cat has the taste I think she has, then I'll have three beautiful women in my life.'"

Theo woke, "Hi. We fell asleep."

"We can see that. How are you feeling?"

"I'm ready to get out of this joint."

"That's what we want to talk about."

"I'm awake." Cat sat up. "We think we might be best in a motel."

"No, you're not. You're coming to stay with me."

"Max, that will put you in danger, and I couldn't do that."

"I want you with me. I couldn't take care of you last time you needed me, I'm going to now."

"Aunty Max, you were there for me and have been ever since."

"Frances flew home this morning but said she will be back Friday evening. She can stay as well."

"And I'm going to hang around, too."

"Great," said Theo. "You'll get to meet Frenchy."

Groaning, Sarah covered her face with her hands. "What is it with you people? Cat's life is in serious danger, and all you can think about is setting me up with this Frances/Frenchy."

Theo, Cat, and Max all laughed. "It's because we all know that you were made for each other."

"We probably won't like each other."

Max said, "Cat, are you going to tell Aroha, Lizzie, Willie, and Cocco about...?" Max couldn't think what to say.

"Yes, I am, the next time we are all together. I don't think I could bear to tell them individually. Plus, if they hang around me, they will be at a certain amount of risk as well, so they need to know. I guess it will have to be tonight as Lizzie is staying with me, and I'll have to tell her why she can't and why she can't stay there on her own."

"Give them all a call, Cat," said Sarah, "and we'll all meet here."

"It will have to be later as Lizzie has to take Danny to soccer practice."

"Why don't we all meet back here at nine? I better go to my office and get the ball rolling on this Corolla character."

Chapter 20

L izzie was the last to arrive, because she had to drop Danny off at Matt's.

"Sorry, I drove as fast as I could."

Sarah put her hand out and said, "It's nice to meet you at last, Lizzie, and don't worry, you've missed nothing. I was waiting till you got here."

"Damn, you had to be gorgeous, didn't you?"

Sarah's mouth dropped wide open.

Cocco said, "Don't worry, Sarah darling, if you're going to be one of us you'll have to get used to Lizzie's candour."

"I don't know where to begin," said Cat. "I love you all, and I should have told you all this before, but I couldn't. It's not because I couldn't trust you or wanted to hide anything from you, it's just to tell you makes it all real."

Cat was sitting on the side of Theo's bed, holding her hand. "It's all right, Cat, they'll understand."

"Cat darling, this is all so melodramatic," said Cocco. "I know, you really a man." Willie was standing over Cocco and swiped him across the head. "Ouch, I'll get welfare on you. I go to Home for Battered Women."

"Will you shut up, Cocco? This looks serious."

"I know, Willie, why you think I joke?"

"Cat, would you like me to start? I've read all the reports from London, and you take over when you can."

"That sounds like a cop-out, Sarah, but yes, please."

Sarah slowly and meticulously went through everything in detail. She thought that once was enough for this story to be told, so she would get it right. There were a few more details she could add after reading the reports. For example, although the police searched the house extensively, the money was never found. "Dean Corolla and his younger sister had inherited a small fortune with the deaths of their father and older brother. This may explain why he was in trouble with the police to begin with, and then after the inheritance, he disappeared."

Everyone was transfixed by Sarah's explanation. Cat interjected occasionally but mostly left it to Sarah. "I've already been in touch with Interpol, but as of yet there's nothing. New Zealand immigration has no record of a Dean Corolla entering the country, so if he is here, and it is him, he is using another name and passport." Max took over from Sarah and told of the intrigue that got Cat to Canada, then New Zealand.

Max then took a bottle of brandy from her bag, saying, "I thought we could all do with a drink around about now." Aroha, Lizzie, Willie, and Cocco all took a drink from the plastic cups they were handed without saying a word. Even Cocco was speechless. Finally, after a minute of silence, Cocco did speak. "Oh, that good, she beats me. I even think she beats Madame Butterfly." Willie looked so angry. He was just about to burst with rage until he heard Cat laughing. They all looked at Cat, then Theo and Max joined in, followed by Lizzie and Aroha. Willie was gobsmacked.

As if to appease Willie, Cocco said, "Well, I'm not the tragic queen any more, Cat is. I happily hand over my crown," and he silently mimicked the removing of the crown and offered it to Cat.

"And I happily accept it, Cocco." She was still laughing, and Cocco bowed.

Lizzie's laughter turned into quiet sobs, "I can't believe what you have been through, Cat. How does someone get over seeing her family killed in front of her?"

"Oh, I was very lucky, Lizzie. I had Max and Callum and a beautiful new country to live in. There was nothing to remind me of my previous life, except Max's family likeness to my mother and I suppose me, but that's kinda comforting. It gave me a feeling of belonging and family."

Max wiped away the tears from the corner of her eyes and silently mouthed "thank you," and when she regained her composure, she said, "It wasn't a one way track. Cat gave us the family we could never have, and we were very happy, very."

Lizzie asked, "So who are you, if you're not Caitlin Craig?"

Theo said, "May I introduce Ms. Catharine Shelly Yates?"

"I'm still Cat, and I think I'll keep Craig. It will make me feel closer to my mother and Max, of course."

"What about your American family, will you try to find them?"

Cat shrugged. "I really haven't ever given it any thought."

"That's because you could never risk applying for a passport, darling. After the police find this Dean, perhaps we could go to America and look."

"I guess we could."

"Meantime, we have to keep Cat safe," said Sarah. "Obviously, she can't go home; so until Theo gets out on Saturday, Cat, I want you to stay with me."

"That's a great idea, Sarah," said Theo, "but are you allowed to do that?"

"Not exactly, but I'll feel a lot better."

"I can't put you in danger, Sarah."

"Well, either you stay with me, or I won't get any sleep because I'll be doing surveillance anywhere you are. Come Saturday, you and Theo move in with Max, and Max said she'll get Frances to stay with you as well."

"Have you met Frenchy yet?" asked Willie and Cocco in unison.

Sarah rubbed her eyes. "No, and I suspect I won't like her at all."

"Yes, you will," came the reply from all.

"Okay, okay, enough. This is serious."

"Maybe I can make a suggestion, Sarah."

"Please do, Max."

"Why don't I pick Theo up on Saturday, and you and Cat can follow, and maybe see if I'm being followed? Then the others can all come out for dinner and maybe work out a buddy system for Cat."

"Oh, oh," said Cocco, "I've got new recipe I've been dying to try out. I'll bring the entrée."

"I think that's a good idea, Max, and I take it Frances will be there."

Everybody except Max said, "Uh huh." Max just smiled.

"It's got to happen sooner or later, Sarah."

"Does Frenchy know you're trying to set us up?"

"No." said Max. "She'd run a mile."

Slightly surprised, Sarah said, "What makes you all so sure that I'm gay anyway?"

"Well, are you?" asked Lizzie. All eyes were on Sarah.

Sarah shook her head in disbelief and said, "Cat, I have to go back to the office. I'll be by in an hour to pick you up. Goodnight all."

Once again in unison they all said, "Goodnight, Sarah."

As she walked down the hall she could hear Cocco's last remark. "Oh, her days are numbered."

Sarah walked to her car. Two days ago her life was as it always was. Now she had potentially seven new friends, a family, and possibly more. Sarah had been with other women when she was younger but the last few years it had been men, simply because it was easier. It was just sex and nothing more, and that's all she wanted. She never particularly liked the men she was with, mostly because they just saw her as a body and never took her seriously. Plus, she wasn't sure she was the two kids and white picket fence type. But lately she hadn't even bothered with men. She was looking for something more, but she didn't know what. Her work usually precluded anything serious, but perhaps it was time for a change. She didn't know whether she was looking forward to meeting Frances or not. She had convinced herself that they wouldn't like each other. "We'll see," she muttered to herself as she pulled out of the hospital car park.

While Willie and Cocco were discussing Sarah with Cat, Theo, and Max, Aroha quietly said to Lizzie, "I need to talk to you outside."

Lizzie obligingly stood and followed as Aroha said, "We'll be back in a moment."

Once in the corridor Aroha faced Lizzie and said, "Lizzie, I'm not ready for you to come home. I'm still hurting and having trouble working out why you did it. You say you love Danny and me, and yet you chose to jeopardize our relationship, our family, as if it weren't important to you."

"Aroha, I don't know why. Do you want me to lie to you?"

"You have already by what you did."

"Aroha, I love you and Danny, and if I could take that moment back I would. Can't you just forgive me, and let us get on with our lives? You know nothing like this will ever happen again."

"Do I?"

"Yes."

Aroha looked Lizzie hard in the face and after a minute said, "I think you had better stay with Willie and Cocco. I'll tell Danny you'll pick him up Saturday for soccer and drop him off at Matt's. Tell the others I'll see them Saturday, and say goodnight for me. I'll see you then, too."

"Aroha, please."

Aroha had already turned and was walking out of the hospital.

When Lizzie returned to the room softly crying, Willie looked up.

"I guess I'm staying with you guys," she said, "for a while."

Willie was on his feet, "You know you're welcome."

Max said, "Would you like me to talk to her, Lizzie?"

Lizzie attempted to smile. "No, it's all right, Max. I'll sort this mess out myself."

"Come on, I'll take you home," said Willie.

Cocco stood. "Yes, I must get beauty sleep. I work in café tomorrow and Friday, so we'll see you Saturday at Max's."

Cocco kissed everyone, and the three of them left.

Cat asked, "Do you think they'll work it out, Max?"

"Well, they have a solid foundation, and if Aroha could just accept it for the stupid mistake it was, I think this could make them stronger. Well, I'll toddle off and give you both a little space till Sarah comes back. I'll pop in tomorrow."

"Hey, Max," said Theo, "how's Ted?" Cat looked at Theo quizingly.

"Oh, he's fine. Fit as a fiddle actually."

Theo smiled and said, "It suits you."

Max smiled back and left.

"What was that all about?" asked Cat.

"I'll tell you when you've grown up. Now tell me, what kind of flat do you think Sarah will have? Modern, cottage messy, or will she be a neat freak?"

Aroha pulled into Matt's driveway, wiping the tears from her eyes. She missed Lizzie so much but just couldn't understand why she did what she did. She tooted the horn, and Danny came running out and jumped in the car.

"Are you all right, Mum?"

"Yeah, I'm fine. I've just got something in my eye."

Danny didn't believe her. "Mum, when's Lizzie coming home? I really miss her."

"I'm not sure, bud. Better get you home and to bed. It's a school day tomorrow, and you'll see Lizzie on Saturday."

Chapter 21

Come on Jemma, you should be word perfect by now. Dress rehearsals start next week."

"Sorry, Miss."

"'Sorry, Miss' is not going to cut it. If you're not word perfect by Monday, Jemma, you're out. I'll put your understudy in. Just because you have a beautiful voice doesn't mean you get away with not learning your lines."

"Okay, no need to be so grumpy, Ms. Beck. I'm doing my best."

Lizzie rubbed her brow, feeling the frustrations of her life and thinking she should not be taking it out on Jemma.

"Okay, Jemma, what say we leave it today, and we'll both return refreshed and READY Monday? Go on, off you go."

"Nerves a little frazzled today, Lizzie? Perhaps I could help you out there and relieve a little tension."

Lizzie lifted her head to find Jojo leaning on the wall.

"No, thank you." Lizzie turned back to her script and continued to read. It was nearly time for first period of the afternoon, and all the kids were making their way to their classes. Lizzie didn't have class for the next period, so she was spending the time making notes to give the kids to take home for the weekend. Things would start to get very hectic when they went into dress rehearsal at the end of next week.

"Oh, come on. Would you like me to massage your neck? You look pretty tense."

"No, thank you." Lizzie hadn't even bothered to turn around. She did so not want to see Jojo, let alone talk to her.

Jojo had her hand on Lizzie's shoulder, "I know you want to."

Lizzie spun around and pushed Jojo to the wall, pinning her there. "I said no! And if you ever come near me again I'll cut your tits off, do you hear me?"

Lizzie was so angry she was shaking. She was so close to hitting Jojo that it scared her. "You've ruined my life, you stupid cow."

She felt herself losing control when she heard Torri Jacobs say, "Lizzie, your phone is ringing." She loosened the grip she had on Jojo. Jojo looked scared.

"Come on, Lizzie," Torri said very gently. "Your cell's ringing."

As if coming out of a trance Lizzie let go and watched Jojo scuttle away. Torri handed Lizzie her phone. Lizzie automatically answered it, "Lizzie Beck speaking. Danny, what's wrong?"

"Nothing. I just borrowed one of the kid's phones as I'm not allowed one."

Lizzie laughed. "You know the rules. Not till you're thirteen and can get a job to pay for the phone cards."

"Stink."

"What's up, squirt?"

"I need to talk to you about something important. Can you come home tonight? Mum says it's okay. I know you and Mum have fallen out, but Mum says it's okay."

Lizzie got that sick feeling in her stomach again. *Oh, god, she's told Danny. Maybe she's starting to prepare him for me never coming home.*

"What's it about, Danny? Are you all right?"

"Yeah, I'm fine, but I can't talk on the phone, I gotta give it back. See, I should have my own phone."

Lizzie realized that it couldn't be too serious if Danny was joking, and Aroha said it was okay.

"Come at seven o'clock?"

"Okay, squirt, I'll see you then."

Lizzie was feeling in better spirits. Lucky Torri came along. *Shit, I was really losing it.* She noticed Torri about to leave the room. "Torri" she called. "Thank you."

"You're welcome."

Then she smiled and said, "And it's Ms. Beck."

Torri smiled and left.

Aroha was having a shit of a day at work. She couldn't concentrate on anything and was so tearful she had to keep excusing herself to go to the loo. Dodgy tummy, she commented to a few who kept looking her way. It was lunchtime, and she could go sit in the sun and eat her lunch, but she wasn't hungry and preferred the quieter office. When the phone rang, she was reluctant to answer it but did anyway.

"Hi, Mum. It's Danny."

Aroha sat up, "What's wrong?"

"Nothing. I just wanted to check what time you'd be home tonight."

"I'm not sure. I've got a few errands to run after work. Seven or eight, why? What's up? Aren't you going to Dad's after school?"

"I've got a surprise for you, and Dad's picking me up later. Can you be home at seven?"

"What kind of surprise, Danny?"

"Well, it wouldn't be a surprise if I told you now, would it? But it is a nice surprise."

"It's not my birthday, is it?"

"No, Mum, you know when your birthday is. I noticed that you've been bummed out lately, what with Theo and Lizzie-mum not being home, so I thought I'd surprise you and cheer you up."

"What a sweet boy."

"Mum!"

Aroha laughed, "Okay, sweetie. I'll be home at seven o'clock on the dot."

"On the dot. Mum, can I have my own phone? I had to give Charlie two bucks for this call."

"No. See you later. Bye."

Danny rushed home from school, giving up all invitations from friends to do stuff. He had to make a stop to buy two candles. "Pink," Cocco said, "and good ones, not cheap, or they'll run all over the tablecloth and you're putting on your mum's best, so don't risk it." He had robbed his piggy bank this morning because he knew he'd have to pay to use his mates' phones and buy proper candles. *This making-up business was expensive.* He made a mental note to always have his girlfriends break up with him. He was embarrassed in the shop at having to buy them, but it was worth it. He had to put them in the fridge when he got home till just before he needed them as Cocco said, "they would burn slower and more even and not drip." *Thank goodness Cocco was sending the flowers.* Hopefully, they would be there when he got home.

With the help of Cocco and Willie, he was going to put everything back together. Cocco didn't tell him everything when he rang him to ask what was up with his mum and Lizzie. Normally, he can get any information out of Cocco. In fact, usually he can't shut him up, but it must be pretty bad if Cocco wasn't telling. He just said, "Lizzie had done something stupid and your mum's having trouble forgiving her."

He got home and waited by the window and checked his watch. Five to four, five minutes to go. The flowers were lying at the back door where Cocco had told the florist to leave them. Two red roses! He shook his head and was pleased he was not a girl. Then he saw the taxi drive up the road. He ran up the driveway and met it.

He opened the back door of the taxi and took out a chilly bin that had kept the food cool and a wine bag. "You've been paid?" he asked the driver.

"Yes, we're good."

"Thank you," he said and closed the car door and went back into the house. He put the chilly bin on the bench and placed the wine in the fridge. He opened the chilly bin and took out the clipboard with written instructions. He trusted Cocco and knew he would have written everything in the order he was to do things.

First, put everything in the fridge and pour yourself a Coke. Danny looked in the bin, and Cocco had included a big bottle of Coke. His mum and Lizzie only allowed him to drink Coke on weekends. When you have finished, wash your hands, and we'll get started. *Why are grown ups so obsessed with hand washing?* Okay, here we go. First, get out your mum's white Chinese linen tablecloth, it's in the linen cupboard in the hall, top shelf. There should be matching white serviettes with it. Now it will probably have fold marks that should be ironed, but we can't risk you burning it, so put it on straight away and it will fall a little bit. The silver cutlery that was your great grandmother's is in the top drawer of the chiffonier. Take out two dinner knives and forks, two dessertspoons, and two bread knives. Boil the jug, and pour boiling water into a Pyrex jug and place the cutlery in it. Don't burn yourself! Dry the cutlery right away with clean cloth and set table.

Cocco had drawn a picture of what went where. You don't have to worry about tablemats as nothing is hot. Get two champagne flutes from chiffonier and place above big knife on table. The serving spoon is the big one in drawer of silver cutlery. Put that in the middle. On top of the chiffonier is a thin silver tall vase. Place two roses in boiling water for two minutes, then chop off bottom inch, place them in vase with cold water, and put on table.

Danny was taking his time and doing everything just how Cocco had written, and he wondered how Cocco knew all this stuff but that made his brain hurt, so he didn't go there. Roll serviettes, and put them in silver rings. They're also in top of chiffonier. He stood back from the table and admired it. From other side cabinet in chiffonier is good white china. Take two big plates and place two of next size on top. Again, Cocco had drawn a picture of how it should look on the table, including the bread and butter plates on the left-hand side. Well done, Danny. It look good.

Now go to CD stack and find Jane Monheit's *Come Dream with Me* and Dianna Krall's *The Look of Love* and put them on ready to go. From the kitchen cupboard, get a small white plate and put a neat square of butter on it. In silver cutlery drawer there should be small butter knife; put it next to butter on table. The champagne bucket is top of shelf in kitchen. At 6:40 P.M., place ice in bucket, put bottle of Bolli in it, and place on chiffonier on top of mat. At 6:50 P.M., place smoked chicken and strawberry salad on table, add citrus dressing after you remove plastic cover. Place sunflower seed and paprika bread on board on chiffonier with bread knife. At 6:55 P.M., take chocolate mouse from fridge and place on long black plate from kitchen cupboard and put on chiffonier. Turn music on and light candles. Smile, you handsome boy, you did it!

Aroha was first to walk in the door. "Danny where are you? I'm ho…" She saw the table. "What's going on?"

Danny had combed his hair; a thing he never did.

"Good evening, madam. Can I take your jacket?"

Aroha was so taken aback that she let Danny remove her little jacket and sat when he pulled her chair out.

"What? Who? How?" and just then Lizzie shouted, "I'm here, squirt. What's so important?"

She stopped in her tracks when she saw Aroha sitting at the table looking just as surprised as she was.

Aroha said, "I smell the works of a particular little Japanese man afoot."

"No, Mum, it was me. Cocco just helped me do what I wanted to do. I know there's something wrong, and you're treating me like a kid and not telling me. All I know is that Lizzie-mum has done something stupid, and you're not forgiving her. I don't understand, Mum. I do stupid things all the time, and you always forgive me."

"It's not that simple, Danny."

"Yes, it is. We all love each other and should be together, well, at least until I'm old enough to go flatting."

They both smiled. A car horn tooted.

"That's Willie to pick me up. I'm staying with them tonight, and Willie is taking me to soccer in the morning. Then he's going to drop me off at Dad's, and when I come home on Sunday night I want you both here."

He picked up his already packed bag, kissed them both on the cheek, and left.

They heard the car door slam, and Willie's car drive off. They were both speechless.

"This looks wonderful. I can't believe he's done all this," said Aroha. "I can't remember the last time we had out the good silver and china." Aroha was examining the cloth, "I think it was when Willie knocked over a bottle of red wine, and I swore I'd never use this cloth again."

Lizzie was on her feet opening the bottle of champagne. "Bolli, what a treat."

She uncorked the bottle and was pouring it into their glasses saying, "That was the night, Cat, who never gets drunk, wasted herself."

"Oh, that's right. We had to help Theo stuff her in the car."

They were both laughing at the shared memory when Lizzie put her glass down on the table and knelt in front of Aroha.

"Aroha, darling, there is no answer to your question why I did it. I've thought of nothing else since it happened and all I can tell you is…" She took a moment to sort out her thoughts. Jane Monheit was singing "Blame It on My Youth" in the background. "All I can tell you is that it was a mechanical reaction that had nothing to do with love. My body let me down and responded to touch. There was no mental connection, no conscious decision, no reality. All I can remember, because it all happened so fast, was the shock of the orgasm, and the realization that it wasn't you. I felt dirty, and I felt abused. And if I were as dramatic as Cocco, I felt raped."

"Raped," said Aroha.

"Yes, I didn't ask for it or want her. My only fault is that I didn't stop her. All I can ask is that you forgive me for being human and not unfaithful. Aroha, I would walk over broken glass for you and Danny. I just had a bad nightmare. I could never willingly be unfaithful. It's you I love and you only."

Aroha was softly crying. "I've missed you so much, Lizzie. I don't think I could live without you by my side. You're my rock. When things are bad at work, I know I have you and Danny to come home to, and that's what gets me through."

Lizzie took Aroha's face in her hands and gently kissed the tears and very softly kissed her on the mouth.

Aroha moaned. "Oh, Lizzie, please don't ever hurt me again."

Lizzie, still kissing Aroha, managed to say, "I'll die first."

"I could do with a shower," said Aroha. "Care to join me?"

Lizzie was on her feet and grabbed the bottle of Bolli and glasses and asked, "What about the food?"

"I'm sure we'll be hungry enough later."

Lizzie, with both hands full, kissed Aroha. Aroha took the opportunity of Lizzie being defencelessness and allowed her hand to wander down her torso while returning her kiss.

"Not fair," mumbled Lizzie.

"Oh, Lizzie, I don't intend to be fair at all."

Ellis Paris Ramsay

Chapter 22

Frances woke early and decided to go for a run along the beach. She had planned to visit Theo this morning as she had some work to do in Wellington this afternoon and would miss her arrival here. She always loved staying with Max. It was so peaceful, unlike waking up in Auckland. She crept as quietly as she could out of the house in the hope of not disturbing Max. Ozzie, on the other hand, missed nothing, and as far as he was concerned wherever Frenchy was going, so was he. "Okay boy, but no barking." Ozzie seemed to understand and was at the door waiting with his tail wagging with impatience while Frenchy donned her shoes.

It was a beautiful morning, and no one else was in sight. She crossed the road to the beach and was doing a few warm up exercises while she decided where to run. Paekakariki was not very large; and Frenchy knew it well as she had often stayed with Max, mostly when Theo and Cat were there, but on her own sometimes, too. She decided to run along the beach, which ran parallel to the Parade, the street Max lived on, until she got to Henare Street. She could cut along there right on to Wellington Road, and at the end of that, right on to Beach Road for a short distance then right back on to the Parade. She reckoned if she did that a few times, that should give her a good workout, which she felt she needed as she was still having trouble taking in everything Max had told her about Cat.

Sleep was elusive for Sarah, so she decided she might as well rise and do something. There had been nothing further on Dean Corolla, and she wasn't sure where next to turn. She decided on a run to clear her head. It was 5:30 A.M., and the sun was just rising. It had been a while since she had been to Paekakariki, so she decided she might as well run there and get the lay of the land in case Max and Theo were followed. Max lived on the Parade between Ocean Road and Pingau Street.

Sarah drove out of Wellington and into Paekakariki, parking around the corner from Max's house on Ocean Road. She spent a couple of minutes studying the map she had in the car. She decided she would run along Wellington Road, going down all the side streets that led on to The Parade and check out places that might have access to Max's property or a view of her driveway. There seemed to be only one other person up and about. A very tall woman with a dog had just passed the end of the street on Wellington Road. She was also running.

Frenchy had nearly completed a second lap that she had set for herself. She was feeling great. Ozzie was happy running alongside her, and at this point, she felt as if she could run forever. There wasn't anyone around, and she felt as if she owned the world. Then she thought about Cat and couldn't believe the danger she might be in. She wondered what this Detective Inspector Adams was like and whether he was any good at his job and whether he was giving this case enough attention. They turned the corner on to Beach Road, and Ozzie got a whiff of last night's fish and chips that had been spilt outside the burger bar, and he took off across the road. "Ozzie!" shouted Frenchy. "Come back!" Ozzie managed to have some of the leftover food from the pavement before he bounded back. "Naughty boy, Ozzie, that's bad for you." Ozzie had the distinct look of 'I couldn't care less' on his face.

Sarah had zigzagged up and down all the streets between The Parade and Wellington Road, and as far as she could see, there were only two points where someone could hide. And the only way anyone could access Max's property, other than the driveway, was if they went through a neighbour's property and over the fence. "I hope everyone has barbecues tonight," she said out loud as if to make it so. She had just turned on to Beach Road and saw the other woman and dog ahead of her. She decided to run along the beach to finish off as she felt she had the layout down in her mind's eye. The tall woman in front of her had a beautiful physique and was obviously used to running. She had a T-shirt and short shorts on, and Sarah could see the sweat mark on the back of her shirt. Sarah, at five foot ten, seldom met a woman taller than herself and never one who ran. She decided to catch up to see if she could keep pace with this woman.

Frenchy was just hitting the beach again when she heard footsteps behind her. She looked back to see a woman running not far away. Ozzie was bored and was now entertaining himself by running at the sea, chasing seagulls, and checking out rubbish bins. The footsteps behind her were getting closer, and Frenchy increased her pace. She always had been able to outpace any woman she ran with, and most men. She could feel a trickle of sweat pour down her face, and her heart rate was increasing. The sand was still damp and easy to run on. She could stay ahead.

Sarah could tell this woman knew she was there as she had increased her pace. *You want a race then? I'll give you one.* Sarah broadened her gait, and within a few steps, she drew by her side. She was able to see a silhouette of Frenchy and liked very much what she saw. *Why can't I meet a woman like this? Her face is strong, and she looks determined. Her skin is naturally tanned, unlike mine that burns so easily.* Sarah lengthened her stride and was half a step ahead of Frenchy.

Who is this woman? I wonder if she lives here. Look at that hair. Why are women like that never attracted to me? All I seem to get are bimbos. Her body is fit, and there's not an ounce of fat anywhere. Her wrists are so thin and delicate. Look at those long fingers. Frenchy dropped back just a little to check out the view from the back and felt her pulse increase, and it wasn't just the running. *Okay, time to leave her for dust.*

She's checking me out. I can't believe it. She's checking my arse. Well then, sister, check this. Sarah increased her speed again.

Frenchy was finding it hard to breathe through the burn in her chest. *No, you don't. Eat my dust.*

They were now neck and neck, and it was obvious to anyone who might be watching that they were racing. Frenchy had never been pushed like this—certainly not by a woman—and not by a woman who was nearly as tall as she. They had passed Ocean Road and Pingau Street, which left Paneta and Tangaho, before they reached Henare at the end of the strip. *Oh, shit, I've got to make it. I hope Ozzie is around somewhere, but I daren't look.*

God, this woman means business. I could do with her on my team. I wonder what she does. She's probably a professional athlete and doesn't look like the type who comes in second. I'm going to end up in a heap. I hope she can do CPR! If I make it to the end of this stretch it will be a personal best. Paneta, two more to go.

Look at this body. I wish I had a camera with me. I'd love to photograph her. Yes, in the morning light just as dawn is breaking and dappled light falls across her face. Maybe I should just ask her. Yeah, that would go well. 'Hi, do you want to come to my place and let me photograph you?' I'm sure she gets that kind of offer all the time. She's not even breathing hard. I gotta get out more.

She's so cool. She's not even acknowledging me. Look at those legs; they go on forever. I wonder what this Frances looks like. She's probably the exact opposite of this woman. Maybe I should just say 'hello,' followed by something really clever like, 'Do you come here often? Do you want to go for coffee?' She probably doesn't drink coffee. Just concentrate on keeping pace.

Tangaho, I'm nearly there. I've never asked you before goddess, but help me make it. Don't let me fall to pieces in front of this woman, and while you're at it, see if you can get her number. Knowing my record, she probably has a husband and two kids. No, take that back; that body's never had kids. Oh, god, my nostrils are on fire, and I'm probably breathing like an old bull. Really attractive.

I can make it; I know I can make it. Focus, Sarah. I can do this. If I keep up with this woman, maybe I can ask to run with her again. Paekakariki is only twenty-five minutes away from Wellington. I can get up every morning at five-thirty, no problem. Yeah, right, especially after a late shift. What on earth makes me think this total stranger would want anything to do with me anyway?

140

Breathe, Frances, just breathe. In out, in out, come on; don't stop. My legs, I think they're going to give way. I think I'm going to throw up first. No, make that faint. Five hundred yards, then you can stop. No, then you can die. She's getting ahead. Come on, you wimp, move it. Oh, god, she's beating me. Move!

Oh, no, she's increasing her speed. I'm in front. I can't let her pass me. She'll probably keep on running, and I can't do any more. She is only half a stride behind. She's not wearing a bra, how can she run without a bra? Wow, look at the size of those nipples, they look like rocks.

Frenchy looked over at her; she knew she was just about finished. She noticed the woman's cleavage showing through her V-neck as her sweat soaked the T-shirt revealing her beautiful breasts. *Man, I have to focus. Keep your mind off her body, woman, or you'll never make it. Two hundred yards to go.*

I should just stop now. This is ridiculous. I'll probably end up breaking a bone or something, then what good will I be to Cat and Theo? And Max, I really love Max. I can't let her down. I suppose she's the mother I never had. Let me die, let me die now, I haven't got any more to give!

Frenchy could hear Ozzie barking and getting closer. *One hundred yards to go.* She also heard another dog barking. *Ozzie must have found someone to play with.* This woman was a stride in front of her. *Come on, Frenchy, do or die.*

Surely, she'll stop at the end here. I know I will have to. What will I say? Think. What if she just continues to run? Think, Sarah, think. I can't. I think I'm going to die.

Frenchy was having trouble; the sand was drier and thicker as they were getting to the end. Her heels were dragging, and the energy and exertion that it was taking to lift her feet was more than she could bear.

Just then, with the end just a few steps away, a golden retriever appeared from nowhere in front of Sarah and sent her flying to the ground. She fell full length and quickly turned herself over, spitting sand from her mouth. The retriever was followed by Ozzie, who in turn knocked Frenchy flying, and she landed on top of Sarah. She was able to put her hands out and stopped inches away from Sarah's face. Frances was breathing heavily as she stared into those eyes—those blue, blue eyes. Sarah was transfixed; she couldn't move. Then she heard a voice off to the side shouting, "Is this dog yours?"

Frenchy knew she should respond, but all she could do was stare into those eyes. They were still both breathing really hard until Ozzie's barking got louder and louder. "Sorry," she finally said and got up. She turned to see a woman trying to hold Ozzie while her own dog was barking at Ozzie. With one look back at Sarah she said, "Sorry, I have to go," and ran to Ozzie.

Sarah was still lying on the sand panting, watching this woman pull the dog away and hold it while the other woman put her retriever back on its leash and walked away. Sarah, lying on her back trying to think of something to say, realized it was too late as her running partner started to jog away with the Blue Heeler. "Bugger!"

Chapter 23

Six o'clock in the morning found Aroha and Lizzie sitting in their dressing gowns eating smoked chicken and strawberry salad.

"Perhaps we should feign a fallout at least once a month, so Cocco can send a mercy package," said Aroha. "Isn't Danny wonderful? Imagine him coming up with this. We've done a great job, Lizzie. He's a wonderful person. I think he'll make some girl a very happy partner."

"Not boys then?"

Aroha laughed out loud, "Not according to the magazine I found under his mattress."

"Well, that puts paid to all those who say gay couples raise gay children. Do you think we should get him his own cell phone for Christmas?"

"What, and break all our own rules?" asked Aroha.

"Yep."

"Bugger Christmas then, let's get him one now."

"Okay."

"Aroha, can we make an agreement that after today we'll never talk about…" Lizzie didn't know what to call it.

"What, the great coming?"

Lizzie went bright red, and covered her face with the serviette. "Aroha, how could you?"

Aroha put her feet up under the table on Lizzie's lap. "I suspect there'll be a fair amount of ribbing at Max's tonight. Cocco will have to get his Bolli's worth, but after that, yes, I will want to."

"I just about lost my job yesterday because of 'she who won't be named.'"

"Why, what happened?"

"She came onto me yesterday at the end of rehearsal and wouldn't take no for an answer. I bowled her up against the wall and told her if she ever came near me again I'd cut her tits off."

"You what?" asked Aroha. "You'd cut her tits off?" Aroha started to laugh. "I'll bloody cut her tits off, let alone you."

"Torri came up to me with my ringing phone. I swear I was going to hit her, and Torri just talked to me quietly till I let go."

"Thank the goddess for Torri then," said Aroha.

"That girl just keeps surprising me. She acts as if we are friends, and the odd thing is I feel it, too."

"I think I like the sound of your little Goth. I look forward to meeting her. What about 'she who won't be named?' Is she gone at the end of term?"

"Oh, yes, just a few weeks to go."

"Good, now what about that chocolate mousse? I'm sure there's one or two cardinal rules we haven't broken today. Let's take it over to the sofa and get more comfortable."

Lizzie sat with her back to the armrest, and Aroha sat between her legs. They were feeding each other mousse followed by a kiss. Soon there was more kissing than eating, and the mousse was put to the floor.

"Hang on," said Lizzie, "we forgot the music that Danny set up."

She rose and turned the music on and returned and sat on her knees between Aroha's legs. She undid Aroha's belt on her dressing gown and slowly opened her gown.

"I don't know if I have any energy left, darling."

"Not to worry, I think the mousse has given me enough for us both."

Lizzie was kissing the inside of Aroha's left thigh while her right hand was lightly massaging her right.

"You always taste so good, your skin, your…"

"You'll have me blushing. Why don't you shut up, and get on with your work?"

"Ah, me thinks the lady doth complain too much." Lizzie pulled Aroha's legs just a little further forward and picked up one of the mousses. With the spoon, she spread some on her inner thigh and dropped a spoonful of it teasingly from her belly button down to her hairline and just a little further past.

"Oh, that's cold."

"Let me warm it up for you. Time for my revenge after what you did to me last night."

"Do your best, sister, but I'm the greatest."

Lizzie had started to lick the mousse ever so slowly from Aroha's inner thigh.

"Challenged am I?"

A very low "hmm" came from Aroha, "again with the talking."

With each lick Lizzie was getting perilously close to Aroha's pubic hair, which was dark and inviting. She parted Aroha's legs further and just when Aroha thought she was there, Lizzie moved to her belly.

"You're a tease, Lizzie Beck," came a very ragged voice. "I'm sure I'm way ahead of you."

"Don't rush me; I have important work to do."

Lizzie's tongue was circling Aroha's belly button and slowly working down. Aroha's breathing increased, and her back arched ever so slightly. Her breasts looked so beautiful; it was a tough choice to stay where she was or move up, but Aroha's breathing told her to stay where she was. Lizzie's tongue finally reached Aroha's hairline, and with ease she parted Aroha and found the pearl she was looking for. She was more than ready. She could no longer discern the moans from Aroha or herself. All she knew was nothing could tear her away from this nectar, and this bliss that was her Aroha. Aroha's body was arching more and more. Lizzie replaced her tongue with her thumb and allowed her tongue to enter Aroha. Aroha's sharp intake of breath told Lizzie she was very close.

"Oh, god, Lizzie, that's so good. Don't stop!"

Lizzie could feel all of Aroha's muscles tense in contraction, and with one last moan, she was there. Lizzie was so hot that she undid her robe, and before she could take it off Aroha had her pinned to the floor and was lying on top of her.

"If you think you're hot now, hang on."

They woke up on the floor at 10:30 A.M., wrapped in each other and their robes.

"There won't be many days like this if we have another child, you know," said Aroha.

She was running her hand over Lizzie's stomach trying to imagine what she would look like pregnant. "Oh, but it would be wonderful, Aroha. We've talked about it long enough, and at thirty-four, I'm not getting any younger. It sounds as if Willie and Cocco would be happy to be coparenting, too. Maybe we should talk to them today. Why don't I give Cocco a call to see if we can meet for lunch and talk about it? We have to thank Cocco anyway. It's a wonder he hasn't called."

"Ah, well, he may well have. I turned the volume right down before I got in the shower last night and turned both our cells off."

"What if Danny had needed us?"

"He went to a lot of trouble last night. He wasn't going to call. Besides, Willie would have come for us if we were needed."

"I can't believe what has happened in a week, Aroha. We nearly lost Theo, I nearly lost you, and Cat is a whole other person who is still in danger."

Dockside was fairly busy, but they were able to get a table. Cocco hadn't taken the smile off his face since they met. "Tell me everything. Was my table looking beautiful? Was the sex good?" Cocco asked.

Willie and Lizzie said together, "What?"

"A girl has a right to know."

Aroha was smiling, "It was the best."

"Oh, make-up sex always best. Sometimes I just fight with Willie for no reason, so we have make-up sex."

"I knew it," said Willie, shaking his head. "I knew it."

Aroha was still smiling.

"Oh, it's so good to see you smile again. You too, Lizzie."

"Changing the subject, we have a gift for you," said Aroha and placed a long, slim designer cardboard box on the table.

"Oh, I love presents," said Cocco. "I open it, Willie."

Cocco opened it and took out a turkey baster.

"Next Saturday would suit Lizzie, if it works for you guys. Wanna come for dinner?"

Cocco started to scream, "Ahh, ahh. I'm going to be mother, ahh, ahh!"

"Cocco, shut up, everyone is looking," said Willie.

"What about Danny?"

146

"School camp," said Aroha.

"Saturday it is then."

"I'm so excited," said Cocco. "What shall I wear?"

This time both Aroha and Lizzie were laughing.

"It doesn't matter what you wear, Cocco," said Willie. "It won't make any difference."

"It will set the mood. I will wear lots of pink, and maybe it be a girl."

"I think there's a little more to it than that, Cocco."

"You have to wear boxers all next week, nothing tight, and keep the boys cold."

Aroha and Lizzie were still laughing, and Willie was just shaking his head.

"Oh, I cook light food, high energy, and we do it two or three times to make it work. I talk to Max, she know best way."

"Cocco, Max is a psychiatrist for god's sake."

"Max know everything, Willie."

Lizzie and Aroha had never been happier.

"So how do you think it will go with Frenchy and Sarah tonight?" asked Willie, trying to change the subject.

"Oh, Sarah so beautiful and her accent. Oh, I just die when she talk."

"I think that they will look like a stunning couple, let alone suit each other," said Aroha.

"Do you think she's gay?" asked Lizzie.

"I don't know, but when she meets Frenchy, I think so, yes."

"What about Frenchy, does she know about what we have in mind for her?"

"No. As Max said, 'she'd run a mile.' She still thinks she's in love with Theo and nobody else knows."

"When does she arrive?"

"Last night, she is staying with Max. In fact, Theo should be there by now."

"This is all so weird," said Willie. "Imagine what Cat's been through, seeing your family killed in front of you. I wonder if Sarah will have any news tonight."

Ellis Paris Ramsay

Chapter 24

Max's pulled her old BMW out of the hospital grounds with Theo safely by her side. It was just after midday. "I haven't a clue what I'm looking for," said Max.

Theo, who looked remarkably well, answered. "Sarah said you don't have to. Just drive home as normal, and she'll be watching. What kind of car is she driving?"

"I think she said a dark blue Holden Commodore. How are you feeling, Theo? You've been through hell, one way and another."

"I feel great, though I've little energy, but I'm just so pleased to be out of hospital, and I think everyone else went through more than I did as I was unconscious most of the time. I feel a bit of a fraud compared to what Cat's been through. I'm just so worried about her."

Max hit the motorway out of the city, and as she reached 100 kph, she was pretty sure she could see a dark blue Commodore five cars back in the other lane.

"Frenchy called in earlier this morning at the hospital. She looked rather odd."

"What do you mean?"

"Like an opossum caught in your headlights just before you bowl it over. She said to tell you that she had some business to attend to in town and just to call her on her cell phone if you need her to bring out anything for dinner. I told her six, is that right?"

"Well, I said six, but everyone knows they're welcome whenever they like. I missed her this morning. She had already left when I got up."

"What a beautiful home, Max," Sarah said, as she walked through the door with Cat. "You must love living here."

"I do, and please, make yourself at home. Did you notice anyone following?"

"No, I didn't. I fell back once or twice and changed lanes, but no, I don't believe you were followed."

"I'm making some coffee, would you like some?"

"Yes, please, black, no sugar. I'll just scout around. I'll be back in five minutes."

"That's fine. Your coffee will be waiting."

Theo and Cat had fallen asleep on the sofa. Cat never slept well when she was not with Theo. Sarah's spare room was comfortable enough, but it made no difference. Theo was exhausted just by the effort of getting dressed, leaving the hospital, and riding the short distance to Paekakariki. The doctor had pointed out that it would take a while to recover and reminded her that she nearly died. Sarah and Max sat at the table and talked as if they were old friends.

"This is so weird for me, Max. I feel as if I have known you for years. As for Theo, Cat, Aroha, Lizzie, and the boys, I feel…" Sarah shook her head.

Max put her hand on her arm, "I know, we all feel it as well. You have a family with us whether you like it or not. I am so blessed, Sarah. Cat has given me so much, my life is very full."

"Do you see anyone? Sorry, I shouldn't have asked."

"Of course, you should ask, and yes, my neighbour, Ted, and I get on very well." Max was smiling. "You'll meet him tonight, he's coming for dinner."

"Max, I'm very nervous about meeting Frances. Everyone is expecting so much. What if I don't like her, or she doesn't like me?"

Again Max put her hand on Sarah's arm. "You have just sat here and told me how you feel about everyone. Do you really think that we could all love someone and you not like her?"

Sarah looked at Max and said nothing.

"I think Frances has been waiting all her life to meet someone like you, and I suspect you have, too. You have nothing to lose, Sarah. The worst that can happen is that you make another new and dear friend. What could be bad about that?"

Sarah thought about the woman she ran with this morning and wished she could meet her. "You're right, Max. What does she do anyway?"

"No one has told you about her?"

"No, just that we are suited."

"You see that framed black and white photograph on the wall over there?"

Sarah turned and looked where Max was pointing. "Wow, is that Theo and Cat?"

"Yes, Frances took it. She's a photographer and not just famous here but in Britain and Europe as well."

Sarah moved over to get a closer look at the photo. They were both sitting on a sofa. The photo was taken side-on; each had her respective arm on the armrest and the same hand holding her chin. They almost looked like a mirror image of each other.

"Did they know this was being taken?"

"Frances said not. She said, 'they looked like bookends.' They are always together in simpatico, but allow people to squeeze in the middle sometimes. At least that's how she feels." Max spent the rest of the afternoon talking about Frances. Sarah almost felt sorry for Frances. She now knew so much about her, and Frances knew nothing of her.

Willie and Cocco had driven to Johnsonville and left their car at Lizzie and Aroha's. They had a Toyota Celica that was too small for four and preferred the comfort of Lizzie and Aroha's Prado. They arrived at 5:30 P.M., as they loved Max's home and spending time there and with her. Cocco had brought the entrée, poached pears wrapped in bacon and cooked in Manuka honey. Max had prepared a lamb curry with a Pavlova for dessert. Cocco had brought enough wine to keep them all floating, and Willie had assumed his usual roll as barman. Ted had arrived, and the house was abuzz with conversation. Ted was happy to be there as all his family was grown and lived a distance away, with one in Australia.

"They keep us young don't they, Max?" He leaned over and kissed her cheek.

The clock struck 6:00 P.M., and Frenchy walked through the door. She was carrying a bottle of wine and a bunch of flowers. Willie and Lizzie were first to see her and stood aside. Then Aroha and Cocco, and they also stood aside. Frenchy noticed the odd behaviour of her friends and wondered why everyone had stopped talking. Theo and Cat walked into the room behind her and Theo said, "There you are. There is someone we want you to meet." Frenchy couldn't imagine whom, as this was a family 'do' to organize Cat's safety. *The Detective Inspector should be here, but surely they wouldn't be making such a song and dance about him. What was his name? Adams, I think they said.*

Just then Max said, "Hello, Frances. Let me relieve you of something."

"Thank you, Max. These are for you," and she handed her the flowers.

Max took the flowers. "Thank you, they're lovely." She turned to the side, revealing Sarah.

"Frances darling, may I introduce Detective Inspector Sarah Adams."

Suddenly, Frances froze, and she knew she had stopped breathing. She dropped the bottle of wine. Sarah reacted very quickly and went for it at the same time as Frenchy. Frenchy's reaction was just as quick but realized that was not a good idea as her blood had already rushed to her head. Sarah got to it inches before it hit the floor. Their hands touched. Frenchy quickly let go, and Sarah picked it up. *Of course, it had to be. I should have guessed, but no one told me she was a runner.* Sarah extended her hand, "Hello, Frances. I've heard a lot about you. It's nice to finally meet you."

Oh, my god, listen to that accent and look at those eyes. Frenchy looked around and saw everyone staring at her with smiles on their faces. *She called me Frances. God, that sounds so good in her accent.* She looked at her hand—she was still shaking. *What beautiful hands.* She knew that she was meant to say something, but she couldn't think what.

Max came to her rescue. "Say hello to Sarah, Frances."

Frenchy looked at Max then Sarah. "Oh, hello. Yes, I eh..." And most unexpectedly, Sarah spoke to her, "Mon français n'est pas terrible, Frances, mais je suis quand meme plus forte que toi. Tu t'es fait avoir par tes amis, ils croient qu'on va devenir de tres bonnes amies. Visiblement elles se réjouissént de ta réaction. Cependant comme toi, je suis etonnée de te voir. Je ne t'ai pas reconnue ce matin. Peut-être qu'on aurait du prendre le temps de se presenter. J'espère qu'on pourra courir ensemble une autre fois, ainsi tu pourras peut-être prendre ta revanche!"

Sarah leant forward and kissed Frenchy French-style, cheek to cheek to cheek.

"Nice to finally meet you, I'll get you a drink."

Frances replied in French, "Merci. Brandy."

"What are they saying?" asked Cocco. They all looked towards Theo. She was the only one who spoke a little French.

"I'm not sure. They were speaking too fast, but I think they were talking about running."

"Running," said Aroha. "You're kidding me."

"Something about revenge and being set up."

"Well, no more French," said Cocco. "House rules. I insist. Did you see Frances' face? She was gobsmacked. Did you see them standing together? They're gorgeous."

Sarah returned and handed Frances a brandy. Frances took it and knocked it back in one.

"Merci."

"No more French," said Cocco. "I don't want to miss out on anything even if it does sound very sexy." Frances coughed as the golden liquid hit the back of her throat. Sarah, who was still standing by her side, rubbed her back and asked, "Are you all right?"

"Yes, thank you."

Willie walked forward, "Allow me to get you another, Frenchy. You look as if you could use it."

Willie took her glass and walked away. He returned with a small one just as Max said, "I think a toast is order. To Theo's recovery, to Sarah, welcome, and to the speedy apprehension of the monster who's after Cat."

"Hear, hear," said everyone.

Dinner was served, and everyone sat informally on the chairs, couches, and floor. Sarah sat by Frances and chatted casually to everyone while Frances was still speechless. They were all relaxing over a glass of wine when Max asked, "How about a song, Lizzie?"

"Oh, yes," said Cocco. "Something sexy."

Theo rose and went to the piano, and Lizzie followed. Theo flicked through a songbook, stopped at one, and placed it on the piano.

"I love this one," said Theo. "Bette Midler sings this on her *Bette of Roses* album. Lizzie looked at Aroha and said, "This one's for you, hon," and started to sing "In This Life."

Theo's harmony was soft in the background and blended beautifully with Lizzie. By the time they had finished Aroha and Cocco were in tears. Cat wished Theo would sing to just her, but that wasn't likely.

Theo was immediately exhausted and held her head while she headed for the sofa. Max helped her, saying, "I can see we are going to have to have a chat about taking things easy."

"I think I'll take Ozzie for a walk," said Frances who was desperate to have a few moments on her own.

"I'll come with you," said Sarah. "I should really have a look around." Frenchy couldn't think how to get out of it, so she had to say, "okay." They crossed the road and walked down to the beach that they had run along that morning, but this time Ozzie was on a lead. The sun had set, and it was a full moon.

"A beautiful night for a stroll," said Sarah.

"Your French is very good, Sarah. Where did you learn?"

"Many years ago in another life, I had a French boyfriend with whom I lived for two years."

"Here in New Zealand?"

"No, in Ireland, before I immigrated here."

Ozzie started to bark. "Quiet boy," said Frenchy. "How long have you lived here?"

Sarah answered, "About ten years, and you?"

"Eleven." Ozzie was barking and pulling on the lead, back the way they came.

"Quiet boy! Probably a neighbourhood cat."

This time Sarah was alert. "I don't know, Frances. Does he normally bark at them?"

"I don't know actually."

They looked back towards the house. It was such a still night that the sounds of Theo and Lizzie's singing were floating in the air. They could see Willie standing on the deck outside smoking, and Cat was sitting in the window seat.

"What is it, Sarah?" Sarah was rubbing the prickles on her neck.

"Something is not right. I think we had better go back..."

Sarah started to run back to the house. She was just about to shout for Willie to go back inside when a single shot ran through the air and shattered the glass of the window Cat was sitting at. Ozzie was really barking now, and Frenchy was having trouble keeping control of him. Sarah was sprinting back to the house, and Frenchy started to run, too. Just then they saw a shadowy figure run from the bushes of the house next door towards the sea. Sarah stopped in her tracks, as if making a decision, and started to follow the assailant. Frances didn't know what to do. Should she follow Sarah or go back to the house to help? She figured there would be enough people back at the house, but Sarah was on her own.

Sarah was shouting, "Stop! Police!" The assailant turned and fired at Sarah. She dived to the ground and looked back at Frances. "Get down, Frances!"

The assailant started to run into the sea, and Sarah was on her feet and following. Ozzie's barking was so loud that Frenchy decided to let him off the lead, but in the heart-pounding excitement, she was having trouble unclipping the lead. She managed finally, and Ozzie went bounding after Sarah and the shadow. The assailant entered the sea, and as Sarah got closer to the water's edge, she could see the outline of a small rubber boat. She was wading into the water while Frenchy was shouting, "No Sarah! Come back!"

Ozzie had caught up with Sarah and was swimming in the water and then they heard an outboard motor. Within a moment, the boat was gone. "Sarah! Sarah!" Frances was ankle deep in the water when a very bedraggled Sarah waded out.

"Shit! Shit! I should have been more alert." Sarah turned to the water. "Come on, Ozzie, come on. He's gone." Willie had caught up with them. "Fuck, was that a real gunshot?"

"Yes, I believe it was."

"Are you okay, Sarah?"

"Yeah, I'm fine, Willie. Anybody hurt?"

"I'm not sure. I came running after you guys."

Sarah tried to run but found it difficult as she was so wet, and the sand wasn't making it any easier. "My cell phone's probably stuffed. Have you got yours on you, Frances?"

Frenchy pulled hers out from her pocket. Sarah was calling the coastguard as they walked quickly back to the house. Frenchy suddenly realized the severity of what just happened and that someone could be hurt. "Oh, my god, Sarah, it's all true."

"No shit!"

Back at the house there was glass everywhere. Sarah reached the house first. "Is anyone hurt?"

Max and Theo were hovering over someone on the floor. "It's Cat."

"'I'm all right, you two. I've just a few cuts from the glass." Cat was trying to stand up.

"Oh, thank god," said Sarah. "I could never have forgiven myself." Sarah stood with her hand over her forehead. "Well, there's no doubt now; I'll be able to get anything I ask for."

They were all looking at Sarah. "What do you mean?" asked Cat.

"I mean I can now protect you. I'll move you to a safe house, and you'll have round the clock protection till we catch this bastard. Also, we will all be armed."

"I didn't think New Zealand police were allowed to be armed, apart from the Armed Offenders Squad," said Max.

"We are, under extreme circumstances and for national security issues."

They could hear sirens blazing on approach.

Willie said, "There are lots of neighbours on the street asking what happened."

"I'll have my officers talk to them in a moment. Max, I'm afraid you'll have to go with Cat and Theo since it's your house the attack was made on."

"Is that really necessary, Sarah?"

"I'm afraid so. Sorry."

"Can I take Ozzie?"

"Not a good idea as he will need walking and could be recognized."

"I'll take good care of him, Max," said Ted.

"I'll give you one of my cards, Ted, and if you see anything suspicious, ring me immediately."

"Certainly, Sarah. We have a good Neighbourhood Watch set up around here."

"Where are we going, Sarah?"

"I can't tell you that now, Cat, as it may endanger the others. We'll stay here tonight. I'll have my people here, and we'll take off at first light.

Frances had been watching Sarah in full mode. She was impressive. Even dripping wet and with her hair lying flat to her head, she looked magnificent. "Will it be far away?" asked a very concerned Theo. Sarah could see Theo looking towards her friends.

"Don't worry. You all have cell phones, you can keep in touch."

"We're going to Lizzie's show two weeks today, Sarah. Nothing will stop us. I will not be held hostage. That family has ruined my life, and it has to end."

Sarah decided not to respond. She could deal with that next week. Right now she just wanted to keep everyone safe.

It was 5:00 A.M., and Sarah was making coffee in the kitchen. She had woken Max, Theo, and Cat and told them they would be leaving in half an hour. They would drive to Paraparaumu airstrip where there would be a helicopter ready to take them where they were going.

"Well, at least I'll be awake for this ride," said Theo.

Frenchy who had been lying on the couch awake all night joined Sarah in the kitchen.

"Will they be okay, Sarah?"

"Yes, they will. I'll be there most of the time except for next Friday. I have a conference in Auckland that I have to go to whether I want to or not. But don't worry; they'll have plenty of cover."

"You can stay with me if you like." Frenchy couldn't believe what she had just said. She never had people to stay. Theo and Cat yes, and Willie and Cocco on a couple of occasions. Lizzie and Aroha had talked about coming but hadn't made it yet. Sarah looked Frances in the eye and said, "Are you sure?"

"Yes," said Frenchy. "I don't cook, but I know lots of great places to eat, and I can take you to the club afterwards, dancing, if you're not too late or tired."

"I would like that, and I think I should be finished by six. What will you do, Frances? Will you stay with the others?"

"I was going back to Auckland tonight, but I think I'll take an earlier flight. I'll leave my car at Willie and Cocco's again and get it when I come down for Lizzie's show."

"Don't book a flight, I'll bring you down. Better get Lizzie to organize an extra three tickets. It looks as if my two guys and I will be going as well."

Frances took a business card out of her wallet and gave it to Sarah.

Chapter 25

The helicopter was waiting at Paraparaumu and flew them to Turangi.

"Where are we going, Sarah?"

"Pukawa. It's on the western side of Lake Taupo. There will be a couple of unmarked cars waiting for us when we land in Turangi. They will stay with us till my boys arrive from Wellington. That will be four or five hours away as I had to organize a woman officer to go to my house and pick up some clothes and toiletries. Doug and John will bring them with them."

The helicopter landed by the two unmarked cars, and within minutes, they were on the road. Max travelled with Sarah, and Theo and Cat were in the car in front. One of the officers in front of Sarah handed her a small black case and a clipboard with a piece of very official looking paper on it. Sarah signed it and gave it back to the officer. Then she opened the case, removed the sidearm, checked the barrel, and looked in the accompanying box to see how much ammo she had.

Sarah looked at Max's troubled face. "Don't worry, Max; I know how to use it."

Max looked at Sarah with further admiration. "Quite frankly, my dear, I'm beginning to think you can do anything."

It wasn't too far to Pukawa. Once they had turned off the main highway and travelled along the road to Tokaanu, they were on their way. Tokaanu is a small settlement with natural hot thermal pools. The smell of the sulphur was strong, and as they drove up the mountain they could see pockets of steam rising from the ground.

"I've been to Lake Taupo hundreds of times, but I've never visited around this side."

When they got to the top, Max gasped at the beautiful panoramic view. "My goodness, it looks quite different from this side."

"There's a view just like this from the house we are staying in."

"Really?" This will be more like a holiday. Have you used this house before, Sarah?"

"Once, two years ago. It's very comfortable. A high-ranking official in the Australian government owns it. He doesn't use it very often and makes it available to us. It's on high ground, with as I said, panoramic views, and there's only one way in unless you're a mountain goat."

Ten minutes later, they arrived. It was a large Lockwood-built home, and the garage was large enough for two cars and a good-sized boat. In fact, if the boat were any larger, it would have to be moored. The house had four bedrooms, three with en suites, two lounges, a kitchen that any chef would kill for, and a deck that wrapped around three sides of the house. The deck itself held a spa pool, barbeque, table and chairs for ten, and a viewing platform with telescope stand.

"Wow, Sarah. This is fabulous."

"Well, it might help the boredom of being incarcerated."

Cat's face darkened. "You mean we can't go for walks?"

"I'm afraid not. But we can, after dark, go down to Tokaanu's hot pools as they have private rooms."

"Well, that's always something," said Max, "and if it keeps you safe, my darling, we'll just have to grin and bear it. The kitchen cupboards and freezers are well stocked, and there's even a wine cellar."

Four hours later, Detectives Doug Spicer and John Fergusson arrived.

"Nice digs, Sarah. How did you wangle this one?"

"I pulled in a few IOUs."

Theo asked, "Isn't this the usual type of place for safe houses?"

Doug and John laughed. "Shit no. We usually get hovels."

"Not quite, Doug."

"Let me put it this way, Ms. Gray. The boss must really like you guys, and for that we thank you."

"Okay, enough," said Sarah. "Go throw your stuff in the fourth bedroom, and over coffee we will sort out a roster."

On the second night, clothed in hoodies, all but Detective Spicer went down to the hot pools. "Sorry to be a wet blanket girls, but I'm going to have to insist on coming in with you." Sarah turned her back as the girls got undressed and got into the pool.

"We are in, you can turn around now."

Sarah sat on the little bench that was several feet away from the pool.

"Do you mind if I ask how old you are, Sarah?" asked Theo.

"I'm forty-one."

"Same age as Frenchy," said Theo.

"What about you guys?"

"I'm forty-two," said Theo, "and Cat's thirty-nine. Aroha and Willie are thirty-seven, Lizzie is thirty-four, and Cocco is only twenty-seven."

"He really loves Willie, doesn't he?"

Theo and Cat just looked at each other and smiled. Theo finally said, "Yes, he does."

"Frances would never have gotten in a pool naked with us. She says she's 'too Presbyterian Scottish' and would rather die first. How about you, Sarah, would you have?"

Sarah grinned. "Well, I'm a lapsed Irish Catholic, and we're not that shy. How did you guys meet?"

"In a gay bar in Wellington," answered Cat. "Theo hadn't been long back from her trip overseas. I was meeting a friend there who was with a whole group of people, and Theo was one of them. Not very romantic, I know, but we hit it off immediately, and we've never been apart since."

"What about you, Sarah. Have you ever been in a serious relationship?"

"Once. I lived with a French guy for two years in Ireland. We would go to Paris every three months or so."

"So that's where you learnt French."

"Sort of. Philip's English wasn't great, so it was a case of having to."

"So come on, Sarah, tell us what you think of Frenchy. What did you say to her?"

Sarah laughed and almost blushed. She was pleased it was too steamy for them to notice. "I think you guys may have been right, and

I don't know that I should be saying this, but I actually met Frances that morning."

"You're kidding," said Theo.

"No, we did, but we didn't know whom each other was."

"How do you mean?"

"I was out running, and Frances was also running, and as it turned out, we pretty much ran alongside each other and sort of ended up in a heap because of two dogs."

"Who was winning?" asked Theo.

"We were just running along beside each other."

"Bull! I know Frenchy. Who was winning?"

"I guess I was slightly ahead."

"Frenchy would have hated that; she's such a control freak."

"Yes, I noticed she tried to take control a few times."

Sarah couldn't take the smile off her face. "Come on, you guys, we had better get back."

Theo and Max were happy to take on the cooking. Although Theo activities were limited by Cat and Max, they tried to make her rest as much as possible. The house had a vast array of games, books, videos, and cards. It was the best break Theo and Cat had had for years and exactly what Theo needed in her recovery.

Sarah was in constant touch with Wellington. There had been some news. "The coastguard found the boat at Plimmerton further down the coast. It had been hired. The officer who spoke with the hire company had said it was a dead end. The man who hired it said his name was Jo Bloggs and paid in cash. After considerable questioning, it turned out that Mr. Banks, the owner, said he told Mr. Bloggs that it would have to be a very large security deposit with a name like that. He paid Mr. Banks an additional $1,000 in cash. The good news is that we did lift a few prints off the boat, and we have confirmed, with the help of Scotland Yard, that they are indeed Dean Corolla's prints. We have the officer who attended the car crash in Napier going through photographs with immigration in the hope of finding the name he is using in New Zealand. We are not hopeful as he could have easily changed it."

Sarah had to go to Wellington on two occasions but returned the same day. She had not been able to talk Cat and Theo out of going to Lizzie's show. In the end, she thought it might be the only way to flush Corolla out, as she was sure he would never find them there. If that weren't enough, going to Auckland and staying with Frances were continually at the back of her mind. She had mixed feelings about Auckland and didn't want to go to the conference but had no choice over that. She did, however, get butterflies in her stomach every time she thought about staying with Frances. *A control freak, huh? Well, it takes one to know one.* She hoped she wasn't hoping for too much. Actually, she didn't know what she was hoping for at all— a night with Frances, then an eight-hour trip in the car, longer if they took a break. That was more time than she had spent with any one person in a long while. *Expect nothing, girl, then everything else will be a surprise.*

Sarah had to admit that she was enjoying the break as well. Not that they weren't keeping vigil. They were keeping a strict routine of checks and shifts, but something had to change soon. Her bosses wouldn't wear her salary and time out of other work for much longer. She was going to have to work out a plan of action for their return to Wellington.

Ellis Paris Ramsay

Chapter 26

Matt wasn't bringing Danny home till 9:00 P.M. It was later than usual for a Sunday; but there was a family dinner on, and an exception was made. Aroha and Lizzie had enjoyed a quiet day at home, each preparing work for the next week. They were really looking forward to Danny getting home, as he didn't know if he had put things back together again. They were in their nightclothes ready for an early night as soon as Danny got in. They had been talking all day about the events of the previous night. The thought of Cat escaping death was unthinkable. Sarah's reassurance that she now could protect Cat was heartening but no less scary.

Finally they heard a car pull up, and a key in the door. "Danny, is that you?"

"Yes, Mum," and a very loud voice shouted, "Bye, Dad."

"Did you have a good time?"

"Yes," said Danny, trying to peer around Aroha to see if Lizzie was there.

Lizzie came out from a door behind him and snuck up and said, "Hi, squirt."

Danny jumped and turned around and hugged Lizzie. "You're home, you're home!"

Aroha moved forward and joined in the hug. "Thank you, you precious boy," and they both started to kiss him.

"Oh, yuk. Enough already, enough." Danny was protesting with a smile on his face, enjoying every moment of his triumph.

"You have to get ready for bed, it's late." Danny bounded up the stairs two at a time. Aroha and Lizzie turned off lights and went to bed; they were sitting up reading and listening to Danny getting ready for bed. When he was ready, he came to their room still smiling and said goodnight.

"Goodnight and thank you."

Lizzie and Aroha sat waiting for Danny to hop into bed. They heard, "What's this?" paper being unwrapped, then thumping steps back to their room. Danny flung himself on their bed in the middle of them both, saying, "You're the best."

"Danny, you make us both very proud." Lizzie started to sing "Danny Boy." Lizzie had sung this to Danny ever since he was a baby. He loved it and used to think that Lizzie had written it just for him, although he had made Lizzie promise that she would never sing it in front of his mates.

"Do I still get Friday after next off school to come to rehearsal?"

"Yes, it's all arranged. Off to bed now, or you'll never get up in the morning." Danny kissed them both and went off to bed. He was well pleased with his phone and its *Lord of the Rings* face cover.

"And, Danny, no playing with your phone in bed, or it will have its first of many, I'm sure, confiscations."

"I won't. Goodnight."

"Goodnight," came the reply in unison. Aroha switched off the light and said, "I wonder where they are."

Chapter 27

The next Saturday, Willie and Cocco arrived at Johnsonville to have dinner and stay the night with the girls. Cocco had spent the whole week planning. Willie was on an extreme exercise program, and Cocco was in charge of everything he ate.

"This I can do, Willie, I know about food. I will have you at peak. No cigarettes either. I will tell Lizzie also not to give you any or get them for you. She want healthy baby, too. And no sex this week, I want you charged and ready like rocket. I think three times on same night and one in morning."

"Cocco, I think the girls are only thinking about once."

"No, no, I no have that. We do it Japanese way, optimum times for best result. I know I can get you to come three times if you at peak and no alcohol. No pub after work, straight home."

"I don't know that the girls will go for that, Cocco."

"I already tell them, and I gave Lizzie menu for week, no problem!"

Cocco was dressed in a shocking-pink tunic over matching pants. He had tied his hair up in a bun with what looked like two chopsticks, but on closer inspection they were two delicate long cones with pink and lavender flowers encrusted on them. Aroha had been instructed to make a salad and a fruit salad. Cocco had brought fresh salmon and pasta and herbs from his own garden. The girls had done their best to make the house romantic and seductive. Aromatherapy candles were burning, as well as oils, and there were lots of candles everywhere. They both wore sarongs and had flowers in their hair. They knew Cocco would be serious and over the top, so they thought they would make an effort, also. They had talked all week about what they might wear to capture the occasion and not be outdone by Cocco, and decided the sarongs they bought in Fiji last year would suit. Aroha also pointed out how easy they would be to remove.

Aroha had decided, before the boys arrived, that there was absolutely no reason why she could not drink, so at every opportunity she took herself off to the kitchen and drank straight from the wine bottle in the fridge. She couldn't see how else she was going to cope with Cocco in full swing. Over dinner, they discussed how the night would go. As expected, Cocco had a plan.

"If this is night of conception then it should be special for Lizzie and Willie. Obviously, Willie will have satisfaction to produce semen, and Aroha, it up to you to make Lizzie happy at point of insemination."

Aroha was having trouble keeping the smile of her face. "And how will I manage that, Cocco?"

"I don't know mechanics of girl sex, that your job. Now, after dinner we listen nice music, and we give Willie and Lizzie nice massage. I brought oils, just right mix for erotic sex."

"We're going to have erotic sex?"

"Don't you make fun, Aroha. This serious."

Aroha knew she could not look at Lizzie. Willie had the look of a browbeaten man and said, "Trust me, best just to do exactly as he says."

"Willie wise man. After we have them relaxed and receptive, we go up to our rooms. You girls better go first and get sexy. My Willie no take long."

Willie had his hand over his mouth, and almost inaudibly, the girls heard him say, "I might tonight."

Lizzie went over to her sound system and tongue-in-cheek popped on the 'Hallelujah Chorus."

"Very funny, Lizzie," said Cocco. "We save that for good news sex. Now put sexy music on."

Lizzie was leafing through her collection and came across an album Aroha and she used to listen to all the time when they first got together—Olita Adams's *Evolution*. She put it on and turned up the volume. Aroha recognized it straight away.

"We haven't played that for ages. Perfect." Lizzie and Aroha started to dance, holding each other very close while Lizzie sang along very softly.

"These not right words, Lizzie," said Cocco.

"I know, but feel the music wash over you and that powerful sexy voice." Lizzie's eyes were closed, and she nestled into Aroha's neck.

"I think we'll move upstairs, guys, any time you are ready is good for us."

Aroha went into the kitchen and took the towel off the handrail and hid a bottle of wine in it. As she passed the living room she said to Cocco, "Don't want to get oil on the sheets," and they disappeared upstairs.

Inside their bedroom, Lizzie said, "You're pissed."

"Oh, I do hope so," said Aroha as she pushed Lizzie onto their bed.

"Cocco will go mad if he catches you."

In between nibbling Lizzie's ear, she asked, "Why?" And in her best imitation of Cocco's speech, she said, "I no inseminated, I just make happy." They both burst out laughing.

"You might have brought a glass for me."

"Who needs glasses?" and she handed Lizzie the bottle. Lizzie was propped up on an elbow drinking from the bottle as Aroha removed Lizzie's sarong.

"We've got to have erotic sex now."

"Oh, good, have you a picture or instructions?"

Aroha was kissing Lizzie's calf, slowly working her way up as she said, "I'll think of something."

Willie was lying on the floor on a towel and Cocco was massaging his back. Willie did not feel comfortable or particularly sexy. The thought of having sex on Lizzie and Aroha's floor was leaving him cold. "I think we should go upstairs now, Cocco. I think I would be more comfortable."

"Okay," and Cocco picked up his bag and led the way. Once in the girl's spare bedroom Cocco removed four turkey basters from his bag. Each was wrapped in plastic wrap.

"We need four, Cocco?"

"I have sterilized each one, Willie, so your swimmers have better chance. Do you want to lie down, sit up, or stand?"

"This is so clinical, Cocco; I wish I could have a drink, I feel odd."

"Don't worry. I know how to get you in mood. Lie down."

"Do you think the girls will hear us?"

"I hope they do hear me make my man happy."

Willie cringed, "Oh, god, Cocco, I don't know that I can do this."

"Of course you can," and with that Cocco took immediate action on Willie's unresponsive cock.

Lizzie had just reached climax when she said to Aroha, "Shit, we were meant to wait for Willie…"

"To come?"

They both started to laugh again covering their faces with pillows. "Don't worry," said Aroha, "we'll just fake it. Men never know the difference."

"Did you only bring one bottle up?"

Cocco had been working on Willie for ten minutes, and Willie's cock was only semi-interested.

"Willie, relax."

"I can't, Cocco. I just feel under a lot of pressure here."

"Okay, time for tricks."

"Oh, oh, Cocco. What are you doing? Oh, my god, oh, my god."

"Oh, oh, wait, Willie! I no got baster over here yet."

"Oh, ahh… Sorry, Cocco."

"Willie, what you do?"

"Never mind what I did, what did you do? You've never done that before."

"I've never had to before, I'll have to go tell girls we be a while."

Cocco knocked on the girl's door. Aroha opened the door expecting to find the baster in Cocco's hand.

"We'll be a little longer, Willie lost control. We have to start again."

Leaning against the door, Aroha said, "Okay, no problem," hoping Cocco didn't notice she was having trouble standing. She closed the door and heard Cocco return to the room and Willie saying, "You didn't have to say that."

"Oh, don't be such a crybaby, Willie, and hurry and get in mood again."

Aroha and Lizzie had to cover their faces with their pillows again. "I'm going to sneak downstairs and get another bottle of wine and a bag of chippies. I've been dreaming about them all week."

Aroha put her finger over her lips and said, "Shh."

Lizzie had to take her time, as many of the stairs were creaky. When she returned, she found Aroha sitting on the bed with the TV on. "Turn that down, they'll hear you."

Aroha's face became very mischievous, "Oh, don't be such a crybaby."

Lizzie picked up her pillow and started to hit Aroha. "I'd rather have you as a lover than a fighter."

Lizzie didn't need any more invitation than that.

"You want me to talk dirty, Willie?"

"No, I just keep thinking about Lizzie lying there waiting on me."

"Look, I tell girls you come three times, it has to be four now. You embarrassment to me, Willie, they think I no good at my job."

"I'm not your job. I'm a man, Cocco, not a baby machine."

"I know, baby." Cocco was massaging Willies temples. "You are my man, my very handsome big Willie. I know! I go doggie. But you have to have more control this time. When you nearly there, I be ready with baster."

"How are we going to get it in there, it isn't exactly a big hole."

"Oh, I think of that, Willie," and Cocco took a small funnel out of his bag, also wrapped in plastic wrap.

Aroha and Lizzie were sitting up on their bed watching TV, eating chippies, and swigging from the wine bottle when they heard Cocco knock on the door.

"Okay, ladies here we go, number one on the way."

Aroha opened the door only halfway, appearing around it and mouthed, "thank you," not daring to trust her voice. She walked back in the room holding the baster as if it were contagious.

"Now what?" she asked Lizzie.

"I guess I assume the position."

Cocco yelled through the door, "Don't spill any."

Aroha started to laugh, "Don't start," said Lizzie, fighting to keep the laughter out of her voice. Lizzie placed a cushion under her bottom and opened her legs.

Aroha said, "Smile, please."

"Get on with it, woman, before I change my mind. You're meant to be making me happy right n…oh, my god, that's cold!"

"Lie still and start making noise."

"Jesus, woman, mind what you're doing."

"I can't see."

"Of course, you can't bloody see, but if you go any further it will be coming out of my mouth."

Aroha fell to the side laughing as the baster stuck out of Lizzie. "Don't leave me like this, do something!"

Aroha was laughing so loud that Lizzie started to make noises in the hope the boys wouldn't hear her.

"Oh, yeah, baby, oh, yeah, uh, uh, oh, yes, yes."

This, unfortunately, made Aroha laugh louder.

Lizzie whispered, "Will you shut up, and take this thing out of me?"

Aroha tried to sit up, but her tears were making it very difficult to see.

"Oh, the pain," Aroha said as she held on to her sides.

"Aroha, you are not being helpful."

"Sorry." Aroha reached over. "I'd better just…" She squeezed the end of the baster.

"Yuck, if that's junior, yuck!"

Aroha removed the baster and said, "You'd better keep your knees up for a while."

"Couldn't I just go to sleep, Cocco?"

"You have a rest, I wake you up shortly. Lizzie sounded happy, I think we make fine baby, Willie."

Fifteen minutes later Willie felt a warm wet sensation and realized Cocco was waking him up in his own way. Ten minutes later Cocco was knocking on the girls' door. They were watching a movie, and the second bottle of wine was nearly empty. Aroha got such a fright when she heard the knock at the door that she spilt the bag of chips all over the bed.

"Guilty conscience?" asked Lizzie.

"You go."

"No, I can't. You said to keep my legs up."

Aroha finally got to her feet, and when she opened the door she just put her hand around.

"Careful, girlfriend, don't you drop precious cargo."

"Uh huh," said Aroha, hoping Cocco didn't hear the crunch of the chippies in her mouth.

"Warm it up this time," said Lizzie.

"How?"

"I don't know. Rub it between your hands like you do a pen when the ink won't flow."

Aroha started to oscillate the baster. "We'll probably end up with a hyperactive kid now. Okay, open up."

"You're meant to make me happy while you do this."

"What do you want me to do, tell a joke or sing?"

"Don't sing. We can't do that to junior."

"There were two lesbians sitting on a park bench. One was a lipstick lesbian, complete with briefcase, high heels, and a designer sandwich wrapped in politically correct brown paper. The other wore doc martins, a plaid shirt, and had white bread doorstop sandwiches in the bread bag. The Doc Martin lesbian asked, "What are you getting your partner for Christmas?" The lipstick lesbian said, "Actually, I'm getting her two presents." "Oh, really," said the Doc Martin one, "What are they?" "A Porsche and a Mercedes Benz." "You're getting her two cars?" "Yes, I thought if she got bored driving the Porsche, she could drive the Merc, and vice versa. What about you, what are you buying your partner?" "Oh, I'm getting her two pressies as well." "Oh really, what are they?" "A pair of slippers and a vibrator." "That's an unusual combination." "Not really. I figure if she doesn't like the slippers then she can go fuck herself!"

Lizzie just about choked on her chippies and as she was laughing, Aroha slipped the baster in, "There you go, and maybe we'll get lucky and have a kid with a great sense of humour."

While Aroha watched the rest of the movie, Lizzie fell asleep. About an hour after Cocco's last visit, there was a knock on the door. Aroha took the third baster from Cocco and quietly closed the door. She looked Lizzie who was still sleeping. *What the hell am I going to do with this? Oh, well, why not?*

At 7:00 A.M., Lizzie heard a knock at their bedroom door. She opened the door to find Cocco looking fresh as a daisy holding another baster.

"You've got to be kidding me, Cocco. It's only seven."

"This could be the one, Lizzie. I had to work hard for this one, so don't waste it."

Lizzie closed the door, saw the two empty wine bottles, looked at Aroha, and realized there was no way she could wake her.

At 10:00 A.M., Aroha woke to find an empty bed. She sat up and saw four basters sitting on the dresser. *Four, I don't remember four.* She held her head and decided it hurt too much to think and went into the en suite to find some Panadol. She wandered downstairs in her robe to find Lizzie cooking breakfast for Willie and Cocco.

"I'm making Willie a cooked breakfast for all his hard work. Would you like some bacon and eggs?" Aroha, who felt like death warmed up, had to pretend she was fine. She smiled at Lizzie, who had a grin all over her face, and between gritted teeth said, "Just coffee, I think, darling."

"If Lizzie no pregnant, we do this all again in four weeks' time?"

"No!" came the resounding reply from Willie and Aroha.

Chapter 28

S arah rang Frances as soon as she arrived at her conference on Friday morning. She wanted to check that she was still expecting her. She left Pukawa at 5:30 A.M. and got to her conference just before 9:00 A.M. She had returned the sidearm to Turangi police and felt the girls were in capable hands. They would be returning to Wellington tomorrow, and it was there that she was more concerned about. *Okay, I've thirty-four hours before I have to start worrying again.*

Frances answered the phone on the third ring. Sarah couldn't decide whether to be professional or not and found herself apprehensive.

"Oh, hi, Frances, it's…"

"Hello, Sarah. You're here."

"Yes, just arrived five minutes ago. Is it still…?"

"Yes, of course. Do you know what time you're free?"

This is easy. "No, but I'll call as soon as I finish and tell you I'm on my way."

"Okay, later then."

"Later."

Sarah was having trouble concentrating and was pleased when lunchtime came, and they were given an hour and a half free time. She chose to go out. The thought of being stuck with a group of very boring old fuddy-duddy Inspectors and curled up ham sandwiches was more than she could bear. Plus, she wanted to see if she could buy something to wear tonight. The policewoman who had packed a bag for her had followed her instructions, but Sarah had forgotten about tonight. She had a few favourite shops she liked to visit when she was in Auckland and let her feet do the walking. An hour later she was sitting in a café drinking an espresso and feeling very happy with her purchases, a new dress and a new pair of shoes.

Frenchy got off the phone and felt as if she were having a panic attack. She was asking herself once again the same thing that she had been all week—*have I done the right thing?* She had changed the sheets on her bed three times today and was already having trouble deciding which duvet cover she wanted. She had changed the spare bed and cleaned the flat twice. And that was after her housekeeper had done it. She had removed her toys from her bedside cabinet three times and put them back twice. She honestly could not remember when she last had sex without them. *Hang on, Frances, whatever makes you think Sarah will want to have sex with you? She has to, but what if I can't without the toys?* There were clothes scattered all over her bed. She had tried twelve or more outfits on. *This is ridiculous; I've never had trouble dressing before. Less is more, less is more, less is more. Yes, but I can't go naked!*

Sarah had been looking at her watch every five minutes since 4:00 P.M. It was now 5:30 P.M., and the conference was finally coming to an end. She was on her feet when she heard, "Detective Inspector Adams, a word please." Sarah turned to find the Police Commissioner standing beside her. *Shit.* It was nearly an hour before she could leave after refusing several invitations to dinner, including one from the Commissioner. She lied and said she had family expecting her. *Let's hope the Commissioner doesn't check my dossier.*

As soon as she got in her car, she rang Frances and said she was on her way. Frances said it would only take her ten minutes. She wasn't far, and Frances gave her instructions to get to her parking spot.

Sarah got out of the car in the underground car park and couldn't believe how nervous she was. Her hands were shaking, and she was sure she was blushing. *This is ridiculous. I'm acting like a school kid. Take a hold of yourself, woman, expect nothing and be cool.* She was waiting for the lift with her eyes closed and almost jumped when she heard the ping of the lift door.

Frances' flat was surprising. She didn't know what she was expecting but not this. It had lots of open space, yet intimate areas had been created with furniture. In one area sat a light blue and white leather chaise lounge on chrome legs, two black and white leather chub chairs on chrome legs, and an Eileen Grey deco chrome and glass table. Further over was an old four-seater couch in charcoal suede leather. On one wall, in front of the old couch, was a plasma TV. The large, black dining table was square and had eight deep aubergine leather chairs surrounding it. On the wall were four black and white photographs, each framed in a thin black frame with a white border. They were all the same size, about two feet square.

Sarah was speechless as she stood in front of them. If she didn't already know so much about Frances, these would have told her all. There was the one of Theo and Cat that she had already seen at Max's. The next one was of Max and Ozzie. She had caught them running on the beach, and both Max and Ozzie were in the air, mid stride. It was stunning, and captured Max to a T. The next was of Lizzie and Aroha. They were sitting opposite each other at a table in a café, drinking coffee from bowls. They were obviously talking to each other, and it looked as if Lizzie was telling a joke as Aroha was laughing; her right shoe was off her foot, and she was stroking Lizzie's leg. There was no denying that they were very much in love.

"Did they know you were taking this, Frances?"

"No, I don't think so. Cocco and Willie's is the only one set up. Cocco insisted on it."

Frances laughed and Sarah smiled. The next was Cocco and Willie. Sarah gasped again. Cocco was sitting naked on a rock like a mermaid. The photo was taken of his back. His long hair was in a tail over his left shoulder and his face was profile looking to the left. His legs were tucked to the right.

"Is that a real tattoo on his back?"

"No, but Willie's is real." Cocco had a large 'S,' similar to the sound hole on a violin, snaking down his back and ending at the bottom of his spine. Willie was standing above him, also naked, but Cocco's head hid his groin. Willie stood looking out to sea in the same direction as Cocco. His arms were folded across his chest, his hair was up in a bun with a feather in it, and he wore a very large piece of greenstone around his neck. Starting on his thigh and continuing down his leg was a Maori motif tattoo.

Frances said, "Cocco is so proud of Willie's tattoo. He says very brave, very brave."

"Frances, I'm speechless. I have never seen anything so stunning. I heard you were good, but I'm blown away."

Frances' face had reddened, and she held it down. "Thank you. Maybe you'll let me photograph you."

Sarah's head flicked round, and she looked surprised. "Okay, sure if you would like."

"Can I get you a glass of wine?"

"I'd better not as I'm driving."

"We'll use cabs. Parking is a nightmare in this town."

"A glass of wine would be great, and then I'd like to change."

"Okay, me, too."

"What a great view, Frances. Are you not drinking?"

"I don't drink alcohol."

"I see. What about at the beach, I got you a brandy? Are your intentions to get me drunk?"

Frances reddened. "No, not at all. That was for medicinal purposes only. My father says brandy is medicine, and I only imbibe in extreme circumstances."

Sarah laughed. "Relax, Frances, I was just winding you up, but it's nice to know I'm an extreme circumstance. Now where can I change?"

Frances showed Sarah to the spare room.

Frances was in her room trying to make a final decision on what to wear. In the end, she went for a pair of black evening trousers and an off-white chiffon blouse. She wore the collar up and decided against the buttons and a bra and tied it at the waist. The sleeves were three-quarter length with open cuffs. She wore a pair of oversized onyx cufflinks, an oversized onyx ring, and a watch, all in black and silver. She went for a flat pair of black sandals.

She returned to the lounge to wait for Sarah. She poured herself a Coke and added some ice. She had booked a table at her favourite restaurant in Ponsonby. She was checking her watch and thinking she had better ring for a cab when she heard Sarah approach. She lifted her head and couldn't believe her eyes. The glass of Coke fell from her hand on to the tiled area of the kitchen floor. It smashed and there was glass everywhere. "Really, Frances, you'll be giving me a complex if you keep dropping glass every time you see me." Sarah was dressed in a sleeveless black dress that was cut straight across the neck and came to just above her knee. She wore no jewellery except for a plain black watch and one silver ring on her right hand. Her legs were bare and she wore a pair of black stiletto heels, which made her about an inch taller than Frances.

Sarah did a twirl and asked, "Will I do?"

Frances didn't trust her voice; she just shook her head. Frances cleaned up in silence while they waited for the cab.

Frances put her bankcard in one pocket and a single key to her flat in the other. She didn't need anything else. She did not want her cell phone with her. She had no interest in talking to anyone else tonight.

Sarah said, "I'm never going to be able to relax, Frances, if I don't take mine, do you mind?"

"No, I'd rather you did."

"I'll just grab my wallet."

"No need tonight is my treat."

"Only if you promise to let me treat when you're next in Wellington."

She wants to see me again. "Sure, I'd like that."

"Okay, I feel naked, but I don't suppose I need anything else."

When they entered the restaurant Frances could feel everyone stare. Only, for a change, this time they were looking at Sarah. She held Sarah's chair out for her and sat herself. She couldn't remember the last time she felt so self-conscious. Dinner was very nice; but Frances couldn't wait to leave the restaurant as it was noisy, and she couldn't talk to Sarah easily without raising her voice, and she wanted to escape the stares. *Now I know how goldfish feel.* At least at the club they could dance, and she would get to hold her; plus, the only people watching them would be other women.

Gerry was behind the bar and could not hide the surprise on her face when Frenchy entered with Sarah. "Good god, Frenchy, this is a first."

Sarah looked at Frances who looked confused.

Gerry put her hand out to Sarah. "Hi, I'm Gerry, owner and barperson extraordinaire and a friend of Frenchy's. And I have to tell you, in all the years Frenchy has been coming here, you're the first woman she has ever brought into the club. You must be very special," still holding her hand. "Actually, I can see you are."

Sarah smiled and shook Gerry's hand, "Thank you, I'm Sarah Adams from Wellington."

"What can I get you, Sarah Adams from Wellington, to mark this auspicious occasion? This one's on the house."

Gerry had automatically handed Frenchy a Coke. "Actually, just a Coke for me, too. I had some wine with dinner, and something tells me I'd better keep my wits about me, especially with the looks I'm getting from some of the young women here. I take it Frances is very popular."

"Oh, yes, and they'll know they have no chance now they have seen you."

Faith Hill was just starting to sing, "If I'm Not in Love with You."

"Oh, I love this one," said Sarah. "Come on, let's dance."

Sarah took Frances' hand and led her on to the dance floor. Frances took Sarah in her arms. The smell of her perfume was heady. She couldn't believe she was holding Sarah. This was the first time in her life she had ever looked another woman in the eye. She was so nervous that she was shaking and nestled herself into Sarah's neck. *Oh, god, what's going on here? I'm losing control.* Frenchy's breathing was becoming louder, and it was making her shake more.

"Frances," said Sarah. "Frances, look at me."

Frenchy reluctantly lifted her head and looked at Sarah. *Those eyes. Look at those eyes. I could lose myself totally in those eyes.*

"Frances, we both know what's going on here. Let's not waste any more time. Take me home. I want to make love with you."

Frances wasn't sure that she had heard Sarah correctly, but she could see the desire in Sarah's eyes and kissed her. The kiss was so gentle and yet electrifying. She felt tingles all down her spine, and she was sure she heard Sarah moan.

"Love me, Frances, love me now." Frances took Sarah's hand and led her off the dance floor.

"Shit, I'm going to have to write this day on the calendar," said Gerry. "Goodnight, girls, and Frenchy," Frances looked back, "don't fuck this up."

They didn't speak a word in the cab on the way home, but they did hold hands, and Sarah nestled herself into Frances' shoulder. It felt like the longest trip of her life even though it was probably only fifteen minutes. They had to share the elevator with other people. *If I don't touch Sarah soon, I'm going to die.* Her hands were shaking, and she could not get the key in the lock. Sarah grabbed the key off Frances, entered it into the lock first go, and opened the door in one clear movement. She took Frances by the hand and pulled her inside while she closed the door with her leg. She pushed Frances up against the door, and before Frances knew what was happening Sarah had undone her blouse, and her hands were on Frances' breasts, and her tongue was in her mouth. Frances' head was spinning. She could no longer discern between reality and fantasy. She had electric currents running through her body, and she had no idea where she began and where she ended. In her head was a buzz that connected her breasts to her groin and every muscle in her body. She was on fire. In her life, she had never experienced anything like this. She held Sarah's head in her hand while she returned her kiss, more for balance than anything else, as she was sure she could no longer stand up.

Sarah took her tongue away long enough to say, "I have wanted to do that all night."

Frances didn't allow her to say anything else as her tongue was inside Sarah's mouth. Her eyes were closed, and she was undoing Sarah's zip. Sarah was not being gentle, and Frances' nipples were as hard as rocks, and the pain was exquisite.

"Will you leave those heels on, please?" was all Frances could manage to say.

"Only if you take everything off."

While she was still kissing Sarah, Frances took off her blouse and undid her trousers, and they fell to the ground. The only thing left was her jockey knickers. "You'll have to do these, my hands are busy," she said as she removed Sarah's dress from her shoulders.

This she opened her eyes for, and was not unhappy with the beautiful lace black bra Sarah was wearing. *Oh, god, this was worth waiting for.* She undid Sarah's bra.

Sarah again took her hand and asked, "Which way to your room?"

Frances pointed as she couldn't speak, and Sarah kissed her while she walked backwards. A few feet away Sarah said, "Fuck this," and fell on the old sofa bringing Frances down on top of her.

Frances then had the opportunity to remove the only piece of clothing Sarah still had on.

"You, too," said Sarah, and as Frances helped Sarah, Sarah was on top of Frances now. She had her mouth on her right nipple while her left hand was rolling her left nipple between her fingers. Her right hand was already between Frances' legs. This was all new to Frances; she was always the one in control. Her gasp was so loud when Sarah entered her; she was shocked.

"Oh, god, Frances, you feel wonderful."

Frances could feel Sarah's long fingers inside of her and never wanted them to leave. She had fantasized about making love to Sarah ever since she saw her on the beach, and right now she was unable to do anything. Sarah was everywhere, and Frances didn't know which sensation to concentrate on. She couldn't tell whether it was Sarah or she who was moaning. Her right hand was holding the back of Sarah's head while her left was keeping Sarah inside her. Electrical waves were washing over her body as it responded to Sarah; she knew the noises she was making were animal, wild. Her muscles tightened, and waves of pleasure were washing over her, but she wasn't there yet. There was a light brightening by the second, and she could no longer hear external noises, only her own heart beating faster, and finally there was an explosion of epic proportion and a rainbow of colours that she couldn't see past.

Then she heard crying—a soul-wrenching, desperate longing.

Sarah was kissing her face, saying, "It's all right, baby, it's all right."

Sarah held her tight and rocked her back and forth. Frances finally realized it was she who was crying and without conscious reason fell asleep or passed out. She didn't know which, but it was only for a few moments.

She woke feeling reborn and saw concern on Sarah's face. *Oh goddess, let me wake to this face every day, and I will happily sell my soul. Please don't give and then take away.* With strength that came from deep inside, Frances stood up, lifted Sarah off the sofa, and carried her to her bed.

She laid her down gently. "My angel, please never leave me. You have my soul; do with it as you please." She could stand the waiting no longer and buried her head between Sarah's legs. Sarah could not remember the last time someone gave her oral sex. It was probably the last time she was with a woman, which was well over ten years ago. Frances' tongue was everywhere. She didn't know there were so many places a tongue could be. Every nerve in her body was responding. She teased her clitoris with the tip of her tongue, with strokes that were inconsistent, and she didn't know when the next one was coming, then it was every second and then back to inconsistency. She was pleading with Frances to let her come, then Frances stopped, and Sarah was in despair. Just as she was about to complain, Frances had moved her fingers inside her and had returned her tongue to the throbbing heart of her soul. She came hard and felt as if her brain was going to explode. Frances removed her fingers but would not remove her mouth. She was back to searching every crevice, and to Sarah's surprise her body started to respond again. It had not been a minute and already she could hear herself moan and beg Frances not to stop. She had often read about this kind of sex in romance books but never believed it was true. She also realized that she could never go back to whatever she had before. *Frances lives in Auckland, what the hell are we going to do?* Then all thought went from her head as her body's animal instincts responded to Frances and wave after wave of orgasm washed over her. Frances fell to the side, with sweat running off her body. Sarah moved to lie by her. "You were very greedy, Frances. Now it's my turn."

Four in the morning found them both in the shower; they had soaped each other's hair and body. Now they were kissing. They just suddenly realized they hadn't been doing much of that, and it was a very nice part. They had been playing a game to see how long they could go without touching. Sarah had won by twenty seconds. The record so far was thirty seconds altogether.

"Things will have to change, Sarah," said Frances, in between kissing every part of her face and neck. "I am the one in control. I'm the one who always wins."

"In your dreams, sister. How on earth are we going to survive a nine-hour car trip tomorrow? No, make that today."

Frances said, "Do you have your car, or did you drive a work car?"

"It's mine, why?"

"Good, I'll go online and book us a flight when we get out of the shower; and you can drive my car in Wellington, and I'll drive yours in Auckland. This way we can go back to bed," Frances arched her eyebrows, "and get some sleep."

Sarah kissed Frances, "Oh, I do like the way you think."

Frances woke a little later and snuck out of bed to get her camera. The early morning light was filtering through the window. Sarah was asleep on her side with the sheet lying in a swathe just covering her thigh. Her breasts were exposed and magnificent. Her right arm was above her head and her left was on the bed. Her head was tilted up and her beautiful blonde hair was lying in curls around the pillow. Frances took the shot and plugged into her computer. *Perfect!*

"Well, if you're so good at sorting problems, how are you going to fix my living in Wellington and you living in Auckland?"

"It's only four weeks to Christmas. We'll fly to each other on weekends. Then after Christmas, if you still want me, we can look at me relocating my business to Wellington. It really doesn't matter where my office is. How do you feel about living on the coast?"

"What do you mean 'if I want to'? What makes you think that you want this more than I do?"

"You couldn't possibly want it more than I do, Sarah," and then Sarah felt Frances' hand between her legs again.

Frances, finally, was able to get online at 7:00 A.M. She booked them flights as Sarah made some coffee.

"How does 4:00 P.M. sound? That will have us in Wellington just after five."

"That's good," she shouted from the kitchen. "I think my men are planning to arrive at six. That will give me time to go to work and draw a sidearm."

Frances pushed her chair back and put her head between her legs.

Sarah dashed in from the kitchen, "Darling, what's wrong?"

184

"I just realized how much danger you could be in, and I could lose you when I've just found you."

"Actually, it was Aroha, Max, Cocco, and Theo who have been looking for someone for you for years, and thank god, they waited till they found me." Sarah kissed Frances. "Don't worry about me, I can handle myself. Plus, now I have a very good reason to stay alive. It's Cat I'm worried about. Corolla has unlimited funds that seem to buy him anything he needs. Now why don't we go back to bed, and I'll show you just exactly who's in control?"

Frances went offline, and her new screensaver came up.

"When did you do that?"

Frances smiled, "It's mine, all mine!"

Ellis Paris Ramsay

Chapter 29

D anny had the day off on Friday, as promised, and had been a great help to Lizzie and her crew. In fact, it had been wonderful to have Danny around. It kept her focused and probably stopped her blowing her top a few times. Danny thought she could do anything, and she wasn't about to blow her cover and spoil that. Last night they had invited the teachers and all the school kids who weren't in the show. It had been the first time the kids had performed in front of an audience. It had gone remarkably well, and they were all very excited about tonight's performance. One thousand tickets had been sold, a school record. Not just to parents and relations but to friends, neighbours, a couple of local presses, and anyone else who wanted to come.

It was well after midnight before they got home. There had been a few lighting glitches, and a few last minute notes. Lizzie thought she was going to have trouble getting Danny up at 7:00 A.M. and was stunned to find him dressed and making her coffee at 6:30 A.M. Aroha had offered to get him and take him to his beloved soccer and back to Lizzie, but Danny had been adamant. "No, Mum, Lizzie needs me, and I told the coach weeks ago that I couldn't play today."

"How are they going to manage without their best goal kicker?"

"They'll be fine. I won't let Lizzie-mum down."

Aroha took both Danny's cheeks in her hand and jiggled them, "You're a lovely boy. What did we do to deserve you?"

"Mummm!"

The school was between Theo and Cat's place in Roseneath and Willie and Cocco's at Hataitai. The show was scheduled to start at 7:30 P.M., and the plan was for everyone to meet at Willie and Cocco's place for an early dinner at 5:30 P.M. They didn't know what time Frances and Sarah would arrive, but Frances knew what the plans were. The police would bring Cat and Theo at 6:00 P.M. and wait for Sarah and further instructions. Lizzie and Danny would come to eat, and Aroha would bring them both a change of clothes. Danny had to have a new pair of black trousers and black T-shirt to wear backstage and on stage as he was part of the scene changing crew. He felt very important and took it very seriously. Lizzie was torn with pride at the realization that their little boy was growing up and soon would be planning his own life and making his own decisions.

The school hall had transformed into a set very well, and Lizzie was very happy with everything and everyone. Jemma was finally word perfect, and if she wasn't careful, Torri was going to steal the show from her. They had had their last rehearsal in the afternoon, and there was nothing more to do by 4:30 P.M. "Okay, you lot, go home, and I'll see you all back here at six-thirty. Tell your parents, if they are bringing you, that there has been a bar organized for early parents in the rehearsal room if they don't want to double up on the driving. I love you all, go."

Cocco had cooked up a storm of mostly finger foods as people would be arriving and leaving at different times. Aroha arrived midafternoon to help, but her idea of helping was sitting on a stool at the kitchen counter, drinking wine, and offering suggestions to Cocco. He didn't mind because he didn't really need her help. He was happy with the company and a chance to gossip, especially about how Frances and Sarah might be getting on. Willie had gone to make sure there were enough seats set up, and Ted would arrive about fiveish.

Willie returned just as Ted arrived, and Ted helped Willie set up a bar. "I can't imagine there being any more excitement and hype if this were a Hollywood production, Willie," said Ted.

"You mean you didn't know what you signed up for, Ted, when you joined this family?"

Ted smiled. "I wouldn't change a thing, Willie. My own early family life was pretty unremarkable. I thought I was destined to boredom and an early grave till I met Max and her entourage. I couldn't be happier and what an education I'm getting. You're never too old to learn."

Cat, Theo, and Max arrived next. Lots of kisses and hugs went around while everyone caught up and heard about their five-star incarceration. There was more speculation about Frances and Sarah, and the excitement was definitely building.

Sarah and Frances got a cab from the airport to Sarah's office. Frances had wanted to wait outside, but Sarah had made her come to her office. "Darling, I won't be long. I just need to pick up my firearm and check for any further developments. There won't be anybody around at this time of day. Besides you told me you were dreading seeing everyone because you'll be given a hard time. Don't you want to see where I work?"

Frances got an immediate smile on her face and asked, "Have you ever, you know, done it in your office?"

This was the first time Frances had shocked her. "God, no, and thankfully, we don't have time now."

Frances came closer to Sarah. Sarah put her arm out and had a definite fearful look on her face.

"Frances, no!"

Frances raised her eyebrow in the manner Sarah had now become accustomed to.

"I'll settle for a kiss."

Sarah smiled, walked to the door, kicked it closed with her foot, and willingly kissed Frances.

Sarah and Frances eventually arrived just before 6:00 P.M. From outside, they could hear the house a-buzz with conversation. Frances hesitated.

"Darling, we'll be fine. I'll be right by your side."

"You promise?"

"Of course, I will."

"No, I mean will you promise to be by my side?"

Sarah looked into Frances' eyes and knew exactly what she meant. It had only been four hours since they had last made love, and it nearly made them miss the plane.

"God, I want you right now, Frances. How am I going to be able to do my job?"

Sarah walked through the door and instantly was in control. She told Doug and John to go home, change, eat, and be back by 7:00 P.M.

It wasn't long, but that's all she could give them. She did not want to change them for rookies at this stage. She just hoped their families would understand. There was a patrol car parked outside, so they should be safe enough for an hour.

There were great screams of excitement when they walked through the door, and there were hugs and kisses all around. Then silence, as everyone stared at them expectantly, till Cocco finally asked, "Well?"

"Well, what?" asked Frances. She was bright red with embarrassment.

Cocco put his hands on his hips, and Frances looked at each of her friends. "How did it go?" asked a persistent Cocco.

"Fine," said Frances, shrugging her shoulders.

Sarah sighed, "That's not what they want to hear, Frances." Sarah stood by her side, took her hand, and said to everyone, while she was still looking in Frances' eyes, "Yes, we are in love. Yes, we owe it all to you guys, and yes, we did fuck our brains out."

She leaned forward and kissed Frances gently on the lips. Frances was speechless for a few moments, and not taking her eyes from Sarah asked, "You love me?"

Sarah was laughing gently and smiling, "Yes, how many ways do I have to tell you?"

"I thought that was just in the height…" Frances looked about, remembering everyone was listening, "You know."

"Yes, I do know, and yes, yes, yes!"

This time her kiss was not so gentle. Everyone was shouting and clapping and feeling very pleased with themselves.

"Champagne, Willie! We need champagne and buckets of it."

Sarah only accepted a mouthful. After all, it was essentially her engagement party, but she was on duty and in the charge of one of her new friend's life. Frances shared her glass, but thankfully it didn't stop everyone else.

Sarah was driving Frances' car, and Frances was taking everyone in Lizzie's Prado after she had dropped Lizzie and Danny off. Cat would stay with Sarah; Sarah and Cat had both insisted that it would be just Cat. Cat didn't want to endanger Theo, and Sarah said it would be much easier for her just to concentrate on Cat without having to watch out for Theo as well. Doug and John would follow in their own car.

They all arrived at the school hall at 7:15 P.M. Cocco had, of course, brought a pillow and marched down to the front row and insisted everyone follow him. Aroha had slipped round back, telling them to keep her a seat. Keeping with theatre tradition, she had brought a big bouquet of flowers for Lizzie and a single red rose for Danny. Both cards read, 'Break a leg. All my love, Aroha.' Cocco and Max had already sent bouquets earlier in the day to the school.

Lizzie was so nervous and was feeling sick. Torri was standing next to her when Aroha found her. "Watch out for that cauldron in Act Two, Torri. I've told the stagehands to make sure it's secure, but watch out anyway."

Lizzie saw Aroha and smiled when she saw the flowers, "Aroha, this is Torri."

Torri put her hand out to Aroha. Aroha ignored it, and instead, handed Lizzie the flowers and wrapped her arms around Torri. She was careful of Torri's makeup and kissed her gently on the cheek, "Thank you, dear girl."

Torri stood with her mouth open but recovered very quickly. She knew what Aroha meant, "You're welcome."

"I'd better go," said Aroha, and she kissed Lizzie. "Break a leg." She waved to Danny as she left; she would not embarrass him with a kiss. Relieved, he smiled back.

Cocco was so excited. He was fanning himself when Aroha returned.

"They should turn the air conditioning up, Aroha."

"Don't be silly, Cocco, schools don't run to air conditioning."

Sarah was sitting beside Cat, and Frances was sitting on her other side. Doug was standing at the back of the hall, and John was outside scouting around. It was a relief for Sarah when the overture started, and the lights went down. *At least we should be safe in here.*

Lizzie was standing in the wings holding Jemma's hand and squeezed it just before she went on stage. She actually cried when she sang "Over the Rainbow." Jemma was in top form. Lizzie peeped through the curtain and saw Theo wipe her eyes. *Yes, if Theo is crying, it's all good.* Feeling a little more positive, she sent her runner for the scarecrow man. She loved "If I Only Had a Brain" and realized this was the last time she would hear it. She would miss the show. Watching the scarecrow, she turned around to see the wardrobe mistress sewing something on the lion's costume. The tin man was on next, "I'm sure he'll be ready by the time he's on stage."

"I see nothing, I see nothing," said Lizzie. The seamstress practically followed the lion on stage, and Lizzie had to pull on her blouse to stop her from going any further. She turned and smiled. "Done! He caught it on a door handle."

The audience was enchanted, and all the kids were having a great time on stage. The lion was playing the audience, bordering on hamming it up. Lizzie was biting her nails, which she hadn't done for years. The lion sang, "If I Only Had the Nerve." *Yeah, you do.* She was relieved when the "Jitterbug Ballet" started, which meant they were nearly at the end of Act One. The curtain fell, and the kids were just hyper, with several of them saying they were going to do this when they left school. Lizzie thought it not the time to point out that New Zealand was too small a country to maintain a professional musical company. They had better think opera, or acting, or going overseas.

"Okay, okay, settle down. We're not there yet, but well done everyone."

Sarah was on her feet when the lights went on, making sure Doug was where he was supposed to be. He gave her the thumbs up.

"I don't want you going outside, Cat. I know it's hot, but there will be too many people out there."

"It's okay, Sarah. I'm sure the foyer will be cooler and a cold drink will be fine."

"Oh, isn't it wonderful?" asked Cocco. "That nasty witch better not stop them from getting to Oz."

"Have you never seen the movie, Cocco?" asked Aroha.

"There's a movie?"

Everyone laughed. "The one with Judy Garland in pigtails, Cocco," said Willie.

"Oh, oh, yes, I remember now. Willie got it out for me to watch when I was sick. I can't remember how it ends."

"Don't worry, Cocco," Max had her hand on his shoulder. "All will be revealed soon."

"What a beautiful voice that girl who plays the part of Dorothy has."

"God, yes," said Theo to Max, "I hope she does something with it."

Lizzie was feeling a lot more relaxed as there was nothing more she could do. It was all up to the kids now. The orchestra was striking up ready for Act Two. *Curtain up, here we go.* Lizzie stood in the wings with her fingers crossed; it was the witch's castle scene, and the cauldron still did not look very secure to her. And as if she willed it to happen, it moved. Torri was a trooper and didn't miss a beat as she stilled it while delivering her dialogue. *God, I like this kid!* Then there was Jemma back to sing "Over the Rainbow" and curtain. Lizzie was pretty shocked to feel tears on her cheek. There were five curtain calls, and then she was forced onto the stage herself; and all the cast, as well as the audience, gave her applause. Torri presented her with a bouquet from the school. She saw Aroha in the front row, and she was crying along with Theo and Cocco. *Wimps, the lot of them.* Lizzie thought she had recovered until she looked to the side and saw Danny clapping, and if she weren't mistaken, he had tears in his eyes. Well, that was all too much for Lizzie, and off she started. This got the whole audience clapping even louder, mostly the front row. Torri was standing beside her and gave her a hug.

"Thank you, Lizzie. Thank you so much!"

The lights were up, and Sarah was on her feet. She had a cold feeling in the pit of her stomach, and Frances noticed. "What is it, Sarah?"

"I don't know, Frances, but this would be a perfect place for an attempt on Cat's life. I should never have agreed to this. There are too many places where someone could hide." She was looking for Doug in the crowd of people. Finally she saw him, but instead of giving her the thumbs up, he shrugged, which meant John had not been checking back every ten minutes.

She said to Lizzie's party, "Stay here."

"Doug, what is it?"

"I haven't seen John for the past twenty minutes."

"Okay. Go look, I'll stay here."

She returned and said, "Okay, everyone into the rehearsal hall. We will wait till everyone else has left. Aroha, can you go backstage from here to tell Lizzie to get everyone to leave as soon as they can?"

"Yes, of course. That shouldn't be a problem as there is a cast party back at the good fairy's house."

"Great. Make sure Danny goes with them, and you can pick him up later. Tell Lizzie to be as calm as possible, have her just say there's going to be a fire drill. Willie, you go with her. Ted, lead the way, please."

Sarah squeezed Frances' hand. "Don't worry. It's probably nothing. Go with them, please; I'll be there in a moment."

Doug returned a few minutes later. "Sarah, I can't find him."

That feeling in the pit of Sarah's stomach just got colder. Sarah took out her gun, checked the ammo, and took the safety off.

"Better call for back up. How long do you think it will take the Armed Offenders Squad to get here, Doug?"

"Twenty minutes, I suppose."

"I'll stay with them," said Sarah. "See if you can get everyone else out as quickly as you can."

Chapter 30

Ten minutes later, Doug returned. "The last few are just leaving now. Willie and Lizzie are just locking up."
"Okay, we are sitting ducks here. Let's make a move. You go first, Doug, the rest will follow. Cat and I will leave through the door around the other side. Frances, bring the car around to that door. Leave the engine running and then return to the others as quickly as you can, please. As soon as she returns, all of you leave. Go to Willie and Cocco's."

Lizzie, Max, Aroha, Theo, Cocco, and Ted were already in the Prado with the engine going. Willie got in the passenger seat. There was just Frances to come. Doug was in his car ready to follow Sarah.

Sarah opened the side door of the hall and saw John lying face down on the grass. She instinctively leant down to feel his pulse. A moment's distraction was all Dean needed, and he grabbed Cat around the waist and held a knife to her throat. "I knew all I had to do was wait till one of you bitches screwed up. Hello, Catharine. Long time no see." Cat was traumatized. Fear was on her face, and her eyes started to roll back in her head.

Just then Frances drove around and stopped abruptly when she saw Sarah pointing her gun at a man who had a knife to Cat's throat. She was half out of the car when she heard Sarah say, "Frances, get back in the car!" Frances just stood frozen to the spot. This time Sarah shouted, snapping at Frances, "Frances! Get back in the car!" Frances sat back in the car; but she left the door open and had one foot on the ground.

"Drop the knife, Dean!" said Sarah. "You can't win. I have a gun, as you can plainly see, and I'm not afraid to use it. You can't win.

You are about to be surrounded. You can't escape. Put the knife down now!"

"Shut up, bitch! I've waited a long time for this, and no dyke is gonna stop me now."

Dean started to walk backwards, dragging Cat with him.

Sarah shot into the air, "Stop right there, Dean!"

Everyone in the Prado heard the shot. "Oh, my god," said Max. Cocco screamed.

Lizzie turned to Willie. "What should we do?" They saw Detective Spicer get out of his car and run around the building.

"Everyone be quiet," said Max. "We will all just wait here. Sarah and Detective Spicer don't need us getting in the way. Just pray that Cat, Frances, and Sarah are all right."

Theo was trying to get out, "Cat, I must go to Cat."

Aroha was next to her and pulled her back down. "Theo, we have to wait here."

Theo started to cry. "Aroha, I can't lose her now."

"I know, sweetheart," and she took her in her arms and comforted her.

Doug stood at the corner and looked around. He saw Dean holding Cat and decided he would go around the building to see if he could sneak up on him from behind. He was wishing the AOS would hurry up. It must be thirteen or fourteen minutes since he called for them.

Dean was slowly backing up to the corner of the building behind him.

"Dean, there is no way out for you. You'll never get out of the country. Let go of Cat now, and I'll put a good word in for you."

Dean was nearly at the corner, and he looked as if he were going to cut Cat's throat.

The light was so bad, and Sarah wasn't sure if she could get a shot off. "Dean, it's all over. I'll lower my gun if you drop the knife."

Dean turned his head quickly as he heard a noise coming from behind him. He tried to pull Cat with him, but she had fainted and he couldn't hold her. She fell to the ground, and Dean ran around the corner.

"Doug! Doug, are you there?"

Sarah heard a car engine as Doug arrived. "He's getting away. You stay with Cat and John till the AOS gets here and call for an ambulance."

Sarah looked back, and Frances, who was kneeling by Cat, said, "She's all right, she's just fainted."

Sarah was running towards the car, and Frances was immediately with her. "I'm coming with you."

"Frances, you can't." Frances was in the driver's seat. "You're wasting time, Sarah."

Sarah was in the midst of getting in the passenger seat when Frances started to reverse the car. The car Dean was driving was just passing the front of the school, and Frances was about five hundred yards away.

"Frances, I can't do my job and worry about you."

"I couldn't let you go on your own."

"Turn left. He's turning into Hataitai Road. I wish I had my siren with me." Sarah spoke into her radio, "Detective Fergusson is down but still alive. Detective Spicer is with him, as is Ms. Craig. She has fainted but is unharmed. I'm in pursuit on Hataitai Road. I'm travelling in a maroon Renault, license number…" Sarah looked to Frances, and Frances gave her number. "Corolla is driving a dark Audi 23E series. I can't see the plate. He's turning right into Mt. Victoria Tunnel."

Frances had to brake and lower her speed in the tunnel. There was nowhere to overtake him, and Corolla was three cars ahead. The noise in the tunnel was loud and added to Frances' increased heart rate. She couldn't speak; she was so focused. She could not get the sight of Sarah with a gun out of her mind, or Cat with a knife at her throat. She was quite sure she would fall to pieces later, but right now her blood was pumping very fast through her veins. Corolla turned left at the end of the tunnel, right on to Rugby Street, and right again on to Sussex, right on to Buckle, and then left on to Cambridge Terrace.

"Where is the bozo going, he's doubling back?" Corolla's car was travelling 100 km an hour down the Terrace, and Frances was gaining. "Shit, where are the police when you want them?" Sarah was back on the radio, "He'll either have to turn left on to Wakefield or right on to Oriental Parade at the bottom here." Sarah could hear sirens in the background. Saturday night in Wellington was a busy night for the police. She just hoped the sirens were for her. She was back on the radio. "He's going left, Oriental Parade, that's Oriental Parade."

Frances' concentration was fixed firmly on the road ahead. This end of Oriental Parade was a very trendy place, and it would be full of diners and walkers. Corolla's car was weaving in and out of traffic. Several oncoming cars were swerving to avoid him. Once Frances drove past the business end of the Parade, the road narrowed and twisted and curved around.

"I think he's heading for the airport, Frances."

"Idiot! There's nowhere to go after there."

Sarah was back on the radio, "I think he's headed for the airport. Hang on, we're on the round-a-bout, we'll know in a moment. Yes, he's heading for the airport. Get the airport police to set up a block."

The road to the airport runs along the side of the runway. As if he knew he was trapped, Corolla stopped his car and got out. He was two feet away from the high fence that surrounded the runway. As Frances drew to a stop, they could see Corolla cut a hole down the wire fence, drop what ever he used, squeeze through, and start running.

"Where the hell does he think he's running to?" Sarah was out of the car and through the fence. "Stay in the car, Frances."

"No fucking way," and Frances was immediately behind Sarah.

Sarah had no time to argue. With gun in hand, she was running like a bat out of hell. Frances had no trouble keeping up with Sarah. *This is not the return run I had in mind.* Frances knew planes were loud but actually being on the runway as they were taking off was altogether something else. Dean had crossed the tarmac and was running on the grass on the left.

Where the hell is he going? They had been running for three or four minutes, and still Corolla was ahead. Sarah could just see the outline of a small plane up ahead and knew she had to pick up the pace or lose him. Frances was right beside her, as they were getting closer to Corolla and the plane. Sarah shouted. "Stop police!" and shot into the air. Corolla was getting closer to the plane, and Frances pulled ahead. She was two feet ahead of Sarah. There was only about six hundred yards left, and they were closing in on Corolla. Frances was pulling ahead even more. *Okay, Frances, you win. Now please stop. I couldn't cope if anything happened to you.*

Corolla was only ten feet away, and with amazing speed, Frances was behind him in four strides. She threw herself at him, and they both fell to the ground. Corolla's knife was still in his hand. He turned over, knocking Frances to the side, and had the knife in the air ready to stab Frances when Sarah shouted, "Freeze, or make me very happy, you piece of shit." Sarah was standing over Corolla, her foot on his leg and her gun just two feet away from his face. Frances moved away and stood up.

Sirens were blazing all around, and soon they were surrounded. Frances watched Sarah. She didn't take her eyes off Corolla for one second. He had dropped the knife, and Frances picked up the blade carefully with two fingers and threw it out of reach. Two police constables got Corolla to his feet and handcuffed him. Sarah saw another couple of police cars approach the small plane. When Corolla was safely in the hands of the constables, Sarah put the safety on her gun and holstered it. She told the constables to take him in, and she would follow in an hour.

Once they were on their own Sarah started to cry, "What the hell did you think you were doing, Frances?"

Frances was shocked by Sarah's reaction, "He was getting away."

"You could have been killed. What would I have done?"

Frances approached Sarah and reached out for her. Sarah put her arm out to stop Frances. Frances still approached and took Sarah in her arms. Sarah's sobs were louder now, and she returned Frances' hug. "Never do anything like that again, promise me, Frances."

Frances kissed Sarah's face, and said, "Okay, baby, okay."

"I'll take you to Willie and Cocco's and see how Cat is, but then I'll have to go in."

Everyone was relieved to see them. Cat had been taken to hospital to be checked out. Theo had gone with her in the ambulance, but both were expected home in a couple of hours. The news on Detective Fergusson was good; he had a mild concussion and would be kept overnight for observation. Max was waiting for Theo and Cat to come home, and then she and Ted were going to spend the night with them at Roseneath. Sarah related the story of Frances' driving and how she captured Corolla. Sarah feigned admiration and said, "My hero." Aroha and Lizzie were leaving to pick up Danny from the party. "Sorry your night was spoiled, Lizzie," said Sarah.

"No, it wasn't. It was a great night. I had a fabulous show, and you two captured the bastard who's been trying to kill Cat. All in all, I say that's a pretty good night."

"I have to go interrogate the bastard now, but hopefully you will all sleep better."

Sarah bid them all goodnight and took Frances' hand and pulled her outside. "You'll stay with me, won't you? I'll drop you off; and promise me, you'll be asleep in my bed when I get home."

"Where else would I be?"

"It could be morning before I get home."

"I'll make breakfast."

Sarah laughed, "I thought you couldn't cook?"

"I can boil an egg and make coffee. What more do you need?"

"Absolutely nothing." Sarah kissed Frances and then drove her home before she went off to work.

Chapter 31

Frances was in Sarah's bed, awakening from spasmodic sleep. The sun was just starting to creep through the window. Something made her open her eyes, and there was Sarah sitting in a chair. Her jacket was over the back of the chair, and her shoes were kicked to the side. Her shoulder holster was empty, and she was staring at Frances. "How long have you been there?"

"About twenty minutes."

"What's the time?"

"Just after six."

"What are you doing?"

Sarah didn't answer for a moment. "I'm just wondering what on earth I'm going to do if you are not there every morning."

Frances was a little stunned, "Oh, no, you don't. I need you more than you need me."

"Says who?"

Frances was up out of bed, and kneeling in front of Sarah. She looked into her eyes and said, "We go through our whole life looking for something, anything, someone to make sense of what were are doing here. Most of the time we just stumble and make do, we compromise because we think we don't have the right to have what we want. Everyone tells us to be happy and then puts obstacles or conditions in the way. We've gotten very good at polishing over the cracks of our life, and when we finally fall apart the only people who are surprised are ourselves. We have a chance at something here, Sarah, and I'm going to take Gerry's advice and not fuck it up."

Sarah looked deep into Frances' eyes. "Maybe Max was right. Maybe we have waited all our lives for each other. But Frances, it's been so quick. What if you can't stand my work commitments or the way I eat dinner?"

"Stop. We are not kids any more. I think that we have to take this gift we have both been given and let our love lead us through our day-to-day lives. At least it won't be boring."

Sarah made a noise that was half laugh, half cry, "Not with our friends, if I may call them mine as well as yours?"

"What's mine is yours, and what's yours is definitely all mine. Come to bed, and I'll have some of mine, all mine."

Sarah woke to the smell of coffee wafting through the house. Frances arrived with a tray with toast, a boiled egg, and a steaming mug of coffee.

"Boy, I could get used to this. What time is it?"

"Two. How did you sleep?"

Sarah's eyes lit up. "Fine, eventually."

"You haven't told me what happened to Corolla?"

"I have asked my office to call everyone to meet at Cat and Theo's at five, so I can tell everyone together. Do you mind waiting and not let him invade our home?"

"Our home?"

Sarah put her hand on Frances' face, "Wake up and smell the coffee. When do you have to go back to Auckland?"

"Not till next weekend."

Sarah smiled, "Really? I've got four days off starting Friday. Shall I come with you?"

Frances returned the smile, "That will only leave three and a half weeks to Christmas."

Sarah and Frances were late arriving at Theo and Cat's; and as it was out of character for them both, everyone knew what must have kept them. When they walked into the lounge where everyone was sitting, they were met with applause and cheers, "Hail to the heroes!" Cat and Theo came forward and kissed both Frances and Sarah. Frances' embarrassment still amused Sarah. They all looked as if they were on to their second drink of the evening. Sarah was handed a glass of wine and Frances a Coke. "What can you tell us, Sarah?" asked Max.

"Not as much as I would like, Max. He isn't giving much away. Okay, here's what we've got. First up, the plane. The pilot does not seem to be involved other than Corolla gave him an inordinate amount of money to have the plane up and running and ready to go. He was paid $20,000 to fly him to an airstrip just by Lyttleton."

"Christchurch?" asked Willie.

"Yes. Apparently he entered the country as a member of a crew aboard a ship and planned to leave the same way. The name he was using was John Smithe. He had a passport with that name on him and a union card with the name of the ship he crewed for."

"Where was the ship going?" asked Cat.

"Canada. The car he was driving was stolen, and we haven't been able to locate any of the places he has been staying. He also had a considerable amount of cash on him. A further $NZ20,000 and $US40,000."

"How did he find Cat?" asked Max.

"That we don't know altogether, but he freely told us that he found out you went to Canada. Unfortunately, the school teacher who helped you was badly beaten and nearly lost his life."

Cat covered her mouth, "Oh, my god, that poor man."

"Max, did he know that it was you who met Cat in Vancouver?"

"Not to the best of my knowledge. He was just told that someone would be meeting her. I guess he could have been told that it was a relative but not who or what name."

"So the trail should have gone cold in Vancouver, but obviously, he found some way to find you, Cat. How are you feeling?"

"I'm fine. Relieved that it's finally over, and I can stop looking over my shoulder and start to think about travelling."

With a smile on her face, Cat said, "Apparently, Theo and I are going to Japan to meet Cocco's mum. Sarah, I don't know how I can ever thank you and Frances. You were both so brave, and all I could do was faint."

"I'm really thankful that you did, Cat, because I truly believe that you would be dead now if you hadn't."

"Oh, my god," said Max.

"It was so dark; I'm not too sure I could have hit Corolla."

"Would you have," asked Theo, "if the light had been better?"

"In a heart beat. The world would be a better place without scum like that."

"Way to go, girl!" said Theo.

"What happens now?" asked Willie.

"He'll be charged with four attempted murders, an assault with a deadly weapon, resisting arrest, driving illegally, and endangering the public. Also, auto theft, entering the country illegally, and a few other charges still to come. He's going to jail for a very long time."

"Will there be an extradition order for him to return to the UK?"

"I'm not sure. Personally, I would be happy to have him out of this country and not be a burden on the taxpayers."

"When will the trial be?"

"He'll be charged officially tomorrow and held over till the trial. There is no chance of bail as he would be a flight risk; plus, he has no address in New Zealand."

"What about the money Jimmy took, Sarah? Did he say anything about that?"

Cat looked puzzled, "The police never found it, and I wondered if he ever did."

"You would have a claim on it if it ever was found, you know."

"I wouldn't want it, Sarah. It killed my mother and brother. It's blood money. I'd want no part of it."

"He said he followed Jimmy that morning, that's how he knew he did it. So I suppose he might have seen where he hid it."

Cat was starting to wane and dwell on the past. Theo was quick to change the mood.

"Cat and I have been talking. It's the American Thanksgiving on Thursday, and we thought that we would have our own thanksgiving and celebrate. So what say you all, to a bloody good knees-up and celebration? After all, we have a lot to be thankful for."

Theo put her arm around Cat's shoulder and squeezed. Cat still looked down but smiled and said, "Yes, please come."

Everyone agreed that it would be just the thing.

"I think turkey, don't you?" asked Theo.

"Oh, I have a great recipe for stuffing," said Cocco.

"Instead of pumpkin pie, I will make kumera," said Aroha.

"I've got a marvellous recipe for homemade cranberry aspic," said Max.

"How about we bring melon and prusciotto for the entrée?" asked Sarah.

Frances' mouth flew open in delight, "Yes, I now have a partner who can contribute. I don't have to feel bad any more about our get-togethers."

She turned to Sarah and asked, with a frown on her face, "You can cook, can't you?" Everyone laughed and Sarah said, "Well, I'm no Cocco, but I can hold my own."

"Of course, you can," said Max. "She can do anything. I found her, you know?"

Aroha had a sharp intake of breath, "I found her."

"No, it was definitely me," said Cocco.

Sarah was laughing.

"It was me," said Theo. Everyone looked at her.

"You were unconscious," said Cocco.

"But I heard all, and I'm sure it was me who said she'd be perfect for Frances."

They all picked up cushions and threw them at Theo. Nobody noticed Frances and Sarah slip into the hall. Theo found them five minutes later, still kissing.

"We have to go now," said Frances.

"Either that or rent a room," said Theo.

They said their goodbyes and left. Sarah went to the driver's door. Frances stood and looked at her. "Hey!"

Sarah shook her head as she unlocked the car. "You said this was my car in Wellington."

"Harrumph."

Frances felt content as they drove to Sarah's home. She had her hand on Sarah's thigh.

"Careful, you'll have me drive into a wall or something."

"I'm not doing anything."

"Yeah, but I can read your thoughts and that would be impossible while I'm driving."

Frances smiled, "I could try."

"No, you don't."

"Thank goodness the nightmare is over for Cat," said Frances. "Why are you frowning, Sarah?"

"There's something not right. Something at the back of my mind, but I just can't reach it. And his gun. His gun bothers me."

"How do you mean?"

"Well, I asked him what was with the knife. I thought a gun was his weapon of choice and asked him where it was."

"What did he say?"

"He said it went overboard at Paekakariki."

"And you don't believe him?"

Sarah shrugged, "Oh, I don't know, Frances, it's probably just me, but I wish I could remember what I can't remember."

"Do you have to go to work tomorrow?"

"Just for a little while. Once Corolla's charged, I can take some time off."

Frances stretched and feigned a yawn.

"Subtle," smiled Sarah, "I don't think."

"Are you objecting?"

"Not at all, my darlin', not at all."

Frances' hand was wandering a little farther. "What else can you do that I don't know about?"

Sarah's laugh was much louder now, and in her best Irish accent she said, "Oh darlin', you have no idea!"

Chapter 32

Cat watched Theo, who had just finished showering, get dressed. Cat had been up for hours and wondered why she couldn't sleep. She should at last be rid of all her demons. Instead, she felt the enormous weight of indecision on her shoulders. As if she had climbed all the mountains, except for the biggest one in front of her. She knew there would be no peace until this was faced. *But how do you talk to someone who doesn't want to talk? There is no opening sentence that will lead, if someone doesn't want to talk. Does this make it my problem if I'm the one who is unhappy with the way things are? Can I go on with the way things are? What are the alternatives, and can I face a life without Theo?*

From the outside we are the ideal couple, and everyone thinks we are exactly that. We are very compatible and at ease with each other, should that be enough? When your partner is emotionally and physically unavailable, do you make do at the cost of losing a piece of your soul? I don't doubt that Theo loves me, but is that enough? Should I accept her indifference to my feelings that she trivializes by not wanting to talk or listen? Am I a mug or a martyr? Am I a fool or a saint? And what makes her willing to accept our relationship the way it is? What is she getting out of it? I feel our life is led on parallel tracks very close together, but only occasionally cross when absolutely necessary. Cat felt her eyes fill up and looked away, but Theo saw her in the mirror. "Cat, whatever is the matter? You're safe now. He'll never get out."

"Max wants me to go back into counselling."

"How do you feel about that?"

Here we go for nothing. "I think the only counselling I need is to talk to you."

Theo looked suspicious, "What do you mean?"

"I mean it's time for us to talk to each other, really talk."

207

"We're all right, Cat. It's just that you have been through so much again in your life; you must still be in shock. We have this house and our work, the rest is just normal day-to-day stuff."

"I don't know, Theo. I don't think that's enough. We build ourselves these beautiful boxes—to put our things into—that we call houses, but these things don't necessarily make them homes. I feel as if I live in a beautiful mausoleum. The only time there's love here is when our friends and Max visit. Most of the time, you hardly acknowledge me. You never want to do anything, just the two of us, and you seem indifferent to me, depressed even, but as soon as we are with our friends, you're happy and carefree. How am I supposed to deal with that?"

"Cat, that's simply not true. I am happy to be with you. I just can't be as demonstrative as you. Sometimes you make me feel claustrophobic because you don't seem to need anyone else. It's too big a responsibility. I feel as if you are watching me all the time, and I can't be myself. You're so contained; everything is so black and white with you. Why can't you be happy with the way things are? I don't know that I can give you what you want. But I can promise to always be here, maybe not the way you want, but as much as I can. I have always seen us growing old together. Most people go a whole lifetime and don't have what we have. I will promise to try to be more attentive, and perhaps you could try not to be so needy. Cat, we do have a home here, not a mausoleum."

"I guess it's that I don't understand, Theo, how you can say you love me but not want to love me? Is it that you're not attracted to me anymore, that you want still to live with me but be someone else's lover? I'm so frustrated on so many levels that I seem to have no defence against you. I need the physical love as well as the emotional support. Is it that, after all these years, that you do want Frances?"

Theo sighed, "No. My love for Frances is no more than it is for Aroha or Lizzie. Yes, I would have enjoyed the dalliance all those years ago, but that's all. Frances and I would never have worked because she is even more obsessive than you, and besides, I need to be the attractive one." Theo was smiling, "I always thought you and I would make it because of your calmness, your stability, and your obvious love for me. I thought you loved me for who I am, not whom you want me to be. Cat, you're scaring me. I don't know why I'm not the person you want me to be. I always thought our relationship was different and that we didn't depend on following a set pattern of what relationships are meant to be, or at least what most people think they're meant to be. I just thought we would embrace each new stage of our life together and give each other room to be who we are."

Cat was looking confused, "What do I get out of this stage of our relationship? This has been going on for a long time; a stage that I neither asked for nor agreed to. You never discussed these changes with me."

"I guess I thought you would just go with it as I would for you."

Cat fell to a chair. "I don't know what to say to that. Does this mean that our relationship is all on your terms, and if I want to stay with you, I have to accept that?"

Theo smiled nervously. She looked like a trapped animal that was looking for a way out. "Lighten up, Cat, you're so serious. I'm going to make some coffee, would you like some?"

"Again, an avoidance tactic." Theo couldn't look at Cat; instead she turned and left the room saying, "No, it's not. I just want coffee."

Why is it that whenever I can get Theo to talk, I'm no further forwards? Nothing is ever resolved; questions are never directly answered. Is it me? Do I expect too much? How do other people relate to each other? Aroha and Lizzie address their problems directly; Cocco never lets Willie get away with anything, but I'm not allowed to judge our relationship by other people's standards. We apparently dance to a different tune.

Ten minutes later, Cat was still sitting in her room when she heard Theo play the piano. Cat smiled. Theo didn't play the piano as much as she wished she would or used to. She remembered when she bought the baby grand. They had only just bought the house, which cost more than they had. Cat had spotted it in an old piano repair shop and had gone in to speak with the owner, a man who found old forgotten pianos and restored them. Cat had borrowed the money from Max on a long-term basis. Max was thrilled. She said it would give her as much pleasure as it would Cat. Theo was blown away, and the house was filled for weeks with music. Theo was more classically trained than Lizzie. Lizzie was best for a sing-along—she has amazing timing and feel—but Theo is the better pianist. Cat went downstairs.

Theo kept playing. She knew Cat was there. She was paying Michael Nyman's "Big My Secret" from *The Piano*. Cat sat and listened to it and was awash with peace. Theo always knew how to appease her. Right there and then she knew this was Theo's way of communicating, just like Ada from *The Piano*, who couldn't speak, so she used music to portray her emotions. This was truly beautiful. She never felt closer to Theo or anyone else as she did at that moment. Not in a lover's embrace, not in deep conversation, but as two souls as one. Cat felt the tears roll down her face. She had no fight left; she had no defence against this woman.

Sad am I, blessed am I, belonging am I. Here, now am I, to quote a poet whose name she no longer remembered: *"And the life that I have, and the love that I have, is yours and yours and yours."*

Chapter 33

Aroha and Lizzie were in the kitchen having breakfast. "How do you think this change of menu thing is going to work?" asked Lizzie.

Aroha smiled, "I think it will be fun with everyone bringing a dish from the country of his or her ancestors."

"Well, at least we don't have to dress in the costume of our ancestral country. I don't do clogs, and I look funny in hats, especially ones with wings. Danny, hurry up," shouted Aroha, "you'll be late." Danny ran into the kitchen and sat down at his place. In between mouthfuls of Weetbix, he said, "I'm bringing my girlfriend tonight. Her grandmother's Italian, so she said she'll bring a pasta dish."

Aroha and Lizzie were speechless, and Danny quickly finished his breakfast, kissed them both on the cheek, and left for school. Aroha and Lizzie were still standing with their mouths open after Danny had left.

"He has a girlfriend?" asked Aroha.

"Willie said he got on well with everyone in the cast. It must be one of the munchkins."

"He's got a girlfriend?" asked Aroha again. "He's not twelve for another couple of weeks."

Lizzie went over and put her arms around Aroha. Trying to keep the laughter out of her voice, she said, "I'm sure it's not serious, honey, I'm sure they're just friends."

Lizzie left the room, not trusting herself not to laugh in front of Aroha. Unfortunately, the bathroom was not that soundproof.

Cocco was standing in his kitchen preparing sashimi. "You got your dish organized, Willie? I no see anything in fridge."

"Don't you worry, Cocco. I'm on to it, got it sussed."

"Are you putting down a hangi at the girls place?"

"Just you wait and see, gorgeous."

Willie knew that would immediately get Cocco off his back. He could organize himself just this once. Cocco wasn't the only one who could rise to the occasion.

Willie went over to Cocco and kissed him. "I'll be home as early as I can. Lizzie and I have a plan. If one of us gets held or caught up, the other will extract him or her with an excuse of a matter of utmost importance."

"Okay then, see you later. Are you sure you don't want me to do a dish for you?"

Willie smiled, "Quite sure. Later."

Max was just returning from a walk with Ozzie when Ted wandered in. "Good morning, beautiful, how are you?"

"Is that your way of getting me to cook something for you to take tonight?"

"No, not at all. I was merely stating the truth."

"Flattery will get you everywhere, my good man. Want some coffee?"

"Sure, I just came to check what time to be ready."

"I think if we leave at four-thirty that will make us just a little bit early in case Theo needs a hand with anything."

"Not Cat?"

"Oh, Cat will be having a lot of fun setting up the table and decorating the house, but knowing Cat, it will all be done by lunchtime, and she'll just be Theo's little helper after that. What is your family background anyway, Ted? I don't think that I have ever asked."

"My parents were English, but I was born in Singapore. We didn't come to New Zealand till I was five. Got out just before the Japanese invaded."

"Interesting. Come sit down and tell me all."

Frances met Sarah in town for lunch. She would rather she had come home as it wouldn't be as easy to touch her in public, not the esteemed Detective Inspector. Sarah said she couldn't spare that much time, especially as lunch at home yesterday had turned out to be without sustenance, well food-wise anyway. And, as of 4:00 P.M.

today, she had four and half days leave. Frances had bought sandwiches, so they wouldn't be tied to a busy café. "Frances, it's just as well I'm having four days off. I'm having real trouble concentrating on my work with the thought of you lying at home in our bed."

"You make me sound lazy," she said with a glint in her eye. "I'm up as soon as you leave. In fact, I had a very productive morning."

"Doing what?"

"You'll see later."

"What are you taking tonight anyway?"

"I thought you would have me do something Scottish or French."

"That's what a little of this morning was all about. Don't worry, darling, I have it all in hand. I won't let you down."

Frances looked at Sarah who was sitting deep in thought. "What are you thinking about?"

"The thought of being all in your hands."

"Sarah Adams, you are a shameless woman…thank the goddess!"

Frances looked sheepish, "I have something to ask you."

Sarah was intrigued, "What?"

"Will you wear your new black dress and your 'fuck me' stilettos tonight?"

Sarah raised her eyebrows, "They worked, didn't they?"

"Oh, darling, I wanted you the moment I fell on you on the beach."

Sarah laughed, "Well, I would have done it right there and then if you'd asked, but you buggered off."

Frances blushed, "I didn't want to, but I had to take Ozzie off that dog. Besides, you would not have done it on the beach in daylight."

Sarah raised her eyebrows again in the way that Frances did. "Okay, but you have to wear that see-through blouse."

Frances feigned shock, "What, in front of my friends?"

"Yes."

Theo walked through to the dining room. "Cat, you've outdone yourself this time. The tree looks beautiful, and the table is exquisite. I took your apple pie out of the oven. It smells divine."

"Thank you. How's the lamb on the spit coming along?"

"Great. I keep basting it every twenty minutes or so. I can't wait to see what everyone else brings."

"You'll never guess. Aroha just rang, and Danny is bringing a girlfriend. Apparently, he just sprung it on them at breakfast this morning. She has an Italian grandmother, so she will be bringing a pasta dish."

"No shit! Oh, Cat, the house looks lovely. It is a beautiful home, is it not?"

Cat stopped what she was doing and looked at Theo. She wanted desperately to take her in her arms and kiss as they used to. Instead, she just smiled and said, "Yes, it is."

Max and Ted arrived first, "Here's the ubiquitous Pavlova. Seeing as New Zealand and Australia can't agree whose it is, I thought it could represent both."

"Your grandmother's Christmas cake, made from her recipe, asparagus and hollandaise sauce, and some Cabernet Merlot from South Australia."

"Thank you."

Ted handed a casserole dish, "A Tiffin, which is chicken curry; it's my mother's recipe from our days in Singapore, and a bottle of gin for the slings."

"This is so exciting." said Theo. "I just feel as if this evening is very special.

Max embraced her. "I think we all feel it. I suppose that niece of mine has the house looking beautiful. What can I do to help?"

"Come baste the lamb with me."

Willie and Cocco arrived next. Cocco proudly presented sashimi, freshly made Wasabi, and a gift of Saki in a beautiful china bottle with six matching little cups. Willie handed over a supermarket bag that held several items, all wrapped in newspaper. "Willie an embarrassment to me. He just went supermarket."

He smiled and handed the bag to Theo, "Six crayfish, cooked. My father and uncle went out this morning over to Riversdale especially and caught them."

"Oh, Willie, you'll be very popular." Then he handed her a six-pack of Steinlager.

Almost immediately, Aroha, Lizzie, and Danny arrived. Aroha's maternal side is Maori, and she has English grandparents on her father's side. She brought roast beef and Yorkshire puddings, a

Kumera vegetable salad, and champagne, as she was not drinking warm beer. Lizzie had brought rollmops, smoked eel, bite-sized pikelets, and salted liquorice. Danny made small paper flags to represent each person's ancestral country that he wanted to place on each traditional dish. He had even rung Ted to check on his contribution.

"Danny, where's your girlfriend?" asked Theo.

"She'll be here soon."

Theo was also delighted to see that Danny had brought his bongo drum with him. Fortunately, he had Lizzie's love for music, unlike his tone-deaf mother. Frances and Sarah were a little late but were forgiven when everyone saw how they were dressed.

"Bloody hell!" said Willie.

"Hear, hear!" said Ted.

Theo took a long look at both of them, back and forth, and finally said to Frances, "She suits you," and to Sarah, "Love the heels."

Max was beaming and lightly clapping her hands. Frances took Sarah's hand.

Cocco was beside himself. "I did this, I did this! CC, they have to sit next to me, all the beautiful people should sit together. Can I try your heels on, Sarah?"

Frances and Willie said "No!" together.

Sarah was laughing, and Cat came over to them both and kissed them on the lips. "Thank you. You are not only beautiful on the inside, but are stunning on the outside. My table will be honoured to sit you." Danny cat whistled, which made everyone laugh, except a stunned Aroha. Frances picked up the picnic basket she had brought, and gave it to Cat. "There is a haggis, courtesy of Gourmet Direct, with a bottle of whiskey, some duck pâté, some pastries, and a bottle of brandy."

Sarah took over, "Also some soda bread that I baked myself first thing this morning, a potato salad, and some bottles of Guinness."

"What a feast," said Cat. "Danny, come help me with this, and you can put your flags on."

Ten minutes later, there was a knock at the door, and Danny ran, "I'll get it." Everyone turned, waiting for Danny's girlfriend to enter the room. It would be a big understatement to say that Lizzie was shocked to the point of being gobsmacked when Torri Jacobs walked in, carrying food in one hand and a violin case in the other. "It's a lasagne, and it will be great. My mother made it, and Danny said to bring a musical instrument, if I played one, as these 'do's' tend to be musical." She handed Cat the lasagne, smiled, and said, "Hello, Lizzie-mum."

Max, as usual, saved the social gaffe by extending her hand and introducing herself. She asked about her style of dress, followed by Cocco. Max was intrigued, and Cocco loved anything dramatic. Lizzie turned to Aroha and said, "She's sixteen, and he's not even twelve yet."

Aroha stood with a frown on her face, but it slowly turned into a smile, "Of course, he would pick Torri, she's perfect for him."

Lizzie looked at Aroha as if she couldn't believe what she had heard. "Did you know she played the violin, Lizzie?" Lizzie, still shocked, shook her head unable to reply.

Frances got Cat on the side and gave her a big box of expensive crackers. "Is it all right if they go on the table?"

"Yes, of course. They are beautiful."

"Could you make sure Sarah gets this one, please?"

Cat smiled, "Yes."

She embraced Frances with a tear in her eye. "I'm so happy for you, Frances. You deserve this."

Frances returned her embrace, "Thank you, Cat."

Willie and Cocco were sent to carve the lamb, and the table looked resplendent with food, flowers, and candles. The house was a-buzz with conversation until dinner was announced. "Would everyone go to the table, please?" said Theo. Cat sat at the top, her usual spot, and was surprised when Theo sat beside her. "I swapped, do you mind?"

"No," said Cat, looking very surprised.

Once everyone was seated, Theo spoke. "Okay, this is a very special evening for me, and if nobody minds, I'd like us to go around the table and give thanks. I would like to start.

Theo closed her eyes, took a deep breath, and said, "I'm thankful for my health, wonderful friends, for Cat's life being saved for the third time, for all the horror in her life being over, and most of all, that she chooses to live her life with me. Thank you."

Max said, "I'll go next. I'm thankful for my health, too, such a wonderful family that Cat has given me, and for my darling, Caitlin, who gave me a reason to go on. I love you, sweetheart, and I'm so glad you're finally safe. Oh, and Ted," Max turned to Ted, "you're a dear man," and kissed him on the cheek. Ted thanked everyone and of course, Max.

After Ted was Danny. "I am thankful for my new phone, and I would like to take this opportunity to remind everyone that my birthday is Christmas Eve, and two pressies are expected, not one. Mum and Lizzie-mum, if you wanted to buy me my own set of drums, that would be cool." Everyone roared with laughter.

Torri said, "I am pleased to be here and look forward to coming to more 'do's.' Danny, I'm a dyke, so I'll be your girlfriend till you're old enough to have a real one, then I'll be your best friend and teach you how to look after your girlfriends, okay?"
Danny shook his head, "Okay."
Cocco said, "Our boy's got his own dyke-hag." While everyone laughed, Torri whispered in Danny's ear, "And when you're old enough, I'll teach you how to kiss, too. Okay?"
"Okay!"

Lizzie was next. *Of course, trust Aroha to work it out before me.* Lizzie stood, "I am the luckiest woman in the world. My beloved forgave me for being a major twatt and nearly breaking up our family. I love you, honey, but I guess you know that. I'm not sure I deserve you, but I'm bloody glad you're my other half. How could we be any luckier with this beautiful boy in our lives?" Danny went red and hid his face, "Mum!"
Lizzie laughed. "I'm blessed with great friends. Thank you all."

Willie was sitting at the top of the other end of the table, in Theo's place. Willie rose and said, "A toast, I think. I'm not really good with words. I just hope that you all know what you mean to me and Cocco." As Willie was getting tearful, he raised his glass, "To life, to love, and to friends." Everyone agreed and raised his or her glass.

Aroha was next. "I can't believe what has happened in all our lives in the last four weeks. I just about lost my best friend, we learned that Cocco and Cat have been to hell and back, and it still went on for Cat, and if it weren't for the heroism of Sarah and Frances, we would have lost her. My other half reminded us all of how much a stupid mistake could affect so many lives," Lizzie looked crestfallen, "and I want you all to hear from me that I have forgiven her, and I never want it mentioned again."

"I'll drink to that," said Willie.

Lizzie mouthed, "Thank you, darling."

"And here and right now, I want it recognized officially, that it was I, Aroha Kiriana, who found Sarah for Frances, and because of that, I feel it's my place to officially welcome this lovely Irish lass to our family and thank her for making our Frenchy so obviously happy. So I ask you to raise your glasses and welcome Catharine Yates back to us, and Sarah, welcome." They all joined in and drained their glasses.

Cocco spoke next, "Danny, close ears! Fuuuuuck, is good job I next, you all too serious. Lighten up, this happy time." Everyone laughed. "I happy I so beautiful and have good taste. I happy I have my handsome Willie, and I guess I happy I have you all, and Max, she the best." When everyone stopped laughing, Cocco added, "I still want to try Sarah's shoes; my legs look good in those."

Sarah was next. She bowed her head for a moment, squeezed Frances' hand and said, "Max told me before Frances and I met that she thought Frances and I had been waiting all our lives for each other." Sarah looked at Frances, then at Max. "What an insightful, wonderful woman you are, Max, and if it had only been you whom I met, I would have been blessed." She bowed her head again and after a few moments, "Whatever has led me to this day and to all of you, I shall be thankful the rest of my life. I have been very lonely and without purpose, but it has been worth the wait." She leaned over and kissed Frances. "You were worth the wait darlin', I love you." She turned back to the table, "Thank you."

Panic was written all over Frances' face, which just made Sarah smile from ear to ear. "I love how you're so sensitive. How can anyone as beautiful and capable as you be so modest and insecure?"

"Well, that hasn't helped any."

"Don't stand," said Cocco, "give me a sore neck looking up so high."

This made Frances smile. "Okay, okay here goes. I don't know what I did to deserve you guys. Because of you I have chosen to live in this country, and I know I have made the right decision. I had no idea you had all made it your mission to find me a partner, I em..." She looked at Sarah. "I want..." She closed her eyes and felt Sarah take her hand. She looked at Sarah, "It feels so good to know that you're there. I can't find the words. Merci, merci beaucoup."

Everyone looked toward Cat. Cat suddenly realized she was next, and last. She looked at every expectant face and was lost. *How can I speak? I feel complete and empty, but at the same time, there is so much I want to say, and I can't think of a thing. Nothing. I feel as if I'm floating over everyone. I want to be here, but I don't think I can. All I can hear is Theo playing the piano in my head, the piece she played on Sunday. How long has everyone been staring at me?*

"Cat," said Max, "Cat, darling, it's all right, you don't have to say anything. Sweetheart, come back to us."

Cat looked at Max, "I'm all right, Aunty Max, maybe later."

Max squeezed her hand, "Okay, dear, okay." Theo looked frightened.

Max said, "Why don't we open these beautiful crackers and start eating all this lovely food?"

Frances was so nervous; her heart was in her mouth. Everyone was laughing at the plastic gifts, hats, and silly jokes that were contained in the crackers. Sarah offered her cracker to Frances and pulled. Instead of a plastic toy, Sarah picked up a silver ring, its setting was like a little pagoda and a large black pearl sat on top. She looked at Frances and gasped, "It's so beautiful."

"I thought it would go with your outfit."

"I love it, Frances," and she slipped it on her ring finger of her right hand.

Dinner was a happy occasion, and the laughter and love were apparent. The men insisted on clearing up, even Danny. Cocco said it would give the girls and him time to enjoy their cigars and talk about the sexy men. Theo wandered over to the piano and started to play. Everyone was pleased just to relax and listen to Theo till the men returned. Willie poured everyone a drink, and Sarah wandered over to the piano. "You play beautifully, Theo."

"Thank you. Do you play or sing?"

"I don't play, but I can keep in tune."

Theo gasped, "Hey, everyone. You know how Sarah can do anything? Well, she can sing as well."

Sarah looked horrified, "I didn't say that."

"Sing us something, Sarah," said Max. "I bet you have a lovely voice." Everyone was calling for Sarah to sing, and Frances, who felt sorry for Sarah being cornered, as she knew how her friends were about music, was trying to think of a way to save her.

Theo said, "Here, have a look in Sir Andrew's book and choose something."

Sarah, now feeling as if she were between a rock and a hard place, realized she wasn't going to get out of it and flicked through the book. She stopped at one, which she handed to Theo; it was from *Tell Me on a Sunday*.

"Perfect, Sarah, just perfect." Sarah looked at Frances, "This is for you my darlin'." Theo started very slowly, just playing a few notes, allowing Sarah to choose her own tempo, and very hesitantly, just above a whisper, Sarah started to sing.

I have never felt like this, for once I'm lost for words, your smile has really thrown me.

Still hesitant and nervous, but a little louder, she sang,

This is not like me at all, I never thought I'd know the kind of love you've shown me.

There wasn't a sound in the room, and Sarah lifted the volume a bit as her confidence was growing.

Now no matter where I am, no matter what I do, I see your face appearing like an unexpected song, an unexpected song that only we are hearing.

Theo picked up the accompaniment as Sarah's voice rose in strength,

I don't know what's going on, can't work it out at all, whatever made you choose me?

220

Her voice was now strong and confident and as clear as a bell, and Theo was thrilled.

I just can't believe my eyes, you look at me as though you couldn't bear to lose me.

Now no matter where I am, no matter what I do, I see your face appearing

Sarah was now singing to Frances as if there was no one else in the room. The atmosphere was electrifying.

like an unexpected song, an unexpected song that only we are hearing.

Torri walked over to the piano with her violin, and as Theo went into full steam on the instrumental, Torri joined in. Danny was already by their sides, ready with his drum to play at the right times.

Sarah had a wide smile on her face as she watched Torri. All three were obviously enjoying themselves; they were playing as if they had always played together. Then Sarah picked up at the end of the instrumental and carried away with the accompaniment, she let fly.

Like an unexpected song, an unexpected song that only we are hearing.

Like an unexpected song, an unexpected song that only we are hearing.

There was tumultuous applause at the end. Max was saying, "I told you she could do anything." Lizzie was over congratulating Torri. Theo could not take the smile off her face, and Sara walked over to Frances. Frances' eyes were clouded over with tears, but she could not take them away from Sarah. Frances was trying to find her voice and eventually asked, "Will you marry me, Sarah?"

Sarah laughed gently, "Well, the Civil Union Bill isn't through yet, so why don't we just live together till then?" She removed the pearl ring from her right hand and put it on her left third finger. "But yes," she kissed Frances, "yes, I will."

Cocco was berating Willie for not ever singing to him. Cat had walked over to Theo and sat down beside her on the piano stool. "That was beautiful, Theo. Your playing was amazing."

"Shall I sing for you?"

Cat looked at Theo in disbelief. "Okay, if you like."

"Hey, everyone. I'm not going to be outdone. This one's for Cat."

She had the Carpenter's songbook out and chose carefully. "This will do nicely."

The room fell silent. Cat went to rise and Theo said, "Stay here," and started to sing, "For All We Know."

When Theo was finished, she kissed Cat softly on the lips. "That was beautiful, Theo," said Max who was standing above them and kissed them both. "Just lovely. What a talented family I have, and Torri, where did you learn to play the violin like that?" Theo sat and looked at Cat and said nothing. Cat returned her gaze and felt peace return to her soul. She felt as if she had been walking around in a daze all week and felt numb, but peaceful. She also felt an overwhelming sense of inevitability.

Cocco, who was sitting next to Aroha, said, "Don't forget Willie and I will be over for Lizzie's pregnancy test on Saturday."

"Where is my bag, Frances?" asked Sarah.

Frances picked the large black bag from behind the sofa and handed it to Sarah.

"God, that's heavy. What have you got in there?"

"Oh, just a few things. You never know when you're going to need them. I just have to pop to the loo, sweetheart, be back in a moment." Sarah took her bag with her.

Cat was in the kitchen with Theo who was making coffee. "I think I'll put the wheelie-bin out now. I don't fancy getting up early in the morning and putting the rubbish out."

"Good thinking, woman."

Once inside the bathroom, Sarah checked her bag. Her gun was still there. She wished she could get rid of this ominous feeling and could remember what it was she'd overlooked. Walking back down the stairs, she saw Cat outside through the stair window. She looked again; there was something not right. Cat was still, as if she were frozen.

"Oh, my god!" Sarah grabbed the gun from her bag shouting, "Nooooooooo…"

222

Chapter 34

*T*ime had stopped. Everything was in slow motion. Surreal. Torri had just started to play my most favourite piece of music in the world. How could she know that? If these were to be my last few moments on this earth and I could only hear one piece of music, it would be this: Mascagni's "Intermezzo" from the opera Cavalleria Rusticana. Was this the reason Torri was brought into our lives, so she could play my death scene? The opening bars are so tentative, as if they're awakening from a dream. Rousing you, teasing you until it has your full attention. Then it's got you, and you're ready to go. The strings wind round your heart and lift you. It's ready for its journey, gathering momentum with its flutes, yearning, gathering up all who are coming with you or are already there waiting for you. Then, in full chorus you're off. Why do angels come to mind? I feel the nozzle of the gun on my neck, I know the voice, I've heard it before.*

"I'll get you. You're dead."
"Kevin, you stupid bastard, I told you not to drive, you're too pissed."

Maria! I should have recognized her voice in Napier. She was more or less the same age as I. I heard it often enough as a child. She was spouting venom about how I ruined her life and took her family away and how long she'd waited for this day. All I could see was my beautiful mother and my sweet brother smiling and waiting for me. I've been living on borrowed time; I should have died with them twenty-six years ago. It's time to pay the piper. I feel amazingly calm; I can't even say that I'm scared.

Oh, that music, I can see a full orchestra of violinists playing just for me, waiting for me, asking me, 'are you ready? It's time to go.' I think it is time for me to go. I feel as if I'm being lifted up, and the peace that has been so elusive for so long is here. Rising to the clouds. My only concern is Theo.

Theo was pouring coffee when she heard a car backfire twice. She hated how that always sounded like a gunshot. She suddenly froze, and a chill ran through her.

"CAT!"

About the Author

Ellis Ramsay was born in Edinburgh in 1953 and was the only girl in a family of four. She started a hairdressing apprenticeship at age fifteen and immigrated to New Zealand in 1973, three months before her twentieth birthday.

While in New Zealand, she was involved in amateur dramatics but in 1978 returned to Scotland and travelled on and off for the next three years.

Returning to live in New Zealand in 1981, she opened her own hairdressing salon and finally convinced the love of her life to live with her. Twenty-three years later they are still together.

Ellis's mother has visited her nine times in New Zealand and on her last visit in November 2003 bought her a computer. After her mother left in June 2004, one of her friends reminded her that she was always going to write a book when she got her own computer.

So, on July 23, she sat in front of her computer, and in between clients, after work, and on weekends, *Journeys of Discoveries* was born and finished six weeks later. Because she loves the characters so much, *Journeys of Tomorrows* was written straight after.

Ellis Paris Ramsay

Other Intaglio Publications Titles

Accidental Love, by B. L. Miller, ISBN: 1-933113-11-1, Price: 18.15
What happens when love is based on deception? Can it survive discovering the truth?

Code Blue, by KatLyn, ISBN: 1-933113-09-X, Price: $16.95 - Thrown headlong into one of the most puzzling murder investigations in the Burgh's history, Logan McGregor finds that politics, corruption, money and greed aren't the only barriers she must break through in order to find the truth.

Counterfeit World, by Judith K. Parker, ISBN: 1-933113-32-4, Price: $15.25
The U.S. government has been privatized, religion has only recently been decriminalized, the World Government keeps the peace on Earth—when it chooses—and multi-world corporations vie for control of planets, moons, asteroids, and orbits for their space stations.

Crystal's Heart, by B. L. Miller & Verda Foster, ISBN: 1-933113-24-3, Price: $18.50 - Two women who have absolutely nothing in common, and yet when they become improbable housemates, are amazed to find they can actually live with each other. And not only live...

Gloria's Inn, by Robin Alexander, ISBN: 1-933113-01-4, Price: $14.95 - Hayden Tate suddenly found herself in a world unlike any other, when she inherited half of an inn nestled away on Cat Island in the Bahamas.

Graceful Waters, by B. L. Miller & Verda Foster, ISBN: 1-933113-08-1, Price: $17.25 - Joanna Carey, senior instructor at Sapling Hill wasn't looking for anything more than completing one more year at the facility and getting that much closer to her private dream, a small cabin on a quiet lake. She was tough, smart and she had a plan for her life.

Halls Of Temptation, by Katie P. Moore, ISBN: 978-1-933113-42-5, Price: $15.50 – A heartfelt romance that traces the lives of two young women from their teenage years into adulthood, through the struggles of maturity, conflict and love.

I Already Know The Silence Of The Storms, by N. M. Hill, ISBN: 1-933113-07-3, Price: $15.25 - I Already Know the Silence of the Storms is a map of a questor's journey as she traverses the tempestuous landscapes of heart, mind, body, and soul. Tossed onto paths of origins and destinations unbeknownst to her, she is enjoined by the ancients to cross chartless regions beset with want and need and desire to find the truth within.

Incommunicado, by N. M. Hill & J. P. Mercer, ISBN: 1-933113-10-3, Price: $15.25 - Incommunicado is a world of lies, deceit, and death along the U.S/Mexico border. Set within the panoramic beauty of the unforgiving Sonoran Desert, it is the story of two strong, independent women: Cara

Vittore Cipriano, a lawyer who was born to rule the prestigious Cipriano Vineyards; and Jaquelyn "Jake" Biscayne, an FBI forensic pathologist who has made her work her life.

Josie & Rebecca: The Western Chronicles, by Vada Foster & BL Miller, ISBN: 1-933113-38-3, Price: $18.99 - At the center of this story are two women; one a deadly gunslinger bitter from the injustices of her past, the other a gentle dreamer trying to escape the horrors of the present. Their destinies come together one fateful afternoon when the feared outlaw makes the choice to rescue a young woman in trouble. For her part, Josie Hunter considers the brief encounter at an end once the girl is safe, but Rebecca Cameron has other ideas....

Misplaced People, by C. G. Devize, ISBN: 1-933113-30-8, Price: $17.99 - On duty at a London hospital, American loner Striker West is drawn to an unknown woman, who, after being savagely attacked, is on the verge of death. Moved by a compassion she cannot explain, Striker spends her off time at the bedside of the comatose patient, reading and willing her to recover. Still trying to conquer her own demons which have taken her so far from home, Striker is drawn deeper into the web of intrigue that surrounds this woman.

Murky Waters, by Robin Alexander, ISBN: 1-933113-33-2, Price: $15.25 - Claire Murray thought she was leaving her problems behind when she accepted a new position within Suarez Travel and relocated to Baton Rouge. Her excitement quickly diminishes when her mysterious stalker makes it known that there is no place Claire can hide. She is instantly attracted to the enigmatic Tristan Delacroix, who becomes more of a mystery to her every time they meet. Claire is thrust into a world of fear, confusion, and passion that will ultimately shake the foundations of all she once believed.

None So Blind, by LJ Maas, ISBN: 978-1-933113-44-9, Price: $16.50 - Torrey Gray hasn't seen the woman she fell in love with in college for 15 years. Taylor Kent, now a celebrated artist, has spent the years trying to forget, albeit unsuccessfully, the young woman who walked out of Taylor's life…

Picking Up The Pace, by Kimberly LaFontaine, ISBN: 1-933113-41-3, Price: 15.50 - Who would have thought a 25-year-old budding journalist could stumble across a story worth dying for in quiet Fort Worth, Texas? Angie Mitchell certainly doesn't and neither do her bosses. While following an investigative lead for the Tribune, she heads into the seediest part of the city to discover why homeless people are showing up dead with no suspects for the police to chase.

Southern Hearts, by Katie P Moore, ISBN: 1-933113-28-6, Price: $16.95 - For the first time since her father's passing three years prior, Kari Bossier returns to the south, to her family's stately home on the emerald banks of the bayou Teche, and to a mother she yearns to understand.

Storm Surge, by KatLyn, ISBN: 1-933113-06-5, Price: $16.95 - FBI Special Agent Alex Montgomery would have given her life in the line of duty, but she lost something far more precious when she became the target of ruthless drug traffickers. Recalled to Jacksonville to aid the local authorities in infiltrating the same deadly drug ring, she has a secret agenda--revenge. Despite her unexpected involvement with Conner Harris, a tough, streetwise detective who has dedicated her life to her job at the cost of her own personal happiness, Alex vows to let nothing--and no one--stand in the way of exacting vengeance on those who took from her everything that mattered.

These Dreams, by Verda Foster, ISBN: 1-933113-12-X, Price: $15.75 - Haunted from childhood by visions of a mysterious woman she calls, Blue Eyes, artist Samantha McBride is thrilled when a friend informs her that she's seen a woman who bears the beautiful face she has immortalized on canvas and dreamed about for so long. Thrilled by the possibility that Blue Eyes might be a flesh and blood person, Samantha sets out to find her, certain the woman must be her destiny.

The Chosen, by Verda H Foster, ISBN: 978-1-933113-25-8, Price: 15.25 - animals. That's the way it's always been. But the slaves are waiting for the coming of The Chosen One, the prophesied leader who will take them out of their bondage.

The Cost Of Commitment, by Lynn Ames, ISBN: 1-933113-02-2, Price: $16.95 - Kate and Jay want nothing more than to focus on their love. But as Kate settles in to a new profession, she and Jay become caught up in the middle of a deadly scheme—pawns in a larger game in which the stakes are nothing less than control of the country.

The Gift, by Verda Foster, ISBN: 1-933113-03-0, Price: $15.35 - Detective Rachel Todd doesn't believe in Lindsay Ryan's visions of danger, even when the horrifying events Lindsay predicted come true. That mistake could cost more than one life before this rollercoaster ride is over. Verda Foster's The Gift is just that – a well-paced, passionate saga of suspense, romance, and the amazing bounty of family, friends, and second chances. From the first breathless page to the last, a winner.

The Illusionist, by Fran Heckrotte, ISBN: 978-1-933113-31-9, Price: $16.95 - Dakota Devereaus, an investigative journalist, is on a mission to uncover the secrets of Yemaya, The Illusionist. However, in her quest for an expose on this mysterious woman, she uncovers more than she bargained for. Dakota is targeted by a power hungry CEO, determined to learn The Illusionist's secret--at all costs-- and a madman intent on fulfilling his perverted fantasies.

The Last Train Home, by Blayne Cooper, ISBN: 1-933113-26-X, Price: $17.75 - One cold winter's night in Manhattan's Lower East side, tragedy strikes the Chisholm family. Thrown together by fate and disaster, Virginia "Ginny" Chisholm meets Lindsay Killian, a street-smart drifter who spends her days picking pockets and riding the rails. Together, the young women embark on a desperate journey that spans from the slums of New York City to the Western Frontier, as Ginny tries to reunite her family, regardless of the cost.

The Price of Fame, by Lynn Ames, ISBN: 1-933113-04-9, Price: $16.75 - When local television news anchor Katherine Kyle is thrust into the national spotlight, it sets in motion a chain of events that will change her life forever. Jamison "Jay" Parker is an intensely career-driven Time magazine reporter; she has experienced love once, from afar, and given up on finding it again...That is, until circumstance and an assignment bring her into contact with her past.

The Taking of Eden, by Robin Alexander, ISBN: 978-1-933113-53-1, Price: $15.95 - Frustrated with life and death situations that she can't control, Jamie Spencer takes a new job at a mental health facility, where she believes she can make a difference in her patients' lives. The difference she makes in Eden Carlton's life turns her world upside down and out of control. A spur-of-the-moment decision sets in motion a turn of events that she is powerless to stop and changes her life and everyone around her forever.

The Value of Valor, by Lynn Ames, ISBN: 1-933113-04-9, Price: $16.75
Katherine Kyle is the press secretary to the president of the United States. Her lover, Jamison Parker, is a respected writer for Time magazine. Separated by unthinkable tragedy, the two must struggle to survive against impossible odds...

The War between The Hearts, by Nann Dunne, ISBN: 1-933113-27-8, Price: $16.95 - Intent on serving the Union Army as a spy, Sarah-Bren Coulter disguises herself as a man and becomes a courier-scout for the Confederate Army. Soon the savagery of war shakes her to the core. She stifles her emotions so she can bear the guilt of sending men, and sometimes boys, into paths of destruction.

With Every Breath, by Alex Alexander, ISBN: 1-933113-39-1, Price: $15.25
Abigail Dunnigan wakes to a phone call telling her of the brutal murder of her former lover and dear friend. A return to her hometown for the funeral soon becomes a run for her life, not only from the murderer but also from the truth about her own well-concealed act of killing to survive during a war. As the story unfolds, Abby confesses her experiences in Desert Storm and becomes haunted with the past as the bizarre connection between then and now reveals itself. While the FBI works to protect her and apprehend the murderer, the murderer works to push Abby over the mental edge with their secret correspondence.

Intaglio Publication's Forthcoming Releases

April
She Waits, by M. K. Sweeney, ISBN: 978-1-933113-55-5
Compensation, by S. Anne Gardner, ISBN: 978-1-933113-57-9

May
Tumbleweed Fever, By LJ Maas, ISBN: 978-1-933113-51-7
The Scent of Spring, By Katie Moore, ISBN: 978-1-933113-67-8
Prairie Fire, By LJ Maas, ISBN: 978-1-933113-47-0

June
Lilith, by Fran Heckrotte, ISBN: 978-1-933113-50-0
The Flipside of Desire, by Lynn Ames, ISBN: 978-1-933113-60-9

November
Times Fell Hand, By LJ Maas, ISBN: 978-1-933113-52-4

You can purchase other Intaglio Publications books online at StarCrossed Productions, Inc. www.scp-inc.biz or at your local bookstore.

Published by
Intaglio Publications
P O Box 357474
Gainesville, Florida 32635

Visit us on the web: **www.intagliopub.com**